PRINCESS DIANA'S
REVENGE

In a full and varied life Michael de
Larrabeiti has worked in the film
industry, as a travel guide in France and
Morocco, as a shepherd in Provence, as
an English teacher in Casablanca and as
a travel journalist for the Sunday Times.
He read French and English at Trinity
College, Dublin, won a scholarship to
the École Normale Supérieure, Paris and
began a D.Phil at Oxford which he
abandoned to take up writing full-time.

He is the author of the much admired
Borrible Trilogy, recently reissued, as
well as several other books. He has three
grown-up daughters and lives in
Oxfordshire.

ALSO BY MICHAEL DE LARRABEITI

The Borribles
The Borribles Go For Broke
The Borribles: Across the Dark Metropolis
The Redwater Raid
A Rose Beyond the Thames
The Bunce
The Hollywood Takes
Jeeno, Heloise and Igamor, the Long, Long Horse
The Provençal Tales
Journal of a Sad Hermaphrodite
French Leave
Foxes' Oven
Spots of Time: A Memoir

PRINCESS DIANA'S REVENGE

Michael de Larrabeiti

First published in Great Britain 2006 by Tallis House
www.tallishouse.co.uk

British Library Cataloguing-in-Publication Data
A catalogue record for this book is available on request from
the British Library

ISBN 978-0-9554622-0-7

Set in 11pt Sabon by Sam Harris & Associates

Printed and bound in Great Britain

*For the inhabitants of Great Milton,
past, present and future,
in friendship and affection.*

Art is the lie that makes us realize the truth.
Pablo Picasso

'Death is down every side-street, just waiting.' Joe spoke out loud even though he was alone. He often did. He should have been feeling happy, joyful even, but he wasn't. He'd filmed in a coal mine once, three months, and the longer he'd spent underground the more frightened he'd felt every time he came out, scared of space. That feeling was with him now and he couldn't move because of it. So he stood where he was.

They'd given him a hard time in prison and they might not have finished with him yet, which only made him miss the closeness of his cell walls and the smell of unwashed bodies even more; he had got used to claustrophobia, come to welcome it, but now an emptiness surrounded him and made him vulnerable. Anything could come from anywhere, from the far side of the cosmos, asteroids aiming for his skull.

Joe spoke again. 'I've seen too many old gangster films, that's my trouble.' He was standing in the black shadows not far from the prison gates. He'd watched hundreds of those films during his time in Wandsworth. Black and white, like the night around him, beautifully lit, glossy pools of dark awash with silver lamplight, everything he dreaded lurking in the shadows – "les films noirs." 'Gilda' with Rita Hayworth; 'The Glass Key' with Alan Ladd.

If the films had been based in truth there should be a car

waiting for him, a long-nosed limousine, one of those old Packards from prohibition days, an elegant hand beckoning him in, the luxurious smell of leather seats, a beautiful woman, his for the taking, a fortune in cash on offer, and thanks expressed for the favours he'd done, and a rich life stretching away in front of him, as smooth as an aristocratic lawn, green pastures for ever, as soft and as tasty as peppermint ice-cream. Dream away Joe. He was broke and the streets were deserted. If there'd been a sound the walls would have echoed, but they didn't. Not even a black cat in the lamplight. He dreamt too much. He shrugged his shoulders and hefted the small attaché case that contained all he owned. It weighed nothing but there was nothing in it but a change of clothing. He walked towards the street lamps and turned towards Magdalen Road, or was it Burntwood Lane, he couldn't remember. The longed for car didn't come, but then no one cared if he was inside prison or out of it, alive or dead. Well, maybe one person, the one person who really would like to see him dead.

He walked on. Perhaps he'd pick up a night bus on Trinity Road, but one thing was certain, he had to book in at the hostel in Kingston by the next day. It was a condition of his parole. And just as important was the probation officer to see once a month. How he'd like to board a bus and simply say: 'A single to the end of the world, please driver, and no return.'

He was alone. Geraldine had divorced him two years before and there were no children. Even if he'd spawned a tribe of kids they wouldn't have wanted him – a failure who had spent no time with them. He laughed like a tinful of nails. Kids who didn't exist and still they despised him. The loneliness was bitter and again Joe yearned to be back in his cell, warmed by the light, comforted by the routine.

Then the car came, a black Mercedes. It pulled into the gutter beside him. It shone like anthracite. Along the pavement were the fences and walls and the houses of Magdalen Road, proper houses with proper people in them; a leafy part of Wandsworth. The front passenger door of the Mercedes swung open and a man's voice said, 'Get in, Rapps.'

Joe knew who it was. There was every chance that if he got

into the car he wouldn't get out alive. He'd been wishing for a role in a black and white film, but not this role. Only one person in the world would send for him, the one person he didn't want to see; you could trust life to spit in your eye, and here it was, spitting. A man in a black sweater got out of the rear nearside door, came up close to Joe and pushed him hard.

'Get in,' he said.

Joe did as he was told, sat next to the driver, and placed his case on his knee. The door was slammed and the man in the sweater got back into the car. Joe looked to his right, but he knew who was sitting there – 'Sunshine' Leary. The man in the sweater was his brother, Ralph.

Sunshine switched off the engine and leant further back into his seat, staring through the windscreen.

'I could have had you killed in there.' He tilted his head in the direction of the prison. 'Should have.' His voice was rough, a throat of sandpaper. Joe said nothing and stared at the walnut fascia of the dashboard. He wondered if Sunshine filed his teeth to points now, like a cannibal.

'I could finish you tonight,' Sunshine continued, 'and who'd worry, who'd come looking for you? Your ex? You want to know who she's shacked up with?' Sunshine left a silence. 'Your brother, that's who. They'd probably pay me to throw you off Vauxhall Bridge.'

Joe held onto his suitcase, waiting. This wasn't going to end easily. Ralph laughed in the back of the car and Joe felt his breath on the skin of his neck. The short hairs of his prison crop bristled at the touch of it.

'You killed my two kids,' Sunshine went on. 'Drove into 'em, drunk. My two kids. What do you think that did to my old woman? And all you got was five, out in three. I don't know how you're still breathing. Do you? I was going to slaughter you...plenty inside would have done it for me, you wouldn't have cost much, two hundred cigarettes at the most...but I was stopped...Ralph said you weren't worth doing time for...you can thank him that you weren't found hanged in your cell...but doing time wouldn't have stopped me, something else did.'

Joe ran his tongue over his lips. He thought about saying he was sorry but then thought again. Sunshine wasn't in the 'sorry' league. Joe had been beaten up regularly inside and a different con had done it each time. Joe knew why; Sunshine was why. The prisoners liked doing favours for Sunshine, they'd drawn lots for it, it was enjoyable therapy, never mind water-colours or pottery. Joe had taken the beatings without complaint, there would have been no point. He had looked on it as part of his sentence. Knowing that he could be killed any day was also part of that sentence. He opened his mouth to speak, to say that he knew.

'Don't you say a word,' said Sunshine, 'you say anything and I'll change my mind, I haven't given up the idea, even now.' There was another silence. 'Here's what you do, Joe Rapps, you get out of London, right out. I don't care where you go, retire, do good works, but if I so much as smell you in the Smoke I'll give you to Cold Ronnie to play with, cut you up nice and slow, he would, you know how much he enjoys it...just get out of London, don't ever come back, not even to be cremated.'

Ralph laughed again, got out onto the pavement, opened Joe's door and pulled him out.

'On yer way, Rapps,' he said, and he slid into the seat Joe had vacated. The car started and drove gently away. Joe watched the rear lights disappear, then crossed the pavement and sat on the low coping that bordered the nearest house. The sweat trickled from his armpits. A comforting trickle, it meant he was still alive. He thought of what Sunshine might have done and shivered. It was like him to let Joe serve his time, making it as near torture as possible, but it would also have been in character for him to have handed Joe over to Cold Ronnie and watch him die. Cold Ronnie, from what Joe had heard on the grapevine, made Torquemada look like a Swiss doctor practising philanthropic euthanasia. Joe had seen Cold Ronnie once, just the once but that had been enough; as charming as a cobra and reliable too – reliable like a quicksand is reliable.

Joe could smell the laurels in the garden behind him. Laurels meant funerals. It was spring, beginning of May, and nearly midnight, and the glow of London was reflected on the low curve of the sky, killing the light that fell from the stars. He hadn't had many visits over the three years. He'd worn his friends out, they'd gone. They'd found him too louche, too much like hard work. A few film people he'd worked with had come to see him, at the beginning that was, but they had drifted away. What did they want with a drunken director-cameraman who had killed two innocent people in a car crash? Someone who'd hit the bottle hard waiting for his trial, and even harder during the trial.

He hadn't looked good in court: grey skinned, his eyes loose in red sockets. Geraldine had come to Wandsworth once, to tell him about the divorce. Then no one. And inside – hell. And no transfer to an open prison. Sunshine must have seen to that. Even the screws knew what the score was and he got all the dirty jobs: how many lavatories had he cleaned, how many hospital bed-pans emptied?

He got to his feet. At least one decision had been made for him. Wherever he chose to go there was no staying in London. But did Sunshine consider that Kingston was London. He had to go to the hostel, to begin with at least. He'd never had a life of stillness, of permanence, you don't get a lot of that in the film business, but London was what he knew; he was Battersea born and bred. Now it was out of the question.

He'd been on location all over the world, but his only real hope of getting a job lay in the capital, though who would employ him now? The film business was a slippery mistress; any time out of it and no one remembered your face, let alone your name. And Joe knew he was rusty. Techniques and equipment change over time. Where to go? He did have a cousin in Devon – bugger Devon! Australia then. Would the probation service permit such a thing? He'd need some money, real money, to get there and set himself up. Money! He had none, just his earnings from the prison. Twenty quid.

Headlights approached up Magdalen Road. Joe thought about running, tightened the grip on his case, changed his mind. What was the point? If it was Sunshine then there was nowhere he could hide. Sunshine would find him whenever he wanted.

The car swerved across the road, the full beam of the headlights picking Joe out like a rabbit. He shielded his eyes.

The car swerved again and came to a halt in the same bit of gutter that Sunshine had parked in. It was a huge car, a white stretch. The driver's door opened and a chauffeur emerged, rising from his seat with an easy movement that said that he was fit and his knees and arms strong. He was dressed in a crisp suit, dark and well cut. He nodded at Joe in a kind of a bow, opened the rear door and inclined his body again.

'Please,' he said. 'I am ordered to take you wherever you wish.'

Joe advanced in a kind of a shuffle, not really knowing what to think or what to do. Getting into strange vehicles was a dangerous game. He bent and peered into the back of the car and saw that there was someone peering back at him; a round red face, grey hair, long sideburns; a heavily built man, thick thighs too. The face beamed and a fat hand waved him forward.

'Ah, Mr Rapps,' said the man in a voice as fat as the hand and as round as the face. 'Allow us to take care of you for a while. We will drive you in any direction you wish to go. Please.' The man leant across the enormous width of the car and pulled a shelf down to reveal a row of bottles. 'I can offer you vodka, Scotch, a Margaux even. I have a little food also, please.'

Joe took a step nearer. The chauffeur held the door and waited patiently, his smile cold. Joe hesitated. The passenger's suit was black and where his shirt should have been there was a spread of mauve material, his collar was white and back to front. He was a churchman: a Bishop.

Joe remained motionless for a moment, then the smell of alcohol got to him as the bishop poured himself a whisky, and he stepped up and into the space of the car, dropped his case onto the floor and let his body collapse into the embrace of the white leather seat. It was as wide as a double divan.

The Bishop poured a Margaux for Joe and smiled again, a smile that could have lit the main runway at Heathrow Airport. 'I know your tastes,' he said, 'or at least I've been told what they are.' He raised his glass. 'Mr Rapps, here's to you, and years of freedom.' Joe rolled the wine over his taste buds. It was his first drink in three years and it hit his stomach like a tsunami. The car moved forward, as silent as a cloud of gas. A screen came down between the passengers and the chauffeur.

'And where would you like to go, Mr Rapps?'

'I have to go to Kingston on Thames, to a hostel. The probation service has to know where I am, I have no option.'

The Bishop nodded. 'But you do Mr Rapps. I have had a word with the Probation Service. They have delivered you into my custody…if you wish it of course. Kingston is a little close to London.'

'I'm more than happy to avoid the hostel,' said Joe, 'I'm told it's only marginally better than prison.'

The Bishop flicked a switch and spoke to the chauffeur. 'Milton Magna it is, Gerard,' he said and flicked the switch again.

Joe leant back on the cushions and took another large mouthful of his drink; it was a superb claret. Maybe he hadn't seen too many old gangster films after all.

*　　*　　*

'What's Milton Magna?' asked Joe. 'Where is it?

The Bishop nodded like he was giving a blessing. 'It's a village of some nine hundred people,' he said, 'this side of Oxford. Quiet and restful. It's a little corner of old England, a microcosm of it. There's a church, a village shop, a public house, The Bull…you'll meet the landlady, pretty racy I'm told. There are rustic houses, thatched cottages and a huge hotel, very expensive, they come out from London in helicopters, just for dinner, it's run by a Belgian, Monsieur Claude de Topinambour, expensive but very good, Michelin rosettes…people complain about the helicopters, there's quite a few every week.'

The Bishop leant forward and refilled Joe's glass. Joe looked through the one-way window; they were heading onto Western Avenue.

'There's also a Church of England school, even a tennis court. A lovely church of course, part Norman…the incumbent is a bit of an odd fish, nothing wrong with that of course, the Church of England likes odd fish – the Reverend Baker...he cycles everywhere on a huge Victorian bicycle, it certainly looks Victorian, he can't drive a car, mumbles to himself all the time and never shaves properly, has little cuts on his face and bits of paper stuck here and there, to stop the bleeding, perhaps his hands shake...but he's got a heart of gold, cycles all the way into Oxford to visit people in hospital...quite dangerous on the dual carriageway. He's storing up treasure in heaven, and he certainly knows his Latin, though I don't know whether that helps up there or not.'

The two glasses of Margaux had made Joe a little sleepy. He yawned. The Bishop reached over to the drinks cabinet and handed Joe a dish of black olives.

'Have some of these,' he said.

'So what are you doing here?' asked Joe. 'I mean, I don't know you but you know I like Margaux. You might have dropped from the sky, especially in that gear. Fancy dress? Are we going to a ball?'

The Bishop laughed. A gentle laugh, self-mocking.

'Not quite. I really am a Bishop, you see, diocese of Aylesbury...retired. There's a seminary and theological college in the next village to Milton Magna, Cuddesdon, up the hill. There's a few of us superannuated old fogeys up there...students too of course, studying theology. They have women as well now, makes life more interesting for the young men. Monks weren't always celibate, you know, especially in the Middle Ages...and I wager our students aren't either.' The Bishop chuckled again, and there was a lot of joy in his voice. He turned his head to Joe and his eyes gleamed, not with lust or concupiscence in this instance, he was simply allowing himself to be amused at the tricks life played.

'You will find some very pleasant restaurants in the area, pleasant country pubs and some delightful churches...Ewelme for example.'

'Well yes,' said Joe, 'but why have you come to fetch me, and why Milton Magna?'

The Bishop shook his head. He was still smiling. 'Oh, I'm not

at liberty to divulge that information…put it this way, someone
has taken an interest in you and I have been employed as a mere
messenger, you mustn't imagine for a moment that this is my
car, or my chauffeur. Someone wishes to help you. They know
your story, they may even offer you employment.'

'What kind of employment?'

The Bishop shook his head again. 'I can say no more. There is
accommodation waiting for you. I suggest you rest for a couple
of days, relax, enjoy the village. You will find the villagers most
friendly. All will become clear in a day or so. Be patient, be lazy
even. After all, laziness is probably the prime mover in human
affairs. We achieve something now, but only so that we need to
do less further down the road. Laziness makes us work hard but
indolence is the future we yearn for. Such a delightful word,
'indolence', it means absence from dolour, absence from the
pain of work. So I advise you, study the word indolence; it is
one of the most beautiful in our language.'

Joe gazed out of the window and watched the white lines of
the motorway flashing by. There didn't seem to be any point in
pushing the Bishop any further. He closed his eyes.

*   *   *

When he opened them again the car had stopped. Joe blinked,
looked out of the window but saw only the indistinct shape of a
house that stood on the edge of the road. It was totally dark
and there were no street lamps. Gerard got out of the car.

'We're here,' said the Bishop. 'It's only about an hour from
London, on a good day.' Gerard opened the door and waited
for Joe to pick up his case and disembark. The Bishop folded his
hands on his stomach and made no move.

'You're not coming?' asked Joe. He suddenly felt lonely, out
on a limb.

'I have to get back to the seminary, lectures in the morning.
I'll be seeing you soon, all too soon I suspect.'

'Yes, but what am I to do?'

'I told you. First you are to relax. Gerard will show you
where to go, it's just here. Your quarters are delightful, better

than mine at the seminary, a trifle monkish for a man of my age. Why not come and see me tomorrow, say? That will make you feel happier, we will talk.'

'Tomorrow?'

'Yes, tomorrow. Mid-morning.'

Joe slid his body across the wide seat, grabbing his case on the way. 'Well, thank you Bishop.' He didn't know what else to say. The Bishop nodded and half raised a fat hand in farewell.

Once outside Gerard closed the door of the stretch and, lighting the ground with a circle of light from a torch, he stepped to the side of the nearest house and waited by the entrance to a narrow alley, about a yard wide. For Joe the alley was threatening, cavernous and dangerous: no light spilling from windows, no light from anywhere, save the torch. Joe hesitated. Blackness all around, a strange man behind him in the car and a muscular young man leading him God knew where. He had no reason to trust either of them. Perhaps he should have gone to the hostel. The torch beam swivelled and shone in Joe's face.

'It's all right, Mr Rapps,' said Gerard. 'Your cottage is just a little further on. It's just that in this village they don't have street lights, the locals think it's too modern.' Joe still didn't move.

The Bishop's window hissed open. 'It's all right, Mr Rapps, I promise you.'

Joe wasn't in the slightest reassured but went forward following Gerard and the torch beam very closely. The path took a sharp turn to the left, then after ten yards or so it took a turn to the right. There was the indistinct shape of a building in the night, then the path turned right again and passed along the length of a long low cottage with one upper storey. Here light fell from behind curtained windows and Joe could see the path and a rough stone wall. Gerard came to a porch and stopped; a security light came on automatically. Joe had an impression of small windows, and a wide area of garden to his left disappearing into more blackness. Gerard pushed at the front door and light flooded out onto the path.

'They don't lock doors here,' he said.

Again Joe hesitated. Where the hell was he?

'Whose house is this?' he asked, taking a step backwards.

Gerard permitted himself a smile. 'Why, Mr Rapps,' he said. 'It's yours.' He gave his little bow again. 'I shall have to leave you now. It's getting late and the Bishop likes his sleep.'

Gerard squeezed past Joe and made his way back along the path, and the beam of the torch disappeared round the corner of the house.

His house? Joe didn't understand. He took a breath and stepped across the threshold and into the bright electric light. The door closed behind him without Joe touching it. Fear gripped him for a second or two. He looked to the right. There was someone standing behind the door and Joe's heart thumped against his rib-cage. He couldn't prevent himself, he threw an arm up to protect his head.

'Oo, don't you be startled, my love,' said the woman, the voice full of affability. 'We don't want you coming to no 'arm, do we now?'

Joe lowered his guard, embarrassed. The woman was built like a barrel, hooped with solid breasts and bands of flesh at the waist, her thighs could have supported the roof of the Parthenon. Her arms were a boxer's, used to keeping a large household in order. She was nearer sixty than fifty, covered in a flowered apron and a black cardigan; only a couple of its buttons were fastened. On her feet were brown shoes like barges. Joe could visualize her at home, solid as a rock, never fazed, surrounded by grand-children of all ages, a kettle steaming on the hob. Her hair was grey and loose about her face, a round flat face, but not in the least bit stupid. Her glance was impudent, she'd seen everything; she had guided so many boys into manhood that she knew men inside out, and her eyes told the world so. She laughed readily.

'I'll be off home now you're here,' she said. There was a slight burr to her voice, a redolence of Oxfordshire farmyards from several previous generations. She took Joe's case from his hand and placed it on the floor of the hallway. 'You must be starving. Anything you don't eat? No, that's good. Now, come 'ere.' She led Joe across the hallway and into the kitchen. On a work surface was a dish covered in foil. There was fruit in a bowl and an open bottle of red wine. 'You likes steak and kidney, I bet. It's in the oven. You looks a steak and kidney man.' She put the dish into the oven and switched it on. 'There's cheeses laid out. You call me Sylvie.'

'I'm Joe Rapps,' said Joe. 'Please call me Joe.'

'I will love, I will. I'll leave you to find your way around, my old man will wonder where I've got to, you lie in tomorrow, you looks exhausted, not surprising, just back from...India, they said.'

'Yes,' said Joe.

'I'll pop in once a day, in the mornings...It was handy having the money in advance. My old man said it was good of you. I know we'll get on. I'll cook you something every morning, something for the evening...and make you a snack for lunch if you want it. Though I says it who shouldn't, I'm the best cook in the village...I do dinners at the big houses, lots of them.'

'Yes,' said Joe again.

'I'll come down later tomorrow and show you the house properly...it's a lovely place, wish I could afford it.' She grinned at her own temerity, unhooked her coat from behind the door and slipped into it. 'Goodnight, then, Mr Rapps, Joe, you'll sleep like a baby down here. You can't hear nothing, not a car, you're away from the road, see.' With that she grinned again and left the kitchen. Joe heard the front door close behind her.

The kitchen was large with a good pine dining-table in the middle of the room. There were wooden cupboards, hand-made, cups hanging on hooks, plate racks, drawers with cutlery and a substantial wine rack. Joe checked the labels and found his favourites. Someone knew what he drank: clarets in the reds, Burgundies in the whites. The open bottle was a Leoville-Barton: Leoville-Barton and steak and kidney pie, brie and biscuits, a bowl of fruit and a bottle of twenty year old Calvados. That someone who knew about his wines knew a lot more about him too. Not the Bishop, he was not the principal in this affair and had admitted as much. 'I'm just the messenger, Mr Rapps,' he'd said, 'Just the messenger.'

The timer on the oven pinged; Joe served up the meal and sat

out to him as sole owner. There was a bill of sale. Joe got to his feet and walked to the window. The bill of sale was for nearly half a million pounds.

Joe was alarmed. Too much was happening and he was finding it difficult to deal with. He'd never made much money in the forty odd years of his life, but he'd lived well; travelled the world, benefit of the film business, and enjoyed it. It had been an occupation that had been good to him and taught him a lot; he'd sailed on destroyers, filmed in steel works, art galleries, done a lot of work with the Royal Family, ridden steam trains across China and India, and drunk a lot of wine.

But never mind the different locations and the ancillary benefits, he'd always been in control of his life, or at least thought that he had, that was until he'd been sent to prison where he'd come under the control of warders suborned by Sunshine Leary. Now he was out of prison and didn't know where he was. He was adrift with no idea of direction. He'd fallen down the rabbit hole and into Wonderland; or was he in Narnia, or in Nutwood with Rupert Bear? He turned and picked up his toast – if he ate it would he grow until his legs and feet and arms grew out of the window, or would he shrink till he couldn't climb the stairs? If he went back into the kitchen would he find the Mad Hatter sitting at the table, dipping a mouse into a teapot? Joe felt his skin shift, a shiver of cold. He wasn't only confused, he was intimidated.

He looked at the deed again. There was no doubt about it, the house was his, desirable residence in Milton Magna, Oxfordshire, and everything in it was his too, presumably.

There was a noise at the front door and a woman's voice called, cheerful.

'Ello, Joe, you there?' It was Sylvie.

Joe put the banknotes and the deed back into the envelope, and wrapped the dressing gown more tightly around his body, tying the belt. Sylvie came into the room and smiled at him as if he were part of her family.

'Ow about a nice drop of breakfast,' she said, her smile still shining. 'Nice English breakfast, bet you 'aven't 'ad one of those for a while.'

Joe looked at her but there was no side to the remark. He remembered the breakfasts at Wandsworth.

'Well, you've been abroad, 'aven't you. They can't do breakfasts over there.'

Sylvie turned and headed for the kitchen. Joe went to follow but noticed a door under the stairs. There was a light switch and when he opened the door the light revealed huge stone slabs, steps into the cellar. The oldest part of the house, seventeenth century.

'What's in the cellar?' he called out to Sylvie. He could hear the bacon frying.

'You better go and see, my duck,' she answered, and laughed her laugh. 'As if you didn't know, eh?'

Joe went slowly down. The stairway turned a right angle at the bottom so he could not see what the cellar held until he had reached the last step. He ducked his head under a low lintel, though the roof of the cellar itself was high enough for him to stand upright. There was plenty of light falling from spots sunk in the ceiling, and a huge beam ran the length of the room supporting the structure of the house. The walls were clean and painted off-white, there were even a couple of grilled windows to let air in from the garden.

But that wasn't it. The cellar was large and in the middle of it stood a full sized snooker table, and against the end wall stood a couple of small armchairs; next to them a score board and a rack with cues in it. The red balls were in their triangle; the baize was deep green and restful. That still wasn't it.

Around the three other walls were deep shelves, newly made, six or seven of them up to the ceiling, the smell of their timber fresh. On the shelves were wine bottles, two or three deep, the bins numbered on printed cards with their names and years. Joe was stunned. There must have been three hundred bottles there. They were mainly wines he knew, or knew of, many of them wines that in the past he simply hadn't been able to afford, even on company expenses: Latour, Margaux again, St Emilion, Pommerol, Graves, and the dry white Burgundies, Pouilly Fuissé, the Montrachets.

Joe made a tour of the cellar, touched the bottles with gentle fingers, drew one or two out and gazed at the labels. Curiouser and curiouser.

Upstairs again he showered and threw his old clothes, the ones he'd arrived in, into a dirty pile on the floor. From the wardrobe he chose a pair of superbly cut casual trousers, a pale blue shirt and a loose sweater, a darker blue, lightweight in cashmere. His shoes were a pair of stout country brogues, and the reflection the full length mirror sent back to him was of a stylish home counties' gentleman.

In the kitchen Sylvie put a plate before him. It smelt like heaven: three rashers of bacon, two lightly fried eggs, just as he liked them, mushrooms, tomatoes, two sausages. As Joe ate she watched him, leaning against a work surface, her arms folded, taking pleasure in watching the food disappear.

'This is just how I like it,' said Joe. 'How do you know my secrets?'

Sylvie moved to the sink and began tidying up.

'Ah,' she said, 'that'd be telling, wouldn't it? I had a letter about you, from Cuddesdon.'

The Bishop again. That must be Joe's first job. See the Bishop and get some information out of him. Shake his teeth loose if necessary.

'Shouldn't I be paying you something?'

'I'm paid to the end of the week,' said Sylvie, 'then it's up to you, if you want to keep me on. I was told to get the place ready and then see what you wanted.'

'Well, who paid you?'

'That Bishop of course. He lives up at the seminary...stacked full of Bishops and clergymen up there...and students...they can't spend all their time praying, can they? Bet they pulls a few strokes. You'd better have another cup of coffee.'

'I'd like you to stay on, at least till I get settled. I'm not much on fridge management, or housework.' What Joe really meant was that he wanted Sylvie near as a presence; a rock in a sea of shifting sand. He needed something ordinary to hang onto while he tried to make sense of the folk-tale he'd been bounced into.

'That's all right. I'll come in mornings, do you a breakfast and something for dinner...I 'ave to go home lunchtimes for my daughter's kids, won't be back in the afternoons...I cleans the school as well and I can't do Saturdays or Sundays, I 'ave shopping and the kids as often as not, my daughter likes to get out with her bloke...she ain't exactly married, as good as. Times change don't they? Couldn't have got away with it in my day.'

'Yes,' said Joe, finishing his coffee.

'Lot of London people here now, new money, not that there's anything wrong with new money...I'd like a pile of it. I'll keep my eye on the washing and ironing and the sheets and pillow-cases...you won't 'ave to worry about a thing.'

Joe stood and put the dirty dishes in the sink.

'Oh, leave them,' said Sylvie. 'Why don't you 'ave a stroll round the village?'

Joe nodded. He was still feeling bemused, as if he were the butt of an elaborate practical joke. He was convinced that at any moment two warders would arrive and take him back to Wandsworth Prison as being in need of serious psychiatric treatment.

'Ain't much to see,' went on Sylvie. 'The shop, the church...few thatched cottages. It's nice down by the river this time of the year. The nearest village is Haseley Magna, in one direction, then Wheatley and Cuddesdon in the other.'

'Sounds good,' said Joe.

'I'll be gone by the time you get back probably. I shan't bother to lock up, 'tain't London here, is it? I've left you a nice shepherd's pie for tonight, all you 'ave to do is stick it in the oven, for half an hour at regulo six...so I'll see you tomorrow...oh, yes, I'm paid Fridays.'

*　*　*

Joe left the kitchen, crossed the hallway, which was bright with wide beams of sunlight, and stepped through the front door. Outside the sun was warm and the air sparkled, a different element to the London sludge his lungs had made do with for most of his life, a sluggish gas that had turned his blood grey over the years.

In front of the house, separated from it by a narrow path, lay the garden. It was long and wide, maybe fifty yards by seventy. It had been well designed, high shrubs and ordered flower beds broke up the squareness of it. To the left there was an apple tree and a plum, espaliered against the remains of a stone wall that must once have been the gable end of a farm building.

The garden ended in a low hedge, with a gap in it that led to a pasture that sloped steeply downwards to what looked like a stream; beyond that the land rose. It was a magnificent view, a view that could not have changed much in two hundred years; not dramatic, but gentle with rounded oaks and small old-fashioned fields with rough hedges dividing them, rising softly to a skyline which was defined by a large copse of tall trees, dark against white clouds. There was a road visible and a fingerpost where the road divided.

Joe stepped across the path and entered the garden. He followed a paved walk that wound between bushes and brought him to an arbour made from green trellises. In the arbour was a hardwood bench, placed to command a prospect of the whole valley. The beauty of the place invaded Joe's heart in a second; it was a lovely spot, worth travelling a lifetime to find. Beyond the hedge that marked the limit of his property and where the field fell away most sharply, Joe could just see the red tiled roof of another house, smaller than his. Joe twisted his head and glanced upwards; his house had red tiles too. There was no other building in sight and the silence was total, apart from the blackbird that sang the blues.

The garden had been lovingly cared for. It was trim and tasteful, but the unknown gardener had left just a hint of carelessness around its edges and in its hidden corners. The effect of it on Joe was extraordinary, as if the beauty of the place was attempting to compensate for his imprisonment; but these feelings only added to his sense of confusion. Again he asked himself the same question: 'What was going on?'

He entered the arbour and sat on the bench. Half concealed in the nearest shrubbery he saw the small statue of a naked woman, sitting with her legs under her, the stance of the mermaid of Copenhagen. She was green with lichen, her smile was mysterious, the breasts perfect, her hair tied up and behind her head.

'Hello, Mildred,' Joe said, and laughed. Why Mildred? He didn't know. He laughed again. Those breasts reminded him again how much he desired a woman. Then he realized for certain that he wasn't lost in a dream, for the one thing that had been missing from the bedroom of his new house was the eighteen year old nymphomaniac, purring patiently for him between the sheets; that indeed would have proved the house unreal and likely to disappear at any moment. No, Pegswell Cottage was real all right, but he was none the less a castaway for all that, and the next bit of terra firma lay a hemisphere away, and over the horizon.

Joe looked at the statue. He had ten grand in his bank account, a house to live in, and one thing was beyond doubt: there was no need to hurry back to the film business, not even if he wanted to. He tried to arrange his thoughts into some kind of order but always came back to the same question. Why was he here? The Bishop had the answer, he knew what was going on, he exuded knowledge and cunning, you could see it seeping out of his pores. He had said for Joe to go and see him, well Joe would, maybe he could get some answers. 'So there you are, Mildred,' he said. 'That's if you don't mind me calling you Mildred...'

'It's not a bad name,' said a voice, and a shadow fell across Joe's face. A man was standing about a yard from him, just outside the arbour. He must have come up the path from the house below. He held his hand out. 'I'm next door,' he said, 'Jack Barrington.'

Joe took the hand and shook it. It was a firm hand, dry, the skin rough. It would be like a club when it tightened into a fist. The rest of the man was big too, tall, broad shouldered, with a rounded stomach on him, wide thighs. He looked about sixty years old; a large face, grey eyes, and hair that had been black once but was now the colour of iron filings, cut short and thick. He looked like someone who had seen a lot of life but could still laugh about what he had seen, and was eager to. He was dressed in a check shirt, with the sleeves rolled back above the elbow to reveal powerful and hairy arms; a pair of yellow corduroy trousers; green hand-knitted socks and an old pair of walking boots that were too comfortable to throw away. His smile was a good one with some sadness in it.

Joe shoved up on the bench and indicated that Barrington should sit down.

'Welcome to Magna,' he said as he sat, 'as distinct from Parva. Milton Parva's a couple of miles away, there's Haseley Magna and Haseley Parva, big and small. Its confusing but you'll get used to it. I live down there.' Barrington waved a hand in the direction of his cottage. 'I see you've snaffled Sylvie Cornish as your housekeeper. You're lucky, best cook in the village...best housekeeper too.'

'Yes,' said Joe, 'she kind of came with the house.'

'Friends in high places,' said Barrington. 'I was after her for months...after my wife died.'

'I'm sorry,' said Joe.

'Two years ago now...so how did you come to pick on Milton?' Barrington's style of questioning was sharp, almost abrasive. It reminded Joe of the way policemen went about it.

'A friend of mine suggested it,' he answered. He didn't know what else to say.

'Bloody expensive, houses here, value never stops going up.' Barrington gave Joe a look which meant he was wondering where Joe had got his money, and how much he might have left. 'I bought mine years ago, before prices went mad. Been abroad?'

'Kind of.'

'Pale though, aren't you? You could do with some fresh air. Nice walks here. I used to be in the Thames Valley Police, Detective Inspector, nothing but fresh air, retired now.'

'The police.' Joe felt the quiver in his voice. His instinct had been right. Just his luck, a bloody copper.

'I'm on the Parish Council,' went on Barrington. 'We deal with planning extensions...you planning anything like that?'

'Not at all,' said Joe. 'This house is more than big enough for me.'

'Married?'

'Not any more.'

Half a smile drifted across Barrington's face. 'Two bachelors, then. We'll be company for each other, keep each other on the straight and narrow.' He gave Joe a Detective Inspector look and took a breath. Joe was positive that it was the first breath he'd seen the man take. Perhaps inspectors didn't breathe like ordinary men.

'Long time without women changes a man,' said Barrington with another of his sagacious looks. Suddenly Joe understood. Barrington didn't need a lie-detector. Ex-copper, still with friends on the force, access to the computer. Barrington knew. Joe nodded. It was his turn to take a breath.

'I've been away,' he tried. 'Three years.'

Barrington nodded his large head, 'I've spent my life with people who've been inside, they get a look about them. Nothing personal, yours will wear off.' Barrington stretched his legs and oddly, unexpectedly, his face broke into a warm smile, all irony absent. 'Wandsworth ain't easy, I know, I've sent enough there, and you're not likely to start stealing money from the church poor-box, are you?' And with these words he stretched out his hand to be shaken again, as if concluding a deal.

Joe shook the hand, felt the rough skin once more and noticed the fingernails, square like shovels. 'I'd prefer if this was kept between us,' said Joe, but thought at the same time; 'Well the Bishop knows, how reticent is he?'

Barrington laughed, and Joe was surprised to hear it so jolly. 'Ha, I shan't be publishing it in the Parish Bulletin...must get you a copy though, bring you up to date on what's going on...village outings, whist drives, planning applications...there's a couple of builders we have to keep our eyes on. And there's the council meeting once a month, very lively...you've dropped into a political maelstrom here in Milton.'

Joe shifted his gaze and looked at the view. 'God,' he thought, 'how long will I be able to stand Milton Magna: whist drives, council meetings...bet there's yoga in the village hall...I'll be bored out of my mind in this backwater.'

'But there's something much bigger than that going on.' Barrington's smile had vanished and his expression had become serious again. 'You could give me a hand perhaps.'

'Well, yes,' said Joe.

'It's all in the Bulletin, there's been hundreds of letters. The dog-owners of these four villages have been up in arms about it, people are very angry, furious...the Parish Council can't find an answer, they're out of their depth...the Vicar's useless...he's only worried because he's got a bloody Yorkshire Terrier, a horrible little rodent that yaps, called Pudding. You see...a person or persons unknown have been shooting dogs.'

'Shooting dogs?'

'Shooting dogs, dead.'

'Would you like a cup of coffee?'

'Not just now, have to be off to Thame. You have one if you want.'

'Shooting dogs?'

'An assassin, or assassins, here in Milton Magna, and in the Haseleys, have been shooting dogs...a crack shot too, either right through the head or right through the heart....Now I may be retired but I want to get to the bottom of it, I'm a problem solver you see, always have been, and this is a mystery that has really got under my skin because I can't solve it, I have to admit that it's got me obsessed...it's been going on for months...I keep my eyes open but I'm on my own...I thought you could give me a hand maybe.'

'Well, maybe,' said Joe. 'It certainly beats whist drives.'

Barrington agreed, nodding. 'It's not that I'm mad about dogs, you understand, or want to save them from an early death, or cats for that matter. In fact I have some sympathy with those people who steal cats to make 'em into fur coats...and dogs do crap everywhere. Have you got a dog?'

'No,' said Joe, 'but if I had one I'd have it put down right away, just to keep out of trouble.' He looked away at the view again. In twelve hours his life had become something he didn't recognise. The previous morning at this time he'd been in his prison cell, trying to make plans, trying to envisage, once he was on the outside, what he would do and where he would go.

But his wildest imaginings could not have transported him to a garden in Oxfordshire where he would listen to an ex-copper discussing how to track down a dog assassin. How crazy was that? One day consorting with murderers and embezzlers, the next talking about the vicar and his Yorkshire Terrier. What would Danny the Dope and Bert Bulldozer have made of this change in his fortunes had they heard of it?

'You know when I was in the job,' Barrington's voice became proud when he talked of his time as a policeman, 'I wrote a paper on dogs.'

'A paper?'

'Yes, a report...we wanted the RSPCA to come into the county and round up the strays...they didn't of course. There's six million dogs in Britain and one person in nine is a dog owner, that means there's at least a hundred dogs in Milton Magna...a hundred.'

'That's a lot of crap,' said Joe.

'Crap! In this country a million gallons of dog pee is squirted out every single day, a torrent of pee. God knows how many tons of shit get squeezed out, and dogs are responsible for twenty per cent of road accidents, they kill more people than terrorists.'

'Okay, so you don't like dogs. Seems to me you could be the assassin? You've got the motive, and the occasion, you've probably got a gun too.'

'I'm not mad about them, but I wouldn't go around shooting them. Anyway, it's not the fact of the assassinations that gets my goat...it's the mystery, I want to find out who is doing it and why, and I want to collar him. It's the detective in me.'

'Fascinating stuff,' said Joe. 'Any ideas?'

'I'm sure it's a villager. There's no doubt in my mind.'

'You can't be sure though, what about someone coming in off the motorway?'

'Motorway! Can you imagine someone coming down from London, Birmingham, flying in from Luton or Heathrow...just to kill a few dogs...besides, it's not happening anywhere else, I've been on the computer...just the Miltons and the Haseleys.' Barrington leant forward, his face animated. 'It's a local killer all right...I want to crack this, really want to crack it.'

'How are you going to do it?' asked Joe. 'It won't be easy.'

'I'll need luck. I've made a map of the area, and I've got flags on the map...it's indoors, I'll show you when you come round. I've got red flags for them that have been shot, about forty so far, and white flags for those that are still alive. There's no rhyme or reason to it. It'll be a waiting game, all right. That assassin skulks over fences and walls, back gardens and bridle paths...sees a dog, and pop.'

'Any clues?'

'It happens at night, mainly; dusk and dawn as well. People let their dogs out for a last minute pee and that's when he strikes. He's got to be local, because he knows where to be and at what time.'

'Could be a woman, of course.'

Barrington tapped the side of his nose with one of his large fingers. He knew. 'This has got bloke written all over it. Some people let their dogs run free, and they've been shot at night. Only one shot in the day, Haseley Magna, old Mrs Downer. Had her dog on the lead. There she was, trotting along, dog behind, suddenly a dead weight where her dog should have been. She's suddenly dragging a corpse by the neck.'

Joe laughed. Barrington turned his head to look at Joe, his expression stern at first. Then he too laughed.

'Poor old cow. He must have shot the dog through a hedge, round a wall. It's a .22 calibre rifle with a silencer. It's powerful enough to kill a human being easily...it's an assassin's weapon all right.'

'Daylight, eh?'

'He's getting more daring, like killers do. But as it's only dogs no one can be bothered except me. I got onto the RSPCA, they think I'm a loony. I had a police surgeon do a couple of autopsies and I've got the bullets. All I need to do is find the rifle.'

'You'd like me to help?'

'Just a bit, you know. It's a bit lonely sometimes. We could stroll around at night, have a few beers, one in the Bull here, one in the Plough at Haseley, the Lamb at Milton Parva. As I said, it's a question of luck. We might stumble on something. If not, well there's no harm done. What do you say?'

'I'm not too sure of my plans yet,' said Joe. 'I may be moving on. Maybe.'

'Oh, you can't do that, you've only just got here. You'll come to love it. It's a special bit of old England here, small, quiet, genteel...'

'Except for the assassin.'

'Okay, except for the assassin...but the people here are good sorts. I guarantee that if you stay a month or two you'll be hooked. Go to the shop for a loaf of bread and you're chatting for hours...I tell you, you won't want to move on.'

'Are you the only one, looking for the assassin I mean?'

'Well, yes. You see I'd look a bit of a fool if I asked someone to help me and by chance it transpired that I'd asked the villain...but I know you aren't the culprit, you've only just got...'

'Back from India.'

'Back from India. And the killings have been happening for some months. There's something odd going on at night in this village, I can feel it. Movement in the dark...I'm not scared, but it would be good to have a bit of company when I'm out, just in case there is a bit of trouble.'

'Okay,' said Joe. 'Nothing regular...an evening or two. I like my sleep.'

'It'll be a pub-crawl with meaning,' said Barrington. He looked pleased, his expression lightened and became jolly. He placed his hands on his knees and pushed himself upright with a gentle groan. 'Gravity's getting stronger,' he said. 'It's been nice to meet you...India, eh?'

'India,' said Joe, and he stood as well.

'Anything you need,' went on Barrington, 'just knock on my door.' He strode back to the path, his feet a policeman's, his gait heavy. He passed in front of Joe's house and was about to turn the corner when he stopped and called back. 'Ah yes, there's garages for the two properties at the back. You may not have seen them last night.' And then he was gone.

Joe sat on his bench again; he looked at the view and then at the garden statue.

'Mildred. You are having me on,' he said eventually. 'A dog assassin! Someone's taking the mickey out of me...Tell you what though, you stop this madness and I'll stop trying to understand what's happening to me. I'll let things go by me for a week or two, and do nothing...I won't even think...and as for you, keep your eyes open. That's your part of the bargain.'

*   *   *

At the rear of Pegswell Cottage there was a rough gravelled track leading down the slope of the hill. To the right of it was an open space of grass, and beyond that a row of village houses stood side by side on the edge of the Wheatley Road. At the end of the track stood a small barn that had been converted into two garages and the name Pegswell Cottage had been painted on the right hand one of the two.

Joe grasped the handle of the up and over door, pulled at it and the door rose and disappeared into the garage roof space, and an overhead light came on automatically. The car before him was the latest model Saab in metallic blue, with a custom built body. Joe peered through the windscreen and saw pale blue leather seats; he had never been able to afford a car of such quality. Whoever had chosen it had gone for something top of the range but devoid of vulgarity; it had discretion, speed, strength and comfort. On the bonnet lay an envelope. Joe opened it and found the log book made out in his name. The car was brand new, the keys were in the ignition. Joe felt like a man with Dengue fever, dizzy and weak with it, only half in control of his mind.

For a moment he thought of taking the Saab out on the motorway, driving it as fast as it would go, but he immediately decided against such a plan. Three long years had gone by since he'd killed Sunshine's kids, but when it came to it he wasn't ready to start driving again. He'd thought about it every day in Wandsworth; it hadn't helped, even now he needed more time, more distance.

Joe closed the garage door; he knew that he was going to

renege on what he'd said to Mildred, he was incapable of sitting back and doing nothing. He would have to find the Bishop and ask questions. If he didn't get an explanation of what was happening in Milton Magna he'd go mad.

* * *

Cuddesdon Seminary was only a couple of miles away Sylvie told him when he went back to the house.

'It's too nice to drive, it's such a lovely walk, Cuddesdon, turn right at the top here, and after the last big house on the right, that's Chiltern Hall, you'll take the footpath, you'll see, it drops down the field, across the brook. 'Aven't been down there since I was courting. There's an old railway sleeper makes the bridge, then up the other side and you come out on the Cuddesdon road, there's an old cowshed. You follows that down to the river, then up to the top, there's a footpath if you prefer. There's plenty in the fridge for lunch, nice brown bread from Thame, the shop delivers it.'

Outside there were few people to be seen: a man and a woman standing outside the post office; a few cars parked; the entrance to the primary school; an old red phone box, and a line of houses scattered along the street. What added to the attractiveness of Milton Magna were the wide stretches of lawn that lay between the houses and the road. The village was quiet, with hardly any movement at all. Occasionally a car went by, faces staring through the windscreen.

In the centre of the village was a large triangular area, the village green itself. A bench had been set there and two or three trees planted to give shade; on the bench a brass plate announced that it was dedicated to the memory of Bernard Cross – "gardener and raconteur." Here the ancient dwellings had survived and gave the village its distinction, flat fronted and thatched most of them – picture postcard cottages. There were also a few Victorian buildings roofed in old peg-tiles. The 1930s semi-detached houses began a couple of hundred yards further on. To one side was the village pub, The Bull, with tables outside. No one was sitting at them, it was too early for lunch. As he passed the pub Joe saw the smudge of a face or two moving in the low, green paned windows. Then someone came to the door and leant against the side of it for a better look at him. A blonde woman in tight jeans and a pink blouse. She smiled at Joe, all-knowing and smug like a slumberous cat, as if he were the least of all the men she had ever known, and then went back inside.

After the pub the road dropped steeply and narrowed, with a high path on the left side, and up on a bank there were more thatched cottages, a whole row of them. On Joe's right there was a high stone wall, the wall of an estate, or a large house. Joe went on and passed a pair of tall wooden gates, a stone column on each side. There was a wrought iron nameplate fixed to the gates: Chiltern Hall. A sensor set into the wall told Joe that the gates were electrically operated.

Opposite, on the other side of the road Joe could see a large square house, also behind its wall; a postern leading into it. As he looked the door opened and a women with grey hair and wearing tweeds came out of it, shutting the door behind her. She carried a trug. That house had a name too: The Old Rectory. The woman smiled at Joe. 'Good morning,' she said. 'Good morning,' answered Joe. It was all very stately. She went away in the direction of the village green.

Then the high wall which Joe was following turned at right angles to the road and there was the footpath that Sylvie had mentioned, the surface of it dry earth and crumbling into dust. A white painted fingerpost pointed the way; Cuddesdon 2, it said.

'That'll be fine,' said Joe out loud, 'two miles is just about right, and I need the exercise.'

The footpath followed the boundary of The Chiltern Hall estate, hugging it closely. To Joe's left the fields fell away behind houses that formed the outskirts of the village. As Joe advanced he entered the pastures that led up to the Cuddesdon road. In them was a herd of black cattle: Aberdeen Angus.

Eventually the boundary wall turned at a right angle. The estate it encircled was obviously a large one, maybe two hundred acres, but the path continued straight ahead, and painted on the mown field that Joe had come into was a large letter H in white. These people arrived by helicopter.

Now the path swept sharply down the field, the thick grass dotted with cow pats, both soft and hard, then it rose gently over about a half a mile, towards a hedge that grew along the side of the Cuddesdon road. Joe turned and looked behind him. He could see the village in its entirety, its houses built along the top of the low rise that he had just descended, the roofs red with old tiles, aflame in the sunlight. The near side of the dwellings spilled down towards him, giving a view of gardens and allotments, separated by untidy fences, the larger boundaries marked by trees; limes and willows and some tall chestnuts. It was a hushed and soothing landscape, a gentle fold in the surface of the planet. The birds sang and there was no sound of traffic. Overhead a red kite drifted on a thermal, sometimes still, resting on the air, searching for a carcass, and the thought made Joe remember Sunshine Leary. He waved a warning arm at the kite but all it did was circle lower.

At last, at the edge of the field, he came to a stile, climbed it and found himself on tarmac, a single track road. Opposite him was an old cowshed, another road and another signpost bearing the legend, Cuddesdon 1.

The Cuddesdon road ran steeply down to the River Thame. The countryside was much as before, rolling fields made small and picturesque by rich hedges, and at the river two bridges, the second crossing the mill race which ran like a torrent by the side of a square mill and its mill house. The water foamed through the remains of a narrow sluice and swirled into a large pool where it slowed and quietened.

By the first of the bridges were two more finger posts, both pointing to Cuddesdon, one by the road, one by a stile. Joe climbed the stile and followed a path that led along the river bank, heading upstream. Here the current was slow and sluggish, the willows luxuriant, the grass rich, the hedges even more ancient, and the sky was blue, high and empty, too remote to worry about Joe Rapps. Black and white cows raised their heads as he went by. Joe began to understand the remark that Barrington had made: 'Stay here a month or two and you'll never want to live anywhere else.'

The river swung round in a huge sweep of a bow bend and Joe followed it, across a pasture and through a five-barred gate and then another field. He came then to a perfect spot, secluded, a flat area of grass with three willows giving shade. This was where the river split into two, one arm being the main stream, the other going on to feed the mill race. A hundred years previously there would have been huge floodgates here, now all that remained were massive blocks of stone that had been washed down from the banks where they had once supported the sluices. The waters surged over these blocks and foamed white, before slowing down and forming a wide, shallow pool where the waters went from silver to green. It was just the place for young men to bring their girls; afternoon picnics, tartan rugs, cooled wine, slow conversation and long caresses. Joe's long incarceration without a woman had turned him into a romantic.

*   *   *

She came out of the shadows on the far side of the pool, where a willow bent low over the surface of the water, and there was a crowd of rushes. She was not abashed by Joe's arrival. She swam well, the American crawl, her head down, hardly disturbing the water, her movements graceful and economical. Her body, long and slightly tanned, was naked. A few strokes brought her into the shallows, she lifted her head and smiled. 'Nice day,' she said, and stood. She came forward a pace or two and picked up her towel which lay on the grass and began to dry herself, unhurriedly and making no attempt at modesty.

Part of Joe wanted to avert his eyes, but not much of him. His throat dried. There ought to be a law against women being this provocative, especially when the victim had been locked away for three years. The girl advanced up the bank, coming closer to him, stroking the towel rather than using it to rub her body. Joe thought her beautiful. He stared and knew that the expression on his face was one of total stupidity, but could do nothing to

43

alter it. She looked about twenty five or six, but might have been thirty. There was no ring on her third finger – the towel slipped to the ground – and no stretch marks on her stomach. She stood naked again. Her breasts and thighs were perfect.

'Don't worry,' she said, laughing at him. 'I was brought up a naturist.'

'Well I wasn't,' said Joe, 'though I think you might have just converted me.'

The woman recovered the towel and made it into a sarong, tying it above her breasts, then took another and began drying her hair with it, shaking her head now and then so it caught the sun, just as Joe knew it would, even waiting for her to do it. The hair was darkened by the waters of the River Thame, the colour indeterminate.

'You've just moved in, haven't you? Pegswell Cottage, Mr Joseph Rapps? Lovely house...the whole village has been agog. Been in India haven't you? You don't look very tanned.'

'Was working in studios most of the time, filming...too hot to sunbathe...how come you know all that about me?'

'I saw Jack Barrington on the way down here. Anyway, no secrets in a village, you know!'

'You live in the village then?'

'I only came last October, I'm doing a D.Phil at Oxford, St Catherine's. There's a row of cottages opposite the end of Pegswell Lane, I rent the end one, Pope's Cottage...so we're neighbours, mind you, everyone in Milton Magna's a neighbour really.'

'I suppose so,' said Joe, still unable to take his eyes from the girl. She found her skirt and pulled it up under the towel and let the towel down, revealing her breasts again. Then she pulled on a light sweater. She pushed her feet into white sneakers and went back to rubbing her hair.

'I'm Erica Sands-Lindsay,' she said, 'you'll have to come over for a drink, when you're settled.'

'Oh,' said Joe, 'I'm so settled I don't think I'll ever move again, and I could do with a drink.' He forced his gaze away from the shifting bosom beneath the sweater as she shook her hair and decided it was time to look at the girl's face. He liked it, he couldn't see the colour of her eyes, he was too far away from her, but they were large, under a broad brow. The face was informed by a bright intelligence, and she smiled easily.

'What's the thesis?'

'Women and Sex in Chaucer.'

Her hair, now that it was drying in the morning sun was taking on a lighter colour, a kind of strawberry blond. She bent and picked up her underwear and wrapped it in one of the towels. She stood and moved closer to him. The eyes were hazel.

'I only know the Miller's Tale. Exams.'

'Men only know the Miller's Tale.'

Her cheekbones were wide and after her swim there was no make-up. She didn't need make-up. The neck of the sweater was wide and hung off one shoulder; her collar bones were fragile. Joe loved collar bones, it was the fragility that attracted him – the ephemeral nature of the human body.

'No, we had to do the Prologue as well...'Whan that Aprille with his shoures soote...'"

Erica laughed and showed her teeth, slightly prominent. Joe liked that too. She shoved her possessions into a small rucksack.

'This is a brilliant place for a picnic,' said Joe.

'It is,' she said, pausing to look around her, then back at Joe. 'You'll like the village. I love it already, friendly...a special place...makes you adore England. I'll invite some people round so you can get to know them. They'll be dying to meet you, you're a mystery man. What did you film in India?'

'Documentaries, and I did some teaching in a film school. Delhi, media studies and stuff.'

She nodded and swung the rucksack onto her shoulder. 'You could meet a few people tomorrow evening if you like, we're talking about doing a play for November.'

'Bloody hell, it's only May.'

'It'll take that long, doing 'As You Like It' with amateurs.'

'They made us read 'Hamlet' at school.'

'I think I prefer the comedies, especially 'As You Like It'. It's characters in a landscape, you know, Forest of Arden and all that, like here really, fields and forests, not that far from

Warwickshire, are we?' She gestured across the river to where the trees grew close together and rose to the Cuddesdon road. 'Dukes and rustics, lovers in disguise, girls dressed as boys, all running around in the woods. We might find you a part. The Old Priory, eight o'clock.'

'No thanks, I don't do acting.'

'Come along anyway, you'll meet Oona Trowbridge.' She half turned, ready to leave. 'And if you don't I'll see you sometime, in the village.'

'Yes,' answered Joe. He was tempted to go back to Milton with her, but the Bishop came first. He was, after all, the only one who could tell Joe why he was here.

He watched Erica walk away, already knowing that the walk would be content as well as form – the buttock beautiful. It was. 'Oh, God,' he said. 'I'm in love again.'

* * *

The Cuddesdon path came out in the middle of the village, passing through a scattering of council houses on the Wheatley road. Joe was standing opposite the seminary, a Victorian gothic edifice constructed in a yellow brick made ethereal by the sunlight. It was adorned with turrets and pretend mullioned windows, a smaller version of St Pancras station. Joe crossed the road, passed through a gateway and came into a gravelled courtyard. It was a confusing building, there were doors everywhere, like the quadrangle of an Oxford college, and there were passageways leading to smaller courtyards. A few students were standing outside one of the doorways; a few more sat on benches; they wore dark clothes, black skirts on the women.

Joe crossed the yard. 'I'm looking for the Bishop,' he said. These youngsters made him feel old. He felt awkward with them; he presumed they all believed in God.

'Bishop,' said one of the young men. 'We have quite a lot of Bishops, we do Bishops. Haven't got a collective noun for them though...a hosanna of Bishops, perhaps.'

Now Joe felt stupid. The Bishop had told him his diocese. 'Aylesbury,' he said.

'Ah yes,' said the young man and there were smiles all round, as if the ex-Bishop of Aylesbury was particularly bizarre. He pointed to one of the gothic archways. 'Aylesbury. Up that staircase and on the first floor you'll find his rooms, there's a card on the door.'

Joe mounted the stone staircase and knocked. The Bishop's voice came immediately. 'Come in,' it said.

The Bishop beamed from behind his desk. 'I thought I might see you,' he said. 'Sit down, Mr Rapps, sit down. I've got some coffee on the go. Did you walk up? Lovely isn't it, the walk, and such a lovely day again.'

Joe felt a sensation of ease flood through him. It was like meeting an old friend after a long separation. They had spent little more than an hour in each other's company the previous evening, but it seemed as if they had known each other for years.

'I'm so pleased to see you, Bishop. It's like old times.'

The Bishop laughed out loud at that, got to his feet and made for the glass coffee jug which was kept on a hot plate in the corner of the room. The sun streamed through the lead lights of the window and on to the Bishop's black suit, the sheen of it green with age, shiny with use. Joe hadn't paid much attention to the Bishop's appearance the night before, in the back of the stretch. He'd been too bewildered. Now as the clergyman stood he could see the whole of him.

He was not tall, his torso was short, fat and wide. The stomach, covered in purple, was well fed and well wined, firm, hard as concrete. The shoulders were muscular, the face square, the expression one of contentment, and the skin was red where the veins were not indigo. The Bishop's eyes were pale blue, but none the less impertinent for that. His silver hair curled extravagantly over his ears, and over his collar. He was like a painting of a romantic poet; he was Keats had he survived into late middle age.

The Bishop returned to his swivel chair. 'And how have you settled in? Lovely little house, isn't it? You'll love Milton, you know. Everyone does, you'll never want to leave.'

Joe took his cup. It smelt delicious; the Bishop knew his

coffee.

'Well,' said Joe, 'I like what I've seen, it's special, certainly, but that's not the point. It's more important to me to know what's going on, and you're the only person who knows why I'm here. I mean, someone sent you to get me, bring me here...what's that about? Why you?'

'Oh no particular reason, mainly because I look reassuring, clergyman and all that, and I'm bribable.'

'Look, Bishop...I've been given a house, the deeds to it, and wardrobes and cupboards full of expensive clothes...even a housekeeper. Things like this don't happen.'

'Ah,' said the Bishop, 'I should not question your good luck too closely as yet. We are all trying to find the back door to paradise, each and every one of us, and you have found yours, so it would seem. A housekeeper too...Mrs Cornish, ah, the lovely Mrs Cornish, and the clothes, a good fit, I trust.' He put his fingertips together and beamed like an uncle at Christmas. 'Good quality, I know they are.'

'You see, you know. I've never had such stuff. That house must be worth a fortune...and there's even a car.'

'Ah, of course. Have you driven it yet? Nought to sixty in the blink of an eye. What a world we live in.'

Joe shook his head in puzzlement. He knew the Bishop was playing with him. 'Oh come on, Bishop. What's happening? Who's doing all this, more importantly, why? I know I'm not a beneficiary of the Church for leading a blameless life.'

This remark truly amused the Bishop and he laughed again, loudly. When the laugh was finished his expression became serious. He sipped his coffee. 'I would like to discuss all these matters, Mr Rapps, but I am precluded by a promise; you wouldn't expect a Bishop of the church to go back on his word now, would you?. I will tell you one thing, you must attend a meeting at the Methodist Chapel this evening at eight o'clock, it's near the old school. You can't miss it, big solid walls, brick corners, tiny slits for windows, impregnable really. Odd little place, nowhere near as attractive as the church, which is in Pevsner, you know. Eight o'clock, on the dot and you will learn all you need to know. All will become clear, and then tomorrow we may talk to our hearts' content...'

The Bishop rose, took Joe's cup, and his own, and refilled them from the pot on the hob. 'But I'll talk about anything else. I can talk for England. You look confused...Mr Rapps, don't be. I have discovered, after a long life, that the world doesn't become easier to understand as we go on, but more difficult, and indeed, crueller, and we have to accept it. We amble through life, we make wonderful friends, then they have the temerity to die off and, gradually, one by one, they leave us to live the rest of our lives alone. Most of those I went to college with are dead or have sailed off to the other side of the world. The world is full of sadness and pain, all we can do is grasp little moments of happiness here and there, waiting our turn.'

Joe leant back in his chair. The Bishop had no intention of telling him why he had been brought here; he might just as well listen.

'God is cruel, the world he has made is cruel. Here we are, planted down amongst all the beauties of life; the use of words, poetry, history, walks by the river, love, the near physical joy of learning, travel...and above all, those friends I mentioned. Then along comes the Almighty and clears the table with one sweep of his arm, takes it all away and we die in pain and loneliness. It's all very well to call it a "mauvais quart d'heure", but what a quarter of an hour, and what comes after...nothing?'

'Quarter of an hour?' said Joe.

'A bad quarter of an hour to get through, Voltaire.'

'You know, you don't sound like a Bishop at all.'

'My dear boy, I'm a retired Bishop. I teach the history of Christianity, I don't ask my students to believe it, but they've got to earn a living, like the rest of us, and earning a living in the Church can be very agreeable.'

'You can't retire from religion, can you?'

'Of course you can, Mr Rapps. I have. I long ago discovered that people take religion far too seriously. They have forgotten all those old fashioned liberal values we used to admire and live by, those humanitarian attitudes that used to sit so lightly upon us. Nowadays there are fundamentalists coming out of the woodwork, making life unbearable...how I long to hear the tumbrels rolling over the cobbles, coming to take them to the guillotine...I tell you, I would be sitting in the front row with my knitting. But the tumbrels will not roll, liberalism has been scared back into its cave by this evil. Christian fundamentalism, emanating from America, has given rise to Muslim fundamentalism, or was it the reverse? And liberalism, the one true faith, will be squashed between them. If we want to get back to those values we will have to fight for them. What you see in the world around you, Mr Rapps, is belief taking the place of thought, and reason being replaced by revelation.'

'You're not really a Christian, are you?'

The Bishop sighed and smiled as he looked back down the years. 'That is true.' He leant forward in his chair. 'And what is more I feel it my duty to criticize all religion, but these days criticism of religion is seen as blasphemy, or Islamophobia or anti-Semitism, and that leads to violence and fatwas. That is truly sad, because religion makes us less human, not more. Nothing wrong with honest blasphemy.'

'But those who believe get so violent.'

'Indeed; they have forgotten their humanity. Theocracy must be resisted to the limit by anyone who cares for democracy, but it's not easy, things are getting out of control. Have you never thought how strange it is that America created a secular state in which self-evident rights would be fought for...and yet that part of the American dream is now being destroyed by bigotry.'

'No, I can't say that I have.'

'Well, you should. It's frightening. The devout are so certain of their salvation: Catholics, Protestants, Muslims, Jews, there's not a shred of good honest doubt amongst them. They bring their children up in certainty, and what kind of education is that? And because they have no doubts we are not allowed to express ours...and doubt is what makes us human. Religion is a poison in politics.'

'Do you believe in God, Bishop?'

'Oh that's irrelevant, really. It's how we live that counts...love, common sense and uncertainty, and the greatest of these is uncertainty. The devout keep up their spirits with a fable of the permanent...that way they don't have to remind themselves that their little lives can be disposed of by death. Our task is more difficult, we are the lantern bearers, bringers of light, but the light is threatened by dogmatism, a disease that would kill us all.'

'But what about the people who run this college? They can't be happy with the way you think.'

'Oh, they don't care as long as I don't preach it at the crossroads. Half of my students think like me anyway, if they think at all.'

'Well, I have no idea what to believe. It's a mad world and I keep quiet in it, stay out of trouble.'

The Bishop laughed, pushed against the arms of his chair and rose. 'Don't be dismayed, Mr Rapps, remember God works on us through the people we meet.' The Bishop laughed again. 'You will not be thinking religion this evening at the Methodist Chapel...Come, let me show you the garden, then you must leave, I have a lecture before lunch.'

Joe followed the Bishop out into the courtyard where the sun was still shining. He was dazzled after the darkness of the Bishop's study.

*   *   *

Joe walked back the way he had come though he could have gone round by the road, an easier walk. The swimming place was deserted: Erica Sands-Lindsay was long gone, but he stood by the flattened grass where she had sunbathed and thought about her body.

Coming into Milton Magna he stopped at the village green. Joe turned to take in the view and saw Barrington sitting at a bench table outside the Bull with another man. They beckoned him over. They were lunching, glasses and plates in front of them.

'This is the new fellow,' said Barrington as Joe sat. 'And this is Dr Vernon Minge, that's a doctor of philosophy, not a medic. Why don't you have lunch with us, the ploughman's decent here.' Barrington stood. 'What'll you drink? The beer's good, Adnams'.'

'I'll have a pint of it then, and that ploughman's. That'll be the first pint since I....'

'...came back from India,' said Barrington, refusing Joe's money as he offered it.

'I understand you've been away,' said Minge, when Barrington had gone. 'India, wasn't it?'

'Yes,' answered Joe. 'Going to take it a bit easy for a while, I had an exhausting job. And you?'

'I'm a fellow of St John's,' said Minge. 'French literature's my subject, mainly the seventeenth and eighteenth centuries. Were you at Oxford?'

'No, Southampton, Media Studies.'

'That must have been interesting.'

About forty-five years old, Vernon Minge was handsome in a delicate way, but not effeminate in the slightest. His hair was black, with touches of grey at the temples, swept back from his forehead and neatly parted in the middle; there was lots of it, and it was washed and blow-dried every day.

His nose was sharp, riding above a ripe plum-like mouth set in a square chin which had a dimple in the middle of it. He was clean shaven and smelt of eau de Cologne. Broad in the shoulders, he took care in the way he dressed; he was wearing a maroon jacket of felt, a handkerchief in the top pocket, and a pink shirt with the top two buttons casually open. Joe couldn't see the trousers but knew they would be snappy, the shoes too.

'You get nice long summer holidays then?'

'As a matter of fact I do summer schools every year, which means that I can avoid going on holiday with my wife and children. That also means I meet a remarkable cross section of American women who come over to study European literature and history...culture, you know. That means they can go back to the middle west and tell everybody they've studied at Oxford, England.'

'Isn't that boring, summer school, I mean?'

Minge released a knowing smile, relishing the slowness of it; it dripped with superiority. 'Not at all. They are unsophisticated young women and easily impressed. I tell them tales of the seventeenth century, Bussy-Rabutin, l'Abbé

Brantôme, L'affaire des Poisons, quite a lot of exciting stuff about. I have a good line on Crébillon, I'm writing a monograph on him. He wrote a thing called "Le Sofa". Minge clothed the words in his best French accent. 'It tells of the soul of a prince imprisoned in a sofa, a chaise longue, and he cannot break free until true love is consummated on its cushions, don't you know.' Minge had a way of saying 'don't you know' like it was a challenge, implying that his interlocutor's intelligence wasn't up to the task he'd set it.

'And guess what I've got in my study at St John's?' Minge winked.

'A chaise longue,' said Joe.

'Exactly, those American girls don't put up much of a struggle, it's all part of their European education.'

'I haven't done French since secondary school,' said Joe. 'I think I'm a bit out of my depth with all you Oxford types.'

Minge raised his glass. 'Well, we're all specialists, I don't know anything about media studies.'

Joe studied Minge as he drank. There was a fox-like look to his face when he moved it, giving him an air of energetic concupiscence. The eyes were tired intellectual eyes, but they shone for sex. He emptied his glass and replaced it on the table.

'I adore women,' he said, 'even though they never get life right: first it's the complexes of puberty, finding out who they are; then pre-menstrual tension, then they worry about not having babies, then they worry about having babies, then its the menopause...it's almost impossible to catch them on an even keel. Still I worship them, they are wonders of nature, and one can gain endless enjoyment from their bodies. I love those soft and soggy sexual organs. I have to get my hands on them before they disappear, they are too rich a gift to be endured almost. They are beautiful clipper ships sailing along, bearing cargoes of the greatest pleasures on earth, and I am a marauding pirate.'

A woman appeared at the pub door carrying a tray which bore three pints and Joe's ploughman's. She was followed by Barrington.

'Ah,' said Minge, 'you are flattered, it is not often that Beryl will bring your drink to the table...she's a bit red hat, no knickers, a good sort though.'

The little procession approached the table and Minge smiled benignly, the sweetest of philanthropists. 'Hello, Beryl,' he said as she placed the tray on the table. She used the time to stare at Joe, her lips pulled back in a strong smile. Her fingers were stained with nicotine and Joe could smell the cigarettes on her. She was truly ripe, like a pheasant hung for a week; her flesh had been forced into tight jeans, the skin of her cleavage was pure butter and her bosoms were escaping from her half open blouse. Her hair brushed her shoulders and was dyed an exhausted yellow, while the mouth was a smudge of pink. Too much alcohol had given her creases under the eyes that were the colour of crushed blackberries.

'Beryl's treated you,' said Barrington, 'to welcome you to Milton Magna.'

Joe was embarrassed. 'Well thanks, that's nice of you.'

'Don't worry, love,' said Beryl. Joe could hear the cigarette smoke and the after hours drinking in her voice. 'We all want you to feel welcome. We need some new men in this village,' she tilted her head at Barrington and Minge. 'This lot are worn out.' She grinned at Joe as if he were a fellow conspirator; then she turned and went back into the pub.

Joe raised his glass and sipped. It was good beer, well looked after.

Minge had been watching Joe. 'Careful,' he said. 'Beryl would pull you apart, like a capon at Christmas. She's too much for you, like going to bed with Mata Hari, Cleopatra and Catherine the Great at the same time. Didn't you get any in India?'

'Well, it was a bit difficult. I was up country a lot of the time.'

'Well you're up country here,' said Minge, smirking, 'but that won't be a problem. Try Norah, at the village shop. She's lively enough. Fellatio's her speciality. Better than the real thing.'

'Humph,' Barrington sipped at his beer. 'There's a school of thought that says fellatio is the real thing.'

'She's been seen in the lay-by at Haseley Parva, with the bus-driver.'

'The bus-driver?' Joe was intrigued.

'Yes. There are two buses a day in, and two buses a day out. They turn round at Haseley Parva, they stay there for half an hour...and so does Norah. He's a nice young Indian fellow.'

Joe cut into his large lump of cheddar cheese, and spread his bread thickly with butter and pickle. Barrington surveyed him closely, like a kind parent full of care, as if Joe, new in the village, was in need of protection. 'Don't worry,' he said. 'We'll find you something.'

'Well,' said Minge, 'a propos of the same subject, I haven't seen Helen for a week or so.'

'Helen?'

'The Norlands nanny from Harrison's Farm, Milton Parva, sweet little thing. I'd arranged to take her out to that new restaurant at Tetsworth...now she's suddenly disappeared. Very odd.'

'Nannies come, and nannies go,' said Barrington, 'you can rely on that, like death and taxes. They never stay anywhere for long, reckon they get touched up too often, they used to at Hazelmere Court, so the rumour went.'

Joe cut himself another chunk of cheese. 'Hazelmere Court?'

'Lord Hazelmere,' said Minge. 'He owns Hazelmere Court, and the estate of course, over at Haseley Magna. The place has been in the family for generations, a baronetcy, the ancestors built a railway or a canal. He's about eighty now, was a bright spark in the London gambling set, in the 'sixties and 'seventies, Mayfair.'

'There's a son too, married,' said Barrington. 'That's why they had a nanny, don't seem to have one now. Viscount Lewknor he is, doesn't have the Hazelmere look though.'

'Ah,' said Minge, 'but there's some bloody good gossip about him...one story has him as the illegitimate son of Philip...Buck House Philip.'

'Wait a minute,' said Barrington, 'that's only hearsay.'

'And there's another thing,' went on Minge. 'The Hazelmere nanny before the last, Christine, I took her for a picnic in the Chilterns, about a year ago...she told me that her room was always disturbed, her underwear drawer, things moved, things disappeared, her outdoor clothes too.'

'Was it the old man, or the son?' asked Barrington.

'Didn't she complain?' Joe wanted to know.

'Yes, of course she did, but Lewknor sat down and wrote her a fat cheque for whatever was missing. She thought it might have been the father, the way he looked at her, stared at her at meal times. Then she left too, never saw her again. Pity. She was gorgeous. Liked doing it in the open air.'

'We get lots of nannies,' said Barrington. 'Some at the Great House, some down at Cuddesdon Mill, and at Manor Farm, Milton Parva. All have had nannies at one time or another.'

'Lonely little things, nannies,' said Minge, and emptied his glass. Joe and Barrington did likewise and on cue Beryl came out of the pub carrying a tray with three more full glasses on it.

'This'll have to be the last,' said Minge. 'I've got to be in college this afternoon.'

'Beats working I suppose,' said Beryl. As heavy as portcullises she lowered her false eyelashes at Joe, delivered the beer, and went back into the pub.

'So the nannies get lonely?'

'Well, yes. They have pretty long days, looking after those upper class brats. Tired and lonely. I do my best for them of course, tell them about Crébillon, take them to the opera in Oxford, a good restaurant or two. I was getting on well with Helen, now she's disappeared. Saw the Viscount yesterday, walking his dog, that Borzoi. I felt like asking if he was still into ladies' underwear, then I thought better of it.'

'He's still got his dog then,' said Barrington, 'I wonder who will be next. There'll be another dog shot soon, I'll be bound.'

'I couldn't care less,' said Minge. 'Not very doggy myself. In fact I dislike 'em.'

'I've got you on my list of suspects,' said Barrington, an edge creeping into his voice. 'Whoever it is I shall catch him before long.'

Minge stood and finished his drink. 'Can't see why you bother, Jack. Going out at dusk and dawn. Who cares? Dogs, good riddance.' He turned to face Joe and extended an elegant hand. 'Goodbye, Joe, may I call you that? Nice to have you in the village. You must come up to my place, Plumtree Cottage, meet my wife if you can bear it, never stops talking, politics mainly. Whatever you do, don't get a dog. They eats 'em in China. That's what you should do, Jack, check out all the Chinese restaurants, that's who's killing them. See you soon.'

Barrington watched Minge walk up the green towards his cottage. 'He's a prime suspect, he is,' he said. He stood and gathered the empty beer glasses in one hand, and Joe's plate in the other. 'I'll see you later, Joe, I think I'll wander over to Haseley, check up on things.'

He went into the pub, leaving the door open behind him.

Joe sat where he was for a while. It seemed like a month since he'd left Wandsworth. The village green lay quiet before him. An old man appeared from one of the thatched cottages and placed an empty milk bottle on the step, looked at Joe and then retreated indoors. Opposite the pub was the garage, its sliding doors pushed wide. Joe could see the rear of car. There was the sound of a spanner clanging to a concrete floor. Then a voice, swearing loudly, and the mechanic came into the open, wiping his hands on a lump of cotton waste. He looked towards Joe, a steady scrutiny.

A car went by the front of the pub. A woman trundled a pushchair along the pavement in the direction of the village shop. The woman stopped and talked to another woman. A crow flapped across the sky, low, just above the roofs, taking an eternity to go nowhere; pigeons gargled deep in their throats, and the red kite returned, turning on the air, still waiting for something to die. Milton Magna was immersed deep in its own beauty, hundreds of years of confidence seeping out of its walls.

Joe sighed and got to his feet and crossed the green towards the garage. The mechanic watched him approach, still wiping his hands although they no longer needed wiping.

In front of the garage the man gave a guarded smile. 'Hello,' said Joe. 'I've just moved into...

'Pegswell Cottage,' said the man. He had a bushy beard and a dour look to him. He wore grease stained overalls of red, and a green woolly hat. 'You've got that lovely Saab,' he said.

Joe creased his brow.

'It's brand new, but I checked it out for you, took it for a spin. Goes like shit off a shovel. Good motors.'

'Who got you to do that?'

'Well, if you don't know how could I? Been in India haven't you?'

Joe nodded. 'Is there a bill, do I owe you?'

'All paid up, no worries.'

'Cheque?'

'No, cash. Came through the letter box in a brown envelope. That's how I like to get paid.'

'Yes,' said Joe. Not only were events puzzling him but they were beginning to annoy him too. He wanted to know what was going on. What he said was, 'My name's Joe Rapps.'

'I know, I'm Tony Merrell. I do plumbing as well, welding, glazing, draw plans. I can do most things, play a guitar too.'

Joe nodded. A dog came from the darkness at the rear of the garage. It was a mongrel with a bit of Alsatian in him, short fur, long legs and an elegant tail. It let its body drop onto the floor as if the twelve or so paces it had walked had drained all the energy from its muscles. It licked its chops, lowered its head onto it front paws and closed its eyes. This was a dog who knew about life and had sorted out its priorities. It would never chase a cat and never bark. It was the only kind of dog that Joe could even begin to like.

'That's Mick,' said Merrell.

'Hasn't been shot then,' said Joe.

'Nah,' said Merrell. 'I don't let him out of my sight, not that he wants to go anywhere anyway. His bark ain't worse than his bite because he don't bark. We get on, better than I did with my ex-wife. Mind you, I ain't easy, but then I can't think of a single reason why I should be.' He turned back into the garage. The dog rose, with an effort, and followed him.

Joe continued along the path, walking in front of a row of houses and bungalows. Then came the shop. Joe hesitated. He needed nothing but remembered what Vernon Minge had said about the woman who worked there – Norah.

Joe pushed open the door and the bell rang. The shop was long and narrow and crowded with merchandise. It was a proper shop, out of the past, out of his youth. There were rows and rows of magazines and newspapers, a freezer compartment with milk and ice creams in it. Shelves of biscuits, tins of soup, batteries, eggs and bottles of wine. In one corner was a window behind which sat a grey haired woman of about fifty-five wearing a red cardigan embroidered with flowers of all colours – the Post Office.

'A book of stamps.'

The woman smiled at him, a welcome to the village smile, and pushed the stamps under the glass partition.

As he pocketed the stamps another woman emerged from the stock room at the end of shop. She was carrying a carton of sweets. Joe watched her walk towards him. About forty the energy in her body was barely contained by it. She was full breasted with rounded thighs, her clothes had been chosen for their tightness. A thin low cut jumper and a short skirt. Her waist was good and her ankles slim. Her hair was thick and black, tied loosely behind her head with a ribbon, ready to be undone and set free at a moment's notice. Her face was joyful, and it had kindness in it. Its expression said that she loved people, men in particular; more than that she was a man's woman, an ally of them in all that they did and wanted. Men inspired her to salacious repartee and sexual innuendo. Joe knew as he watched her approach that she knew intuitively that he needed a woman, and she knew that he knew she knew. This was indeed Norah, the postman's wife.

Norah came to stand close to Joe, nudging him with the carton of sweets. 'You must be Mr Rapps, you've bought Pegswell Cottage, 'aven't you? All on your own, eh? Though not for long, I'll be bound.'

'I certainly hope not. Call me Joe.'

'Yes,' said Norah, 'and you must call me Norah. Been away a long while, haven't you? India, they said. I'd love to travel to exotic places...film business too. How glamorous.' She pointed her nipples at him.

'Yes, I've been away a long while.'

'Well, you won't be lonely for long, we're very friendly in this village, by and large. Now what can I do for you?' Her eyes glinted just in case Joe hadn't understood what she meant.

'I'd like to order a Sunday Paper, The Observer, and maybe the local daily.'

Norah trotted behind her counter, unburdened herself of the carton of sweets, reached down and took out an order book. She took longer than necessary bending, and then straightened, smiling, the smile acknowledging that the bending had been for Joe's benefit.

'The boy will deliver them,' she said, writing in the order, 'today's Oxford Mail isn't in yet.'

'Thanks,' said Joe. He moved towards the door. 'See you again.'

Norah put the book away and smoothed her skirt over her hips. 'Sooner rather than later,' she said and Joe left the shop.

Immediately opposite stood the old school, now a private house, and next to it, the Methodist Chapel. The chapel was a solid building, stone built with brick corners, the windows were tall and narrow, Victorian gothic. The door to it was as massive as a drawbridge, oak planks with wide strap hinges of iron. The chapel stood on its own, surrounded by a small rectangular tarmac yard.

Joe crossed the road and went up to the door; it was locked. This was where he was meant to be at eight o'clock that evening: this was where, according to the Bishop, he would learn why he had been brought to Milton Magna.

He turned away. The entrance to Pegswell Lane was fifty yards further on. Opposite was the row of white painted nineteenth century cottages where Erica Sands-Lindsay, the mermaid from the river, lived. He counted up the people he had met in this one day. He had never lived in the country before but he supposed that was how it was: a small village, a small population, he was bound to get to know people quickly and all at once. He'd lived in a flat in Clapham for years and never met a neighbour. In Milton Magna, in spite of the threat of whist drives, he hadn't yet had time to get bored.

He came down the lane and to the gable end of his house. His house! He still found it hard to believe that he actually owned it. He went into his garden, past the arbour where he had sat with Barrington, and contemplated the view. It was indeed superb. He was facing south, and the fields and hedges were spread out to the east and west. The slight valley dropped away before him, then the hillside rose to the sky line, beyond which, and in the next valley, lay the River Thame, not visible though the village of Cuddesdon was, the church with its squat square tower high on its hill. It was classic England, something you could fall in love with effortlessly. It was certainly better than anywhere else he had lived. He remembered his days as a young cameraman and assistant director; the flat in Clapham: miserable bedsits shared with girl friends for a month or two; a semi detached in Tooting when he'd been married. And then prison had come along and put him in limbo, had changed him utterly. Joe had always yearned for some class, and now at last, if Pegswell Cottage was truly his, he had found some.

Suddenly someone was standing beside him, grown out of the ground.

'Hello,' said the man. He was young, maybe early thirties, sharp features, black hair slicked back and his face computer pale. He wore brown corduroy trousers, brown brogues and a kind of bomber jacket in green. His movements were precise; he could have been a lawyer's clerk out of a Dickens novel.

'Hello,' said Joe. He'd given up being surprised by Milton Magna.

'Mr Rapps. I'm Dudley Mackintosh. I publish the village Bulletin.' He offered Joe several sheets of printed paper stapled together. 'Thought you might like to have a copy, it's last month's, but it will give you an idea of what we do. There's the minutes of the last parish council meeting, the times of church services for both parishes, Haseleys and Miltons, the vicar's monthly news letter. You'd be surprised how well he writes. Lots of adverts – you know, electricians, builders and decorators...even massage in Wheatley, lovely girl does that, I can recommend her, she's fully qualified, reflexology too. And we'd like you to write something for us, your adventures in India for example. That would be excellent.'

Joe took the flimsy magazine and flicked through its pages. 'Parish Council News.'

'Oh, yes. There's some very pungent letters about the dog assassin. Tempers are rising, we don't know who it is, you see. Still, Inspector Barrington's on the case. Then there's the pond over there.' Dudley Mackintosh gestured towards the view. 'Halfway down the slope. It's just been bought, the field, by a man called Greenaway, he's an incomer, only been here about ten years.'

'Ten years!'

'Well it wasn't a pond really, just soggy ground, now he's dug it out, some people are calling it a lake, letters about that. Very difficult to define a lake, or a pond for that matter.'

'Perhaps there's some kind of legal definition.'

'Precisely. If it's a lake the Parish Council doesn't like it, kids may fall in and drown. Mind you the river's been down the road for a few million years, we always went there after school, in the summer, jumping and pushing each other in, no supervision. Then we're having trouble with people dumping their garden waste on the allotments instead of taking it round to the dump...very anti-social that. More letters from disgusted of Umbrage Wells...it's got to stop.'

'Yes,' said Joe, 'I suppose it has. Where are the allotments?'

'Other side of the village, by the recreation ground. Do you want one? There's a couple free.'

'I don't think so,' said Joe. 'Don't get on with earth and manure.' He waved the magazine in the air. 'Think I'll take this in and read it.'

'It'll help you get settled,' said Dudley Mackintosh. 'Think about writing something. My telephone number's on the back page. I live down by the church, in Lychgate Lane. Handy for funerals I always say.' With that he ducked his head and disappeared around the end of the house as silently as he had come.

Joe went indoors leaving his front door open. The weather was warm and kind. Sylvie Cornish had done her work and the whole house shone clean and bright and smelt of furniture polish. In the kitchen was a note, 'Nice fish pie in the fridge for tonight. Then ice-cream and fruit salad. Got to keep you healthy after all that foreign food. See you tomorrow. White wine in the fridge. Muscadet.'

Joe shook his head in admiration. She really was a treasure. He went upstairs; the early business of the day had exhausted him and he decided to lie on the bed, and read the Parish Bulletin. Milton Magna was a village that demanded close study, and there must be much to learn.

He fell asleep before he'd read the first page; the warm air coming in through the open window caressed him into a dreamless slumber. The blackbirds and thrushes still sang but Joe didn't hear them. As he drifted into unconsciousness he could feel the coarseness of prison life seeping out of him; and all the years of living on his own, the dull locations in factories and the anger of his short marriage, all left him. He was being renewed, it was heaven.

And then he did dream, a delightful fantasy; Norah from the shop, a soft hand on his face, under his shirt, stroking his chest, his thighs. His shoes were removed, his clothes were slipped from him and then a mouth did to him what only a mouth can do.

When he did wake it was into pleasure. Three years of prison had evaporated up into the eaves of his brain. His mind was free, rested and clear; the tension of sad thought gone. Such a dream. He opened his eyes slowly. The sun was lower in the sky, the evening filling the room with a dusty light. He was indeed undressed, completely naked and Norah was sitting at the end of the bed, her face suffused with a physical greed and a triumph of satisfied desire; her bright lipstick smudged, her lips moist. She beamed happiness at him.

'I bet you didn't get woken up like that in India,' she said. The slight Oxford burr in her voice added a degree of carnality to her words. 'I brought the local paper over...and I couldn't resist it, you're pretty handsome you know, you looked like a little babe in the wood...someone had to welcome you to the village, 'adn't they? So I decided it should be me.'

The air was turning cool and Joe slipped under the covers. He didn't know what to say so he said nothing.

'I see you're reading the Bulletin. Strange about them dogs, my old boy, my husband, he's the postman for both parishes...he reckons there's something odd going on over Hazelmere Court...we do steams open the occasional envelope. It ain't at all what it seems over there...people drifting about early in the morning, and they used to get through nannies like they's going out of fashion. Not now though. Strange old world, it is.'

Joe closed his eyes; lotus eating in Oxfordshire. When Joe opened his eyes again Norah was beginning to remove her clothes. 'I don't know if I can do it again right now,' said Joe. 'No more tadpoles.'

Norah grinned a greedy grin. 'You leave that part of it to me,' she said.

*　　*　　*

Joe drank the Muscadet with the fish pie. Norah had laid the table for him and then gone to get her husband's supper. 'He likes me to be there when he gets back from Oxford,' she'd said.

When he'd finished his meal Joe took the wine through to the sitting room, sat in the most comfortable of the armchairs and attempted to contemplate the day and what had happened in it. It took him only a minute or two to realize that contemplation was a bad idea; there was too much to think about. The day had been too full, the village too crowded. He would leave reflection until the next day. Besides, he still had the evening to get through, and a visit to the chapel, where he would find out who and what had brought him to Milton Magna.

After some moments of relaxation Joe took the envelope from the coffee table and began to look through the deeds to Pegswell Cottage. As far as he could see the documents looked water-tight, but then he was no lawyer. It might be a good idea to pay a visit to the Wheatley solicitor later in the week and go through the documents with her, to make 'assurance doubly sure.'

Joe put the deeds back into their envelope and looked at his watch. It was nearly eight o'clock, time to change into a suit and be on his way.

Dusk was falling as Joe emerged onto the road from Pegswell

Lane. He had chosen a light grey suit of cotton, a silk tie of pale blue, pale blue socks, and black shoes. It might be overdressed for Milton but then he didn't know what to expect; better to be too smart than too casual.

Joe walked slowly as far as the old school playground and going into it came to where the Chapel stood. He could hear no noise but a golden light came from the tall gothic windows and from the door which stood half open. Two large men stood on either side of the door: their shoulders massive, their hands, like bundles of sausages, held together in front of them, faces round, heads shaven. Joe hesitated. They looked just the sort of men that Sunshine would have protecting him. Sunshine Leary was never far from Joe's thoughts; an angel of death.

Joe went forward. The men looked at him but said nothing. He went between them and now he heard something: a recorded version of the song that Elton John had sung at Princess Diana's funeral – Candle in the Wind.

As Joe crossed the threshold he entered the warmth of candle light, a hundred candles, solid and thick. Not very Methodist, was Joe's first thought. At the back of the chapel, where there would have been an altar if it had been a church, were banks of flowers rising halfway to the ceiling, as high as the high window sills, and on into the corners and halfway along the side walls, expensive flowers: lilies and roses, gypsophila and hortensia, and there was greenery too. And in the middle of the display stood a column, as tall as a man, and on it a carved head of Diana, the Roman goddess of hunting – original polished stone, no plaster copy here.

There were benches arranged across the width of the building, with an aisle running down the middle of them. The benches were full, with more women present than men, all well dressed as if out for the evening, lounge suits for the men, frocks and dressy coats for the women. To one side was a small organ and even a pulpit though there was no one in it. The song played on and the congregation, if that's what it was, stood silent, heads bowed.

One of the big men from outside came through the door, motioned Joe into the nearest bench, then went away; the door closed. Joe took his time and inspected the forty or so people standing before him, but recognised no one. Then a head turned: Erica Sands-Lindsay, the mermaid.

Joe waited for something to happen. The music ended, the congregation sat. Nobody went to the front, nobody went to the pulpit. There was silence apart from a cough or two. Then Joe noticed a poster-picture of Diana, Princess of Wales, deceased, on one of the side walls: beautiful, alluring, sexy and distinguished at the same time. Those huge doe eyes, a still maybe from the interview she had given on television about her marriage breaking up. 'There are three people in this marriage.'

Joe turned his gaze away. She wasn't his favourite royal. If he liked any of them, which he didn't, it would be Princess Anne. She was a real cow, throwing bread at parties, swearing like a trooper and getting pissed, and tipping her detective into a swimming pool on a visit to the States. He remembered an American secret service agent being obliged to dive into the pool to retrieve the British detective's automatic from the bottom. Joe knew it for a fact because he'd been the cameraman on duty that night. He'd been on more than a few royal jobs and seen more bad behaviour than most, enough to make everyone in the country a paid up republican.

Still Joe waited. Nothing, the chapel was silent. Then a woman stood. She was dressed in an expensive coat, her hair piled on top of her head. Her face was not visible to Joe.

'Joanna,' came the woman's voice, 'Hampshire. I come to these meetings because I know I am going to meet people who think like me, people who know that we've been robbed of our princess, people who know that our royal family has let us down. The most beautiful person in the world has been taken from us in a dire conspiracy, the kindest, the loveliest woman. I am bereft and I know I am not the only one. Everyone I speak to has the same sense of loss. Something unique has been stolen from us.' The woman sat, the silence returned.

A young man stood then. He was in the front bench, so he turned to face the audience. His face was pale and shone with passion and Joe began to comprehend what was happening. He was present at the equivalent of a Quaker meeting – those whom the spirit moved stood and gave way to their feelings. Joe had heard of these groups. They worshipped the departed princess, and they existed world wide – they called themselves the 'Friends of Diana'.

The young man spoke, his voice heavy with emotion, a romantic lover. 'I have been thinking of this new Duchess, this so-called second wife, and my heart is distressed. How could there be a Queen Camilla? Unless we do something there will be, as sure as we are here. Diana the goddess, Camilla the hussy. All over the country members of The Friends are appalled...we all know that there was a conspiracy to take Diana away from us, she was too loved and admired, she stood in the way of the second marriage. And it is well known that Henri Paul, the driver on the night of the fatal accident, was an agent for both French and British Intelligence...I have spoken to Diana, through a medium, she knows now what she previously only suspected. Why did one of her detectives die in a traffic accident? Diana spoke to him, also through a medium, before she died, because she knew...' The young man's voice trembled and tears came to his eyes and he could go no further. He sat and lowered his face into his hands and Joe heard him sob.

There was no pause this time. A couple stood hand in hand, and half turned. Both were slightly overweight, but cleanly dressed like godparents at a christening, their cheeks scrubbed. The woman spoke, staring hard at the Diana poster, while her husband stared at her and held her hand tightly, nodding from time to time, encouraging her.

'We feel,' began the woman, 'that our princess was a reincarnation, she returns to us through the ages, though that does not make her loss any the easier to bear. She is Isis of the Egyptians, Artemis of the Greeks, daughter of Zeus, sister of Apollo, she is Diana of the Ephesians, her temple at Ephesus was one of the seven wonders of the world...there is a carved head of her in the museum at Nimes in southern France...we have been to see it, it is Diana, our Diana. From early times she had a temple at Rome...she protected slaves and plebeians, like us. That is why the royals detested her. How could Charles be so cruel to her, how could he not love her...?' The woman became angry. She took her hand from her husband's and pointed at Diana's picture.

'...the symbol of all love? Her spirit is not happy. She is not at peace. She demands a sacrifice before she will come amongst us again.' The woman finished, buried her face into her husband's shoulder and his arms went round her in comfort, and they sat.

Another woman stood. 'Elizabeth from Maidstone.' She was young, in her thirties. 'Can you remember the love and pity that flowed from us, over the whole of the country when she was murdered? Were you there outside Kensington Palace, do you remember the flowers and the tears? How we all felt the same pity, how strangers embraced each other, talked to each other...and at St James's Palace, waiting to sign the book, all of a single mind. We should have marched then against the royal family, that cold family that couldn't understand her love, her compassion. What did they know except their own self-interest? We know who killed her and we know why. They should pay the price.'

There were cries of 'Yes! Yes!' from the audience, and there were sobs.

A middle-aged man sprang to his feet 'Visions of her have been seen from Kosova to Althorp and from Lourdes to St Petersburg. There was a sighting of Diana in Liverpool, in the blue and white robes of the Virgin Mary, in America too, a Helen of Troy in her beauty...and at the fountain in Hyde Park people have drunk the water as holy. The Friends of Diana have meetings like this regularly all over the world and it will go on...She will live for ever...she loved children, she had no fear of Aids, cuddling those who had the disease because she knew her purity made her immune. She could walk among landmines and fear no evil. Had she lived she would have done great good, she was the Queen of all our Hearts...killed at the age of thirty-seven...In classic times human sacrifices were made to Artemis and Diana...we too need a sacrifice...'

Joe was glad he was near the exit. He could stand no more of this rhetoric, and it was obvious that passions were going to rise, the temperature moving up into the red zone as speaker after speaker gave free rein to his or her emotions.

Joe caught Erica's eye and tilted his head, hoping that she might follow him as he moved towards the door. She did not. Another votary began a panegyric of Diana's attributes, and Joe retreated, opening the heavy door quietly and stepping out into the dark.

Then he remembered why he had been asked to attend this meeting. 'All would be made clear,' the Bishop had said, but Joe had learnt nothing. He was no nearer understanding why he had been brought to Milton Magna. He already knew about Diana worship and the strong body of public opinion that was convinced she had been murdered. He himself didn't believe a word of it but was well aware that conspiracy theories had a long life, centuries sometimes. Theories about Diana's death would last as long, if not longer, than the theories about President Kennedy's assassination.

He pushed the thought from his mind. It was good to be outside, the air cool and fresh after the candles in the chapel. Joe made a small decision: whoever wanted to contact him would have to come to Pegswell Cottage. He would make no more effort. He half turned, poised to leave, and saw the two bouncers emerging from the blackness at the side of the building. They stood close to him, very close.

Joe felt his heart bang against his ribs. Again he thought of Sunshine Leary. If it happened it would happen like this, with no warning, a bullet in the back of the head, a knife at the throat. Joe stiffened and stood still. He felt a strong hand on his arm as if he were being taken under control by a meaty shop-walker. The second bouncer walked behind. Perhaps they were taking him out of the village to a secluded spot where his cries would not be heard.

He was led across the school yard and out onto the road. It was darker there. No street lights in Milton Magna, he'd seen it in the Bulletin: the Parish Council was against it, this was a village, not Piccadilly. There was a car parked by the phone-box and a door clicked open. The inside light came on and Joe saw a third man sitting at the wheel. They were taking no chances; he wasn't walking away from this one.

Joe was pushed into the back seat of the car, a bouncer followed him in and the other one came in on the opposite side; 'I feel like an Oscar winner,' said Joe. None of the three men said a word. Joe studied the car. It was not the stretch of the previous evening, it was something low and fast, a Mercedes maybe, Sunshine's car.

Joe put his elbows on his knees and his hands over his face, covering his eyes. Well, it had been a lovely day, plenty of incident and new people, and at least Norah had been nice to him. She must have done her degree at a lollipop university. The sex had been a welcome gift from God after years of abstinence.

The car advanced slowly. Joe uncovered his eyes. He was still in the village but it was too dark for him to see where. The car swung to the right and Joe was tilted against the body of the bouncer on his left. There was no give in that body; it was a brick wall.

Joe saw two square pillars, and wooden gates opened under the action of automatic sensors. He heard gravel under the wheels. He hated the sound of gravel, it was funereal, churchyardy, and it also made him feel poor, reminding him of his early upbringing. He had taught himself to forget that upbringing eventually, and lose the chip on his shoulder. Just take what you could when you could – 'cop it and hop it', as they said in the film business.

The drive wound left and then right. Joe saw a blur of tree trunks and thick bushes. The drive turned one last time, windows became visible, security lights came on. There was a high wide porch, supported by two huge pillars, and the car drove into it and slid to a stop, silent, as if it were sighing. There were two large stone lions, recumbent on either side. The bouncer on Joe's right opened the car door and jerked his head, indicating that Joe should disembark. He said nothing. Joe did as he was told and the car drove away, continuing round the side of the house, where more security lights came on. The car disappeared.

Joe felt relief surge through his body, not quite champagne in the blood, more like cream soda, but it was a good feeling. He turned to the door, a large door, divided into two halves with glass panels. There was a huge handle hanging in front of his face, the handle connected by rods to a bell inside the house. It was a bell from a horror movie, but before Joe could pull on it half the door opened and a man stood in front of him. Not Sunshine Leary, not even Cold Ronnie, but Gerard, the chauffeur who had driven him from Wandsworth the previous evening.

'Am I pleased to see you,' said Joe. 'You've got more style in your little finger than those three who brought me here.'

'Please follow me,' said Gerard, stepping to one side so that Joe could enter the building. Joe did and the door closed behind him, and was locked.

Joe found himself in a spacious hallway with a high ceiling and lit by a small chandelier, the light muted. There was the most exquisite Persian carpet on the floor, the colours gorgeous and properly dimmed by years of use. There were a few armchairs, a Pembroke table or two and polished doors of dark wood. Opposite Joe was a wide staircase rising to a landing and then dividing, right and left. Joe drew a long breath in over his teeth. There was a lot of money here, not just well-off money, train loads of it.

'Follow me,' said Gerard again.

Joe examined the chauffeur closely this time. He was a good-looking man who kept himself fit; wide shoulders, clean shaven and dressed in a suit that was as well cut as any that Joe had found in his wardrobe. He walked light on his feet, ready to spring, like a hopeful young actor in Los Angeles. His face was expressionless, giving nothing away, a robot waiting to be programmed, and intimidating because of it.

Joe mounted the stairs, noting the graceful way in which Gerard moved. The carpet was thick and there was no sound of footsteps. They turned to the left where the staircase divided and went onto a landing. Here they went right and along a short corridor with doors on either side and one at the end. Gerard stopped before this door and gave that gentle bow of his, deceptive and dangerous, indicating that Joe should go on alone. Then he turned and retraced his steps.

Joe didn't move. He had no idea what to expect on the other

side of the door, but then he hadn't known what to expect at any time since his arrival in Milton Magna. The previous twenty-four hours had brought him so many surprises that it seemed pointless to query anything. He was Alice Through the Looking Glass. All he could do was go forward and deal with the madness as it occurred. Stuff happens.

He opened the door, telling himself that he was ready for anything, but knowing that he wasn't. He found himself in an enormously long room. Again, the carpets were a magnificent collection of Persian, top quality. Joe made the judgement easily. He had done a documentary on Persian carpets once, like he'd done documentaries on most things.

Down the left hand side of the room, at what must have been the front of the house, were huge square windows, huge if the size of the embroidered drapes was anything to go by. Most of the room was taken up by large and comfortable armchairs, Victorian in the main, gathered in convivial clusters. Two thirds of the way along the room the floor rose in three steps, leading up to a more private space set apart for the intimate entertaining of friends. Half filling the back wall of that space was an Adam fireplace, on either side of which were two matching armchairs, upholstered in a crimson plush, deep and welcoming. By the fireplace stood a woman, tall and elegant, and as far as Joe could see, in the low lighting, extraordinarily beautiful.

She tilted the glass she held, meaning that he should approach. It was a long way and Joe knew she knew it was a long way. She watched him closely, judging him. He got as far as the three steps and hesitated, then went up.

She was even more beautiful close to than from a distance, unlike those girl-friends you hadn't seen for ten years who grew uglier with every step you took towards them. She sat, and indicated the chair opposite her. There was a small table by its side and on it was a glass of white wine, a bottle too, standing in a terra-cotta wine cooler.

Joe said nothing, wanting her to speak first. For something to do he stooped and half-lifted the bottle from the cooler to read the label: Puligny-Montrachet, his favourite white. She knew.

Then suddenly Joe knew, it wasn't difficult. He knew who had bought the house, who had stocked the cellar, who had paid for the suits and who had chosen the car. She had. He let the bottle sink back into the cooler and he sat.

She crossed her legs. Joe could have watched the movement for ever. The dress, cream-coloured, was cut on the cross so that it swirled across her body. She tossed her hair, fair against the red plush of the armchair. Those gestures were pure, straight from God. Watching her you saw sexual energy, so powerful that there was no criticising her. You would believe anything she said and do anything she suggested. She was as aristocratic as Joe had ever seen, her body and face did the work.

Joe gave up waiting for her to speak. He wanted to say something smart, really smart. 'So it was you,' was all he could come up with.

She smiled and it was a couple of thousand volts.

'It's been enjoyable, Mr Rapps,' she said, 'but I thought we ought to meet at last, we have things to talk about.' Her voice was a mixture of Greta Garbo talking and Marlene Dietrich singing.

'Enjoyable, yes, but it's been a puzzle, a very expensive puzzle for you.'

She waved a hand about shoulder height, and the wave was patrician. It dismissed money, not as something vulgar but as something unimportant, non-existent even.

'It must be a relief for you to be out of prison.'

'It's cured me of drink-driving.'

'You were unfortunate in the accident and the people you killed were well connected.'

'I didn't think I'd see another day. He has a quick way with people who cross him.'

'Yes. Sunshine Leary. A lovely name.'

'His nature's not half as sunny. I don't know your name.'

'My full name...the Countess Woronzov-Zinoviev, but I'm English, née Fleur de Malet, Lady Fleur de Malet. The Malets came over with the Conqueror, posh but poor. I married a Russian oil tycoon...'

'A good career move,' said Joe.

'He certainly knew how to make money and didn't care how...I never asked. He bought the Woronzov title, White Russians they were, lost everything at the revolution, completely sham the dukedom, but then my husband had absolutely no style. But he was the richest man I knew...seriously rich...'

'Could have bought two football clubs,' said Joe. Was that remark smart enough?

'I was glad when his business rivals took a dislike to him. They knew I couldn't be bothered with a divorce, they did it for me. They poisoned him, on the Black Sea. His skin went thick, ravaged, like yesterday's cold porridge, so I was told. I inherited the lot, so much I don't know where it all is or even how much, billions. There was a pay off, cheap really, all I have to do is stay out of their business operations. No hardship, as I detest business.'

Joe poured the Countess another glass of wine, and one for himself. So this was what an out of body experience was like. He was conscious of where he was and what he was doing but he was seeing actor Joe as the stand-in for a film sequence, while Joe the director was looking down on him from a high gantry. He was floating above the village of Milton Magna with the most beautiful woman he had ever seen, a woman who was also richer than anyone he had ever known. So what did she want? It wouldn't be a bagatelle, not for the money she'd laid out.

'Countess,' he said, and the word stuck on his tongue. Never, in his whole life, had he said it out loud before. 'I have come from Wandsworth Prison to Milton Magna; I have a house, a car, ten grand in the bank, the softest suits, the best housekeeper in the western hemisphere and a cellar full of my favourite wines, and even a probation officer who's been straightened. Somebody wants something, something big, like a lifetime of my blind devotion.'

'Not that.'

'Look, I'm not a crook, I'm not a safe blower, I don't know any Hollywood producers and I know nothing about drugs, except the occasional joint. I am, in a word, just a very ordinary guy who's of no special use to anyone.'

She held out her glass. Joe rose and refilled it.

'You underestimate yourself. You have been in the film business.'

'I've been inside for three years. I have lost all my contacts and no one came to see me. I was HIV positive as far as my friends were concerned. I have an address book as big as a dictionary and everyone in it is dead.'

'Yes, but you have an area of expertise which might be useful.'

'And if it isn't? The house, the ten grand, the suits...What then?'

The Countess laughed and her hair glinted once more against the red plush. 'Those are yours, outright. Payment for this meeting, if you like.'

Joe took a sip of his Montrachet and tried to look relaxed. He failed. 'They are all mine?'

'Yours...You did a lot of work with the royal family, you followed them around?'

'Just before I went to prison I spent most of my life doing royal stuff...Buck House interviews, documentaries, Windsor, foreign trips, the houses in Gloucestershire, they even got to recognise me, became used to me.'

'That was my information. I want you to do another interview, Prince Charles this time.'

Joe looked at the colour of his wine; ancient gold. 'Well okay, but why me? You could hire a dozen technicians for a fraction of what you've laid out, you could set up a whole telly series. There's something going on here.'

'Well yes, Mr Rapps, of course there is. An interview with Charles was arranged months ago and it will be an interview with a special crew in possession of very special talents. You see, I want you to bring the Prince home with you, kidnap him.'

Joe didn't want to hear what he'd heard, but the words got to his brain second time round. This was why so much money had been aimed in his direction. The Countess smiled, uncrossed her legs, and then crossed them again on the opposite side. The movement was as sensual as before but Joe dismissed the lechery from his mind. He had other things to think about now. He rose, filled his glass, and sat down again. The bottle was empty now. He shook his head.

'It's madness,' he said, 'it can't be done.'

The Countess laughed. 'This project has been three years in the planning. We have been given the go-ahead from the very top. There are important people behind this, and you have not the slightest idea how important. It can't go wrong, we have been waiting for you to return from India, you see. We could do it without you, but it goes better with you...you know the ropes and you are known.'

'That's part of the trouble, they'll know exactly who they are looking for.'

'I promise you that will not be a problem. No one will be looking for you.'

'Oh, yeah? I've just spent three years in jail. I won't do that again...and for lèse-majesté, it'd be the block on Tower Hill. Sunshine Leary would do the job for nothing.'

'Mr Rapps, I can't tell you the details yet, but I can promise you that no one will be looking for you.' She leant forward in her chair, and now Joe could see her green eyes clearly, enthusiastic and full of desire, but not for him – for the madness of the scheme.

'I've enjoyed my time in Milton Magna,' he began. 'The house is wonderful, Sylvie is a diamond, I walked to Cuddesdon and met a river nymph, but I'm prepared to return everything you've given me and live in a basement flat in Birmingham, rather than risk my freedom. Next time I go to jail Sunshine may not be so generous spirited in his choice of minions...it was hell enough last time.'

'There'll be no jail, and I can take care of Sunshine.'

'Nobody takes care of Sunshine, he's a vulture.'

'Money takes care of vultures,' said the Countess. She rose from her chair. The dress swirled round her thighs. She leant against the mantelpiece and stared at Joe. There was a silence, a long silence. This was an impasse, thought Joe, then the Countess broke through it.

'How does a million pounds sound to you, Mr Rapps?'

Another silence came, longer and deeper than the previous one. Joe felt his mouth go dry. He looked at his glass. It was empty and he knew there was no wine left in the bottle. He closed his eyes and let the silence continue, using the time to think what he could do with a million pounds.

A million pounds meant very little to the Countess, but it meant an awful lot to him. It would change his life, put him beyond care, beyond Sunshine Leary even. That kind of money fuelled escape velocity – it was a magic potion that gave the men who had tasted it the lustre of a Greek God, gave them balls of iron, cocks of fire and spermatozoa of molten gold.

'I could certainly indulge a whim or two,' he said, opening his eyes to stare at the Countess, 'but to offer me that much money means that this is a dangerous enterprise...I could take anything but not a long sentence in prison, and for doing royalty I'd get eternity with no remission. They'd find me one morning hanging behind the door of my cell. No, I'd rather die penniless.'

The Countess smiled, walked a few yards from the mantelpiece and turned. Joe wondered if he'd ever get into bed with her. What would she be like, how would the conversation go? He got rid of the thought; he wasn't even in her league.

'I want you to think about it, Mr Rapps. We will have dinner together soon, and talk more. There isn't much time, there is a plan in place and it can't be delayed. If not you it will be someone else, but we want you. A lot hangs on your answer. As I said, a lot of important people are involved...they cannot wait.'

Joe stood. It was time to go. 'What was all that in the chapel?' he asked, 'the Friends of Diana, are they nutters?'

The Countess's face hardened, she was not amused. She not only looked angry, she looked dangerous. She was a woman who was used to getting her own way, used to being listened to, someone who knew how to use all the money behind her.

'They are in fact reasonable people,' she said, 'but they have been hurt. They love Diana, the memory of her and her manifestations through time. She was Artemis; she was Isis.

They are sincere and full of affection. You have seen only one small group but there are groups like that all over Britain, all over the world, hundreds of groups with thousands of people in them. They are little people, but don't underestimate their power and determination. They meet, they talk, they exchange ideas – together they can achieve whatever they want to achieve. A lot of those people met outside Kensington Palace, laying flowers at the gates, signing the book of remembrance at St James's, lining the route at the funeral. They were wounded in their hearts and they came together, and then they came to me, asking for help. For them, as for me, there is only one guilty person. There was a conspiracy, Mr Rapps, now they want revenge.'

'Revenge! It's crazy.'

'Not at all, Mr Rapps. When you have learnt a little more you will see that the plan is more than reasonable.'

'Even if you got The Prince out of the palace the whole country would be up in arms. Special Branch, the protection squad, MI5, anti-terrorism. It would make what's happened since nine-eleven look like a picnic. You wouldn't get further than the back door.'

'I've always remarked,' said the Countess, sitting again, 'that people in the imagination business have no imagination. You are no exception. You just can't see how it could be done. Some of the best brains in the country have been working on this. It can be done, if you have the right people.'

'How?'

'I have to think about you, Mr Rapps, I'm not sure you are ready to hear all I have to say.'

'And what do you do with Charles once you've got him?'

'Nothing much. The Friends of Diana will want to talk to him. They'll want to get at the truth, we believe we know it already. He will discover what it is to live in the real world, for a while at least. He has played the petulant brat for too long.'

Joe shook his head. The door at the end of the room opened and Gerard appeared. He stood motionless, waiting.

'I will send for you soon,' said the Countess. 'We'll have

dinner and talk further.' There was a threat in her voice, soft, but a threat nevertheless. 'Remember, money can achieve a great deal, it can keep Leary away...but it can also bring him back. You have some serious thinking to do, Mr Rapps.'

Joe's out of body experience ended there. He was suddenly back in his shrivelled heart. He shook the Countess's hand, descended the three steps and trekked the length of the room towards Gerard, who stepped aside and allowed Joe to pass through the door. As he arrived on the landing Joe glanced to his left where the stairs continued upwards. He saw a tall suited figure disappearing into the shadows of the next floor, black shoes catching the light from below.

Gerard guided Joe to the heavy front door and opened it. Lights came on in the drive.

Joe looked at the quiet face. 'I suppose you'd push me off the planet on her say so, wouldn't you?' There was no answer. As Joe went out into the night Gerard gave his little bow. 'Good night, sir,' he said, and Joe left him.

Joe listened to the sound of his shoes on the gravel. If he ever got her there would the Countess still be calling him Mr Rapps in bed? How did women like that talk when making love? Would she be ordering him what to do, and when? Would she talk at all, and in that cut glass accent? What was not in doubt was that the de Malet barons had been scattering their seed for centuries, and only raping the best-looking women and stealing the richest inheritances. There were enough beauties amongst the toffs to prove it, though those that had come over with the Conqueror must have been a bit rough to start with. 'Bloody Normans,' said Joe and walked on, deciding not to entertain ideas above his station. He had enough to worry about.

*　　*　　*

Joe woke late the next morning. The jazz-bird was in full voice and he could hear Sylvie making kitchen noises. In a little while there was a knock on his bedroom door and Sylvie came in with his breakfast on a tray, and the local newspaper.

She drew the curtains, and turned to face him, her fists on her hips. 'You're getting into bad habits already,' she said. 'Out gallivanting, no doubt, and missing the best part of the day...it's lovely in the garden. Drinking too, I bet...I'm making you a nice salmon pie for tonight...all you have to do is put it in the oven.'

'I'm so glad you're here,' said Joe. He pulled himself upright in the bed and leant against the headboard. 'I can't stand shopping.'

The rest of the day passed in lethargy. Joe sat in the sitting room, then in the garden, relishing the experience of being 'maître de maison', though he was still dazed by the events of the previous evening – after all, a woman he didn't know had offered him a million pounds.

Sylvie brought him coffee from time to time and he let her talk to him all morning as she moved about the house. Her talk was good solid mother earth talk, ongoing for ever, sinewy: births, marriages, christenings, holidays. She was wreathed round in an aura of joy and common-sense and made him realize, not for the first time, how competent women like her were. She could do everything, much more than men: sewing, cooking, certainly, but she could care for the human body and the human mind also, could nurture and calm troubled spirits; she made life seem reasonable instead of menacing. There were whole families implicit in her conversation, generations of them. She knew their names, the houses they had lived in, the children who had moved on and those that were still in the village. Joe was at ease with her. Sylvie was an angel brooding over Milton Magna with love to spare. She looked at him across the ironing board at one point, smiling like she understood all men, much better than God did.

'I'll soon find you a nice marrying girl,' she said, 'I know where to find 'em.'

'What's the gossip about the Countess?' asked Joe. Sylvie had brought him a slice of shortbread in the garden, in the arbour, and they sat for a while, looking at the view.

'She's been here quite a long while now. Big house, ain't it, Chiltern Hall. She bought it off some pop star...no don't ask me who, can't stand all that umpty-dumpty music, give me Bing

Crosby and Frank Sinatra any day of the week. She must be worth a lot, but she's good with it. She put money into the cricket pavilion fund, helped with the playgroup. But then, if you've got stacks you don't miss it, do you?'

Joe thought of a million pounds.

'They say her husband was something in the Russian Mafia. She has visitors. They stops you in the street sometimes and they ask you the way to the shop...some can hardly speak English, snow on their boots we used to say. Her husband was killed, it was all in the Daily Mirror. She's as English as they come though, Lady something or other...she speaks to you, but we hardly see her. She always sends that man of hers down to the post office, chauffeur he is, and creepy, gives me the shivers...I couldn't live in Russia, could you? Only three weeks of summer in Siberia. She bought the Methodist Chapel when it was all falling down, saved it, the roof leaking, did it all up, lets 'em use it, Sundays. Brought her own workmen in too, Russians they were, the local builders didn't like it...that Colin Putt, he had a thing or two to say, but he shut up when she gave him some other work...'

And so the day went on, agreeably, the hours barely moving. Sylvie brought a bacon sandwich out to him at lunchtime, then abandoned him to fetch her grandchild from school. Joe read the paper and tried not to think of the money he was being offered. He didn't need much. especially if the Countess was serious about giving him the house, and the ten grand in the bank. A few wedding videos would keep him ticking over, stills too. But he was not free of the Countess yet, not by a long shot. The hint she'd dropped had landed like a ton of bricks narrowly missing his feet – Money could keep Sunshine away, certainly, it could also bring him back.

Midway through the afternoon Joe went into the sitting room and ran his fingers along the shelves of the bookcase. There it was: 'As You Like It.' He had known it would be – Pegswell Cottage came complete. The book was a school edition with plenty of elementary notes, which was just what he needed. He carried it out to the arbour and read it through the afternoon, marking certain passages with a pencil, speaking out loud those lines he had never seen or known but half remembered nevertheless; "All the world's a stage..." So that's where it came from.

*   *   *

The sun sank below the trees. Apéritif time, six-twenty-nine. Joe went to the cellar and brought up a bottle of St Émilion. He was in the kitchen pulling the cork when Barrington's face appeared at the window.

'Timed that right, didn't I?' he said.

Joe sniffed. 'I never had this trouble in London,' he answered. His third floor flat hadn't been conducive to casual visits. In Milton Magna the whole village seemed ready to troop through his life. Joe put two glasses on the window ledge. He hadn't known Barrington for long, twenty four hours, but he was pleased that he'd met him. Even though he was an ex-copper, he wasn't graceless with it. Life had given his face good laughter lines, and he was just the sort to have in the trenches with you.

Joe filled the glasses. 'I guess wine doesn't have time to breathe in this village.'

Barrington didn't waste time with a sip, he took a healthy gulp, rolled it round his mouth and sucked air over it. 'Very good,' he said. 'I like St Emilion. I went there once, on a wine-appreciation tour...there's a church dug into the rock, with a steeple above.' He took a another gulp and narrowed his eyelids to look at Joe over the glass. 'I've been thinking,' he said. 'I'm on the prowl tonight, on the dog mystery...I'd really like it if you came along...do you fancy it?'

Joe didn't fancy it very much at all, but after the encounter of the previous evening with the Countess, hunting a dog assassin with an ex-copper seemed positively staid. He was also slightly flattered by the invitation.

'I like my sleep,' he said.

'Oh, it wouldn't be for long. A couple of hours. We'll go about ten, over Haseley way, behind the Vivaldi hotel, there's been a few shot over there. Then we could pop into The Plough as well.'

'Why me?'

'Ah.' Barrington raised his glass and Joe put some more wine in it. 'Well mainly because you aren't a suspect, whereas everybody else is...and you've been round the block a few times...is that good enough? It'll be fun, the two of us.'

Joe relented. 'All right,' he said. 'Be nice to catch the bugger, eh?'

Barrington raised his glass again.

Joe did likewise. 'Here's to us...The Bow Street Runners.'

'Look at that,' said Barrington, 'the bottle's empty. You drink as much as I do.'

It was odd, thought Joe. He knew there wasn't a million pounds in this amateur sleuthing but finding the dog assassin had an attraction about it that kidnapping Prince Charles did not possess.

'Where's The Priory?' he asked.

'Turn left in the road, couple of hundred yards on the right, opposite Tallis House, that's the place with bay windows and black railings. They've roped you in for the annual play, haven't they?'

'Not really, just thought I'd take a look. Meet people.'

'That's how it starts, they'll drag you in all right. It's fun though. I'm in it as well. Watch out for Oona.'

'Oona?'

'She's the director. A wide woman, big thighs and I swear she eats aphrodisiacs like liquorice allsorts. She'll have you for breakfast.'

*   *   *

At eight o'clock that evening Joe walked out into the village and turned left, a direction he hadn't yet taken. Barrington had been correct; The Priory wasn't far.

It was a stone built pile, of three storeys, steep roofed in slate and with tall narrow windows. Half hidden by high stone walls it was for ever captured in a loose net of unmovable shadow cast by huge mature trees, a dozen of them, a mixture of beech, cedar and yew. There was a vast rookery in the topmost branches above the house, a score of nests like shaggy-haired, severed heads stuck on pikes, and the rooks quarrelled loudly as Joe approached, as if they hadn't yet decided who was sleeping where.

The Priory imposed itself on that north end of the village, it loomed, long and large. The grass of its garden needed cutting, and unkempt bushes swirled along the edge of the uneven drive. It was a Boris Karloff residence.

The evening was warm and the front door, wide and heavy, stood open, as did most of the windows.

There was a sheet of white paper pinned to the door. The message on it had been written with a fountain pen in pale blue ink; the hand loose and generous.

'We are at the end of the garden, the wine is poured. Oona.'

The drive continued to the right and then on around the building. The garden at the rear was dishevelled; the shrubs encroaching on the drive with an Amazonian abandon. The drive soon dwindled to a path, and the trees closed in, as mature and as high as those that surrounded the front of the house. Joe pressed ahead through the bushes, and the terrain sloped upwards, steeply, so much so that on occasion two or three stone steps had been cut into the ground to aid progress. Abruptly the bushes ended, in a straight line, and there, at the very end of the property, was a wide lawn and, at the back of it, a raised terrace, as wide as the lawn, with steps on either side, bounded at the rear by a stone wall. It was an outdoor stage, a pastoral theatre.

In the middle of the lawn were some half a dozen people relaxing on wrought iron chairs. On a matching table were several bottles of red and white wine standing in ice-buckets. Oona Trowbridge saw Joe first and rose from her seat. Erica stood also. The others turned their heads as Joe went towards them.

'Ah Erica,' said Oona. 'Here's your Mr Rapps. He's handsome, isn't he? And just the right age. Where on earth did you discover him?'

Erica laughed; 'Oh, I found him under a tree like a dropped acorn.'

Oona was an outgoing creature, and large, her flesh delicious, soft and much massaged by men who had enjoyed losing their hands in it; she wore a flowing white skirt which had been chosen to dissimulate the vastness of her thighs, and a loose crimson blouse which performed the same service for her unsculptured bosoms. Her face was long, her eyes were wide set and her black hair, parted in the middle, fell straight to her shoulders.

'Come and sit by me,' she said to Joe, indicating a place on the bench beside her. 'White or red?'

Joe did as he was told. A horde of women were traipsing into his life and organising it.

'Red,' he said.

Oona filled a tumbler with wine and pushed forward a plateful of cheese biscuits. A grey light filtered down from the trees in a dust of powdered graphite, and half a dozen candles, set on the table, glowed yellow in it.

'This is Joe Rapps,' Oona said to everybody, 'just arrived from India.' She pointed round the table. 'That there is Martyn Troy, head of our primary school...never trust a man with two y's in his name. Then there's Jane Medrowska, she'll be playing the harp in this production, she also leads the church choir, sings like a bird, but doesn't say much. The man next to her, with the long hair and the sharp nose is Mattie Juffkins, runs the bookshop in Thame, a sly rogue...and the Japanese fellow is Makoto, he's the pastry cook at the Vivaldi, can't speak English yet but will do by the time of the production. I'm giving him lessons – one to one of course. He'll be a scene shifter and dog's body. 'Bout time the Japanese did something for us, reparations are certainly in order.'

'Oh, Oona!' said Jane Medrowska, and that was all she did say.

'Where had we got to?' asked Martyn Troy.

'Choosing the parts,' answered Juffkins.

'Right,' said Oona. 'Rosalind to be played by Erica; because she's so pretty. Celia by that rather blousy lady who runs the hairdresser's in Wheatley.'

'Duke Frederic?' asked Erica.

'Well it's all type casting, the whole play: Duke Frederic is Vernon Minge, and Duke Senior by that man who works for Radio Oxford, and lives at Monkery Farm.'

'But he's got an American accent,' said Martyn Troy.

'I know, dear,' retorted Oona, 'but you have to take what you can get when it comes to male parts, if you'll excuse the expression. You Martyn are to play the lovely Orlando, whom everyone fancies...there's type casting for you...you do have a bit of a reputation amongst the yummie mummies. I'm sure you've been up to hanky-panky.'

'That's why my school is over-subscribed.'

'Jacques? He's important.'

'That's Juffkins.'

'But he's got an Irish accent.'

'Celtic melancholia, my dear, the twilight.'

'Oliver?'

'I think I've got Barrington, it wasn't easy but he'll be just right. Heavy and solid. Besides, he's a good drinker. Touchstone's a problem. We need some of the smaller parts now...Silvius and Phebe, Audrey...think we'll get those without too much trouble...I think Joe could play Silvius very well, don't you?'

'Oh no,' said Joe. 'I'm being shanghaied here.'

'It's only a short part, Joe,' said Erica. 'Silvius is the love sick shepherd, who is treated so badly by Phebe, his woman. You could moon about the stage, and look sad and bereft, waiting for things to happen, type casting yet again.'

'Yes but who would play Phebe to his Silvius?,' asked Jeffkins.

'Aha,' Oona's shifted along the bench and her body touched against Joe's. 'Beryl from the pub would be ideal, but she's too busy...it'll have to be Cordelia Minge, she's got just the necessary inbuilt disdain and exaggerated idea of her own worth, and she loves acting, does it all the time.'

'Hang on,' protested Joe. Oona poured him another tumbler of wine and her hand brushed his. 'I've never acted in my life,' he said, 'and I certainly don't want to start now. I wouldn't know where to begin. I'll stage manage if you like, sell ice-creams.'

'Oh it'll be all right,' said Martyn Troy, 'there are plenty of men in the cast...it's great fun and it's very good for the village. We did 'Old Time Music-Hall' last year, very vulgar. We were rolling drunk every night. You'll have us for company, not to mention Makoto.'

'We won't take no for an answer,' insisted Oona, 'we've heard such good things about you from Erica, and Silvius hasn't many lines.'

'Yes,' said Martyn Troy. 'Imagine playing opposite Cordelia Minge. A destiny not to be sniffed at.'

'Indeed,' said Oona. 'We'll have a preliminary read-through with the whole cast in a month's time.' She tilted her glass and the others did the same.

'Oh God,' groaned Joe, clinking his glass against Oona's as he felt her massive thigh, alive, pushing against his with the strength of an anaconda. He hadn't been in Milton two minutes and now he was in a play, and drinking too much.

'Don't worry, Joe, you'll piss it,' said Oona, leaning further into him. 'Remember, 'All the world's a stage.''

At that everyone, except Makoto, and Joe, roared with laughter, and the line was repeated by the group at the table.

'All the world's a stage,' they said, raising their glasses in Joe's direction. 'All the world's a stage.'

*   *   *

Joe was not quite sure how he got back to Pegswell Lane, given the wine he'd drunk that day. It was nearly dark when he left the Priory, and he was shown the way by Martyn, the school teacher, who, fortunately, carried a torch.

'The others'll be drinking till gone midnight,' he explained. 'But I've got a yummy divorcee to visit. Kids aren't doing too well at school, that's why I got away early.'

He left Joe at the top of Pegswell Lane where Barrington was already waiting. 'You're only a little bit late,' he said, 'anyway it's better to go at dusk.' Night glasses were slung around his neck.

'I wonder if I should still go.' Joe staggered a little.

Barrington laughed and ruffled Joe's hair. 'Come on,' he said, 'you'll soon walk it off.'

They went through the village without speaking. Lights were on in the windows, curtains were being drawn. The heat had been oppressive all day and although the sun was long gone the evening was close and sultry, as if promising a storm, but there was no noise in the sky save a distant hum from the motorway over to the north.

The lights were on in the Bull public house but Barrington strode on past. Behind the pub were two or three houses and the track leading to them dwindled rapidly into a scruffy path with stinging nettles on each side.

'This path's called the Grove,' explained Barrington. 'It's a short cut to Haseley Magna. It goes behind the Vivaldi.'

A hundred yards along the path they came to a stile, which they climbed, entering a wide field where the darkness lay in long hollows under the hedges. Joe stared into the gloom and made out a flock of sheep, dispersed over a large area and bedded down for the night. He heard one or two of them cough, sneezing snot from their nostrils. The hotel, floodlit, glittered across the night about half a mile further on. The two men stopped for a while and looked at the distant building, its turrets and towers standing out against the sky.

'It used to be a manor house,' said Barrington.

'It looks like the chateau out of Puss in Boots,' said Joe.

Just then there was a movement on the far side of the field and to the right, a figure in white gliding along by the boundary that separated the pasture from the grounds of the hotel. Barrington raised his binoculars. 'It's a woman,' he said, 'with long hair. She's moving fast though…floating over the grass, like a bloody ghost.' The figure hesitated, stopped for an instant, disappeared, reappeared, moved on and then disappeared again. The whole episode had taken no longer than thirty seconds. The two men stood silent and unmoving for about as long again.

Barrington broke the silence. 'A woman alone across the fields at ten, very strange.'

'And a woman in white,' said Joe, 'You said you thought there were things going on in Milton after dark.'

'We'll go down there,' said Barrington, 'take a look.'

The two men went forward over the tussocky grass as quickly as they could without running, disturbing several drowsy sheep who, with much effort, got to their feet and trotted away in search of a quieter place in which to sleep. Joe and Barrington came at last to the hotel's helicopter pad and went through a small iron gate which led directly to herb gardens and greenhouses. The sky was properly dark now and the night lay in one uniform gloom across the fields.

Joe followed Barrington between low box-wood hedges, past bronze and marble statues of swans and milkmaids, and across a stream by a tiny bridge until they came to an ornamental lake surrounded by a terrace laid with York stone slabs. There was a small row-boat floating on the lake, looking more magical than real, for now the moon was up and, away from the floodlights, its beams shed silver everywhere.

'Very King Arthur,' said Joe, 'Bet you could find Excalibur in there.'

He halted for a moment, tipsily romantic, paying a homage to the gardens in which he stood. The scents of the night were changing, though the air was still charged with the fragrance of an endless spring day; it was a mixture of mown grass, rich like top quality hay, clear water, dark leaves and cherry blossom. The tower of the church, which stood just beyond the hotel, was caught in the moonlight and loomed over the cemetery wall. An owl swooped, and there came the squeal of a tiny mammal as it perished in hard talons.

On the far side of the lake was a flight of stairs which Barrington and Joe climbed. They passed underneath an archway and emerged on to a wide expanse of lawn cut as close as carpet. Before them stretched the hotel in its luxury, lights gleaming from the huge windows of the dining room, and there were more lights shining down from the first and second floors.

Barrington led Joe to the shadows under a cedar tree. They sat on a wooden bench and spread their legs. The moonlight had settled now into its own boundless quietness and Joe felt at ease in it.

'We'll take a rest,' said Barrington. 'We won't find our assassin here, but I'd like to know where the woman in white went. I didn't recognise her...and I know most people in these villages, just from the way they walk.'

'One case at a time,' said Joe. He gazed in at the restaurant windows, the waiters moving behind them, the diners at table, the women in their best dresses. Barrington nudged Joe's arm and shoved a silver hip flask in front of him. 'I take this on my patrols,' he said, 'keeps the inner man going. Have a swig.'

Joe took the flask and raised it to his lips. It was good brandy, Armagnac by the smell and taste of it. A fine odour to add to the smells of a spring evening.

'What did you think of Vernon Minge?' asked Barrington.

'I don't know really...he seems typical Oxbridge. He's good looking in a square jawed, florid way, I suppose. Certainly fancies himself...loves women, and tries to make love to them all, would do if he had several life times. Mind you, that doesn't make him a bad person. I'm told that college lecturers get through a fair number of students.'

'Summer school is where he scores.' Barrington sounded envious. He took the flask from Joe, drank and then returned it. 'Those poor little American girls come over for a course in European civilisation and get Vernon Minge crawling all over them.'

'Nice work if you can get it,' said Joe, and gave the flask back to Barrington.

'He's very partial to nannies is our Vernon, as you know.' Barrington took a deep pull at the Armagnac but he wasn't mean with it. Joe took the flask from him. The brandy began to reignite the wine he had consumed earlier.

'Norland nannies preferably. Top of the league he says they are. Classy girls, good families. More satisfaction in seducing them, that's what he says. He loves their uniforms too, white and brown, starched aprons. There's plenty for him to get into round here.' Barrington gave a fruity laugh. 'I smell like a Christmas pudding.'

Joe laughed too. He would be more than tipsy soon. 'Aren't

they a bit young?'

'Well, I think that's what he likes.'

Some figures in the restaurant moved across the windows; the lights gleamed golden and welcoming.

Barrington changed the subject. 'Costs a fortune to eat in there. They fly down from London by helicopter: celebrities, television people, Arab Sheiks. Bottle of Margaux costs eighteen hundred quid, so I've been told.'

'Obscene.'

'Not if you've got it, it ain't...tell you what though, if we catch the assassin we'll treat ourselves to a slap up meal in there.'

'Done,' said Joe. 'There's nothing left in the flask.'

'I bet there isn't. We could go inside for one, the bar's not bad. We might see the woman in white. Follow me, old chum.'

Entering the hotel was like entering a church. The silence was reverential, the carpets yielding. Barrington turned left, away from the restaurant, and a corridor led them past two or three sitting rooms to a small bar where a barman waited, all alone. He smiled like a tombstone.

'Two vodka martinis,' said Barrington without asking Joe what he wanted. Joe knew then that there was trouble ahead. They sat at a low table, and after a little while the drinks arrived.

'That Vernon's been caught with his trousers down a couple of times. I was out looking for the assassin a couple of months ago, sitting on the village green, could have been two in the morning...very dark, and he went by with a ladder on his shoulder...I'm not kidding you...' Both men sniggered. The vodka martinis were strong enough to fuel Russian rockets. 'He was keeping to the side of the road, in the darkest part. I followed him...I still have an open mind about him being the assassin or not...'

'He must be too busy doing nannies to go round shooting dogs.'

'The criminal mind is a complicated piece of machinery,' said Barrington, his voice beginning to slur. 'He's an intellectual, so there's room in his schemes for all kinds of skulduggery.'

'Nannies, American students...and dogs...can't wait to read his memoirs.'

'Anyway, I followed him with his ladder. Past Chiltern Hall, on the other side of the road, there's another big house, Queen Anne style, Alden Manor. Big estate too. Stables at the rear, large grounds. The nanny slept first floor back. Vernon used the ladder to get over the wall, then into the window of her bedroom...'

'Got to admire his gall,' said Joe. He took a sip of his drink and felt it slide directly into his blood stream. While he was dealing with that Barrington ordered two more. They appeared on the table immediately. The thought of Vernon, immaculately dressed, stealing down the village with a ladder on his shoulder was too much for Joe and he began to laugh again, a laugh that was close to being uncontrollable. Barrington was in the same difficulty.

'I followed him into the property. There's a gate at the back which had been left open...I saw him get to the top of the ladder, the window opened and I saw her white arms wrap around his neck. It must have felt like heaven. They kissed while he was still on the ladder. I don't know what he's got but he must have it in spades.'

'Then?'

'Then nothing. I went home to bed. He did tell me about it later. He told me him and the girl had been discovered by the housekeeper, a real harridan. I've seen her in the village shop – she could curdle milk at five hundred yards. She didn't say much on the night but she cornered him one day and threatened to tell his wife unless...' Barrington went into a spasm of laughter.

'...unless?'

'Unless he visited her in the same way and for the same purpose. You should have seen his face when he told me...pitiable it was...'

Barrington's laughter was catching, and Joe was swept along by it.

'He was caught, you see. If the housekeeper had told Vernon's wife he'd have been dead. Cornelia, that's his wife, is a fearsome creature, flashy, but she can handle Vernon all right...face like a haunted house, red hair down to her shoulders.'

'So?'

'So Vernon was nice to the housekeeper. She was happy for a while I suppose, or perhaps she was disappointed in Vernon's performance. Anyway, that was the story I was told. The nanny, she went a few weeks later...Vernon does a big turnover in nannies.'

They laughed again, louder than before. The barman frowned. He lodged in the village and had seen Barrington in action in the pub. He was not the right kind of clientele for the Vivaldi. Behind the bar he pressed a button.

Barrington banged the table with the flat of his hand, for emphasis. 'I don't know how he got out of her clutches, it must have taken him weeks...it was only last year. Might still be performing for all I know – The Flying Dutchman of the double-bed.' Now he raised his hand at the barman. 'Two more,' he said.

The barman hesitated, was about to refuse, when a man wearing a dinner jacket came to the bar entrance and stood for a while surveying the scene. He was overweight, about five feet six tall, bearing a round stomach which, although giving an appearance of solidity, seemed to have a life of its own, and moved left and right as the man shifted his gaze. His hair, the colour of dirty straw, surged back from his forehead in two cresting waves. He had a large nose for sniffing out embezzlement amongst his staff, his ears were large and creased like some kind of sun-dried fruit; his coarse skin was a net of red veins. This was Monsieur Claude de Topinambour, owner and master chef of the Vivaldi.

'Oh my God,' said Barrington, 'We're in for a wigging...he's Belgian, you see.' Both Barrington and Joe found this remark hilarious. They leant back in their seats and laughed until the tears ran.

Topinambour advanced until he stood looking down at Barrington. 'I shall have to ask you gentlemen to leave,' he said. 'You aren't residents and in any case you are making too much noise...this isn't the village pub. You can be heard in the restaurant, and you are disturbing my clients.'

'I'm a client,' said Joe, 'and I ain't disturbing me a bit.'

'Aw, come on Claude,' said Barrington, 'one more and we'll be on our way...and tell us about the woman in white who we saw creeping in here...is she your bit of crumpet?'

'I've had nothing but disturbances with you,' said Topinambour. 'You have brought the most disreputable people here in the past, and from what I have heard of this gentleman...' he sneered at Joe and stretched, trying to gain a foot in height...'your new acquaintance is no improvement on your other friends...just back from India, is it? I'm surprised that they let you into the country.'

Joe wasn't too good in his cups; he lost his temper and sprang to his feet, knocking the low coffee table with his knee and sending the glasses crashing to the floor, breaking them. He made an attempt to grab Topinambour's tie so that he could pull him onto a punch, but he missed.

'You Belgian cough-drop!' he shouted, knowing that it wasn't much of an insult. 'And how did you get into the country? In a banana boat?'

Topinambour stepped back, his red face turning pale. Two chunky waiters appeared in the bar, they took a few paces forward.

'Leave it, Joe,' said Barrington.

'Yes,' said Topinambour, the crimson flooding back into his face. 'That damage is going on your bill, Barrington. Now leave before you end up battered.' He chuckled at his little culinary joke. He waved the two waiters further into the room. The barman picked up the pieces of broken glass.

Barrington and Joe began to make their way towards the door, none too steadily. Topinambour got out of their way, a sarcastic smile on his thick lips. 'And, Barrington,' he said, 'don't bother to come back here, with or without your new friend...I'll have you thrown out before you get in.'

The two men were escorted to the front of the hotel, and pushed out into the night air, which hit them like another dose of vodka. The two waiters followed them across the gravelled courtyard and onto the road. They watched as Barrington and Joe, arms around each other, swayed, as if tectonic plates, miles beneath their feet, were preparing for a serious earthquake.

'Bloody 'ell,' said Joe, 'we've taken some on board tonight.'

'Courage, my friend,' said Barrington, 'the devil is dead.'

'I wouldn't eat in his restaurant if I was still in Wandsworth,' said Joe. 'How did that little Belgian cough drop know about my trip to India?'

'Easy,' replied Barrington. 'All his waiters and receptionists lodge in the village...gossip goes round like wildfire...You're a fellow of great interest to everyone, someone to talk about over the supper table.'

'This is the first time I've been pissed since I returned from the orient...' said Joe, suddenly. 'But then I've only been out two days...and it's bloody wonderful.'

'You're a good fellow,' said Barrington, 'for an old lag. I nearly choked when you called him a Belgian cough-drop, bloody marvellous.' He slapped Joe on the back. 'Come on, we haven't finished yet, we've got to get to Haseley... dammit, we should have filled the flask at the Vivaldi, we'll be sober if we don't watch out...we'll get to the Plough before it closes and get a refill...they never close till midnight...and not even then.'

They came to a stile and helped each other over it. They were at the back of the hotel again and, in the moonlight, easily found their path. Once more the sheep got to their feet and ambled out of the way, still coughing and snorting snot, but peevishly, doubly annoyed at being disturbed twice. At last Barrington led Joe across a main road, picked up another path that took them behind a tractor factory and on by a half ruined windmill. Then they passed between two fields until the path became a track that led them into the village of Haseley Magna.

* * *

There was only the slightest glimmer of light showing from the Plough, and only a few cars in the car park. Barrington tapped on the door at the rear; 'Nobody cares anymore,' he said. 'Licensing hours are a thing of the past.' He pushed at the door,

which was open anyway, and a rectangle of light slanted out
into the darkness and Joe followed Barrington inside.

He found himself in a long narrow bar. The lights were dim
and there were large areas of shadow in the corners of the
room. There were about ten people present; half a dozen
standing, and four sitting at a large round table, playing
dominoes.

There was silence and the ten heads turned to see who the
newcomers were, then conversation was resumed as they
recognised Barrington.

'Hello, Jack,' said someone. 'Found who's killing your dogs
yet?'

Barrington was used to the jibe. He smiled and ignored it. He
jerked a thumb at Joe.

'This here's Joe Rapps,' he said, 'bought Pegswell Cottage in
Milton Magna.'

Another man came through a curtain and stood behind the
bar. A young man with thick curly hair, wearing jeans.

'What'll it be?' he asked.

'Two vodka tonics, we're off drink.' said Barrington.

The young barman placed the drinks on the bar and waved
the money away when Barrington offered it. He looked at Joe.
'Call it a welcome drink,' he said. 'India eh?'

'Yes,' said Joe. He had come to like the idea of India.
'Name's Joe.'

Barrington put some money down. 'Give us a bottle of vodka
anyway,' he said.

The barman laughed. 'You're still out looking for whoever's
killing them dogs?' he asked, 'and you've dragged this poor
bloke into it as well. You'll never catch 'em.'

'There was another dog shot yesterday,' said one of the
drinkers, 'over Haseley Parva...it was an 'orrible Jack Russell
anyway.'

'Whose was it?' asked Barrington.

'Ole Miss Hatt's, it was found behind the telephone box.
Nice clean shot. Bob Wise told me, he seen it.'

'Miss Hatt was right put out about it. She'd had that dog
since it was a pup, took it everywhere, bed and all. "Whisky",

that was its name. She drinks enough of it.'

'Who's killing these dogs though? It's an odd business.'

'Someone off his rocker.'

'That could be anyone in this bloody parish.'

Joe only had to smell his drink to feel it attacking his brain, but he took a sip nevertheless.

Barrington slipped the bottle of vodka into his jacket pocket. 'We got aimed out of the Vivaldi just now,' he said. 'D and D.'

'You coppers are all the same. Dipsos.'

Joe ordered, and paid for, two more drinks.

'Old Topinambour was it? Fancies himself, that one. Helicopters, telly stars, royalty, and some pop stars.'

'They say the Queen Mum used to come down regular.'

'On our bloody money,' said a voice from the domino table. Joe turned to look. He didn't need to be told it was Norah's husband – the postman who steamed envelopes open – he was still wearing his uniform trousers. ' 'Bout time them parasites was put down. I'd like to see 'em swinging a pick in a three foot seam, all of 'em, 'cept we ain't got any coal mines any more.'

'She liked her gin,' said the barman. 'Used to keep it in a silver tea pot by her bed when she went visiting.'

'Shame them Hanoverians has to live in tied cottages,' said the postman, 'Balmoral, Windsor and such, just like my mum and dad over Haseley Parva. Take us for mugs they do, and that's what we are for putting up with 'em.'

Barrington and Joe finished their drinks and made for the door. All heads turned to watch them leave.

'Steady as you go,' someone yelled.

'Mind you don't get shot yourself, Jack,' said another. Barrington waved, Joe opened the door and the two of them were back out into the night.

'Now,' said Barrington, 'on we go.' He patted the vodka in his pocket. 'We have provisions, and we'll be off to Haseley Parva.'

'We won't find anything there,' said Joe, 'if there was one shot the other day.'

'That's just what they'd expect us to think,' said Barrington tapping the side of his nose, 'so that's where we'll go.' And stumbling slightly Barrington led the way into another footpath, the moon bright enough to throw clear shadows of the two men across the ground.

*   *   *

They went by the winding road to Haseley Parva, taking nips from the bottle of vodka now and then to make sure they didn't decline into sobriety. The air was still and they found nothing and saw nothing, only a few streaks of cloud occasionally dulling the bright moon, and the looming shapes of black trees leaning over to threaten them. The night was silent too except, from time to time, for the echo of a screech owl resounding across the empty fields. After an hour or so Joe and Barrington returned to Haseley Magna by way of a bridlepath and came to the gates of a huge eighteenth century house, set well back from the road. There was a drive, a high wall and massive balls on tall pillars.

'You know you've arrived when you've got balls on your pillars,' said Joe, and snorted, sending vodka up the back of his nose.

'You do here,' agreed Barrington. 'This is Lord Hazelmere's gaff...Hazelmere Court.'

At the very moment he said this they both saw the figure in white again, some three hundred yards away. This time they had a clearer view of it. Barrington gave Joe the bottle to hold and put the binoculars to his eyes. 'It's a woman,' he whispered, 'a long white raincoat, long skirt underneath and blond hair...looks like a woman, tall though, takes long steps, slithering along.'

'Let's get after her,' said Joe, keen to make a capture, and both men began to run forward immediately, staggering more than running, along a path that followed the perimeter of Hazelmere Court.

'Come on Joe,' yelled Barrington, 'faster.'

The figure in white heard Barrington's shout and began to run, ahead of them on the same path. Then, once again, she disappeared. Barrington and Joe tried to pick up speed but the night's intake of alcohol was working against them. At last they came abreast of a postern gate set in the wall. It was open. They burst through it and, now only two hundred yards away, they saw the woman in white again, just disappearing into a small stand of trees.

'Come on,' yelled Barrington, louder this time, 'come on.'

'We're trespassing,' said Joe. He was breathing hard, and the blood was beating violently in his heart. He was at pains to keep going.

'Bugger trespassing,' said Barrington, 'citizen's arrest, you'll see. I'll give her trespass.'

They were into the trees now where it was too dark to see the path, though their feet found it easily enough. Then they were out into the waning moonlight, pushing ahead as fast as they could. The woman in white was not moving easily either and was visibly slowing, limping even.

'I've got her this time,' Barrington was panting, 'and all these months I thought it was a man...and at Hazelmere Court as well...there's a turn up.' He gasped: 'My God I'm out of condition.' He stopped for an instant and took three or four deep breaths.

But now the quarry had come to the side of the great house and gone into a shadow darker than the rest. The pursuers took up the chase again. 'Mustn't let her get away,' said Barrington.

The woman ran on, close to the wall of the house, and then, arriving at the back of it, turned at a right angle, disappearing as she did so.

'Dammit,' said Barrington, 'she's gone again. Quick.'

Both men forced themselves to pick up speed, came to the corner, turned it, and stopped. The woman in white was nowhere to be seen. The marble terrace was long, wide, elegant and empty. A balustraded staircase in stone led down to the gardens, there were plants in pots, and a swing seat or two...but no human figure.

Barrington and Joe came to the stonework of the balustrade. They leant forward, hands on knees and gasped for breath.

'That was terrible,' said Joe between huge gulps of air, 'it's made me feel quite sick.'

For a while they sat in one of the swing seats, not speaking. Then, when their bodies had recovered, they retraced their steps to the postern gate, walking unsteadily. Barrington was inconsolable. 'We nearly had her,' he said. 'We were that close. I wonder where she could have gone?'

'I don't know,' said Joe, 'probably tucked up in bed now like we ought to be. It's bloody three o'clock in the morning, and we're seriously pissed.'

'Okay,' said Barrington. All the fire had gone out of him, but that didn't mean he had sobered up. 'The only thing we can say in our favour is that we might have narrowed the field to Hazelmere Court...might have.'

*　　*　　*

The moon had gone and the sky was lightening in the east. Barrington followed a footpath that led along the side of Haseley churchyard, and then into it. Joe, exhausted now, kept close behind him. They passed through a kissing gate, and it swung on rusty hinges. Joe thought about saying, 'Give us a kiss, Jack,' but decided against it. The mirth had faded from the expedition. There was now enough light for Joe to see the gravestones and crosses that were close to him, and the nave of the church had become a looming shadow, distinguished in the way that Norman churches are; a square tower and one low roof set into a higher one.

'Got lovely brasses in there,' said Barrington, without any interest. The vodka had done for him. 'People come from all over...' Suddenly he yelled and Joe saw and heard him fall over. A heavy disastrous sound. 'Well fuck it!' Barrington couldn't contain his anger. He swore again and again. A broken ankle at least.

'Are you okay?' cried Joe, 'are you okay?' He darted round the prone figure of Barrington and crouched so that he could get close and speak to him. The swearing continued. Then he saw why. Barrington had tripped over a dead dog, set deliberately across the path, a large dog.

'That bloody woman in white,' cursed Barrington. 'Led us on

a wild goose chase, and all the while she had set this up. I'll kill her when I catch her, a gang rape would be too good for her. I'll throw her over to the whole of the Metropolitan Police Force.'

Joe, realizing that Barrington was in no danger, stood and took a step back, his knees aching, his head dizzy from rising too quickly. As he did so his right foot slipped from under him and he fell sideways, twisting into an open grave. His head banged against the lip of the tomb and the breath was knocked from him as he landed six foot down. He lay flat on his stomach, surprised and stunned, feeling pain in spite of the alcohol he had consumed.

Barrington got to his hands and knees and looked at the dog. 'Another red flag on me map,' he said. 'There'll be trouble over this, it's Sir Beasley's Red Setter, Belcher's Farm. He'll be livid, it's a bloody thoroughbred. Shot just behind the shoulder...we didn't hear a thing, did we? I told you, a silencer.'

Joe lay without moving, sure he was going to be sick. He tried to draw a decent breath but could only manage a series of shallow gasps.

'Joe,' said Barrington, still on his knees. 'Joe, where the hell are you?'

'I'm down here. Somebody's dug a grave.'

'They do, in graveyards.' On his hands and knees Barrington crawled over to the pit and looked down, swaying dangerously. 'Whoa,' he advised himself, 'steady. There must be a funeral tomorrow.'

Joe lay still a little longer. The smell of the earth was pungent, agreeable in a way. He was so tired, so drunk that he could have gone to sleep just where he was. The sky was streaked with mother of pearl now, and dawn was edging across the fields. A beetle crawled over his hand; he felt like sneezing. He sniffed; he could smell something else apart from Oxfordshire earth. He dug his fingers into the ground and began to push his body up so that he could get his legs beneath him. The earth was loose and shifted, his hands found little purchase and sank several inches deeper. That was strange, he thought. He would have thought the bottom of a grave would have been harder clay maybe. His fingers touched something,

something round, something slippery, something that gave under pressure but in a different way to the way the earth gave.

He scratched a layer of dirt away. He raised his head a little so that he could look. There was something white, a dress. Joe scratched a little more. It was white all right, a sleeve and there was a human arm in it – a woman's arm.

Joe screamed then, a scream that came from his guts. He didn't do dead bodies. Getting to his feet was no effort now. He didn't know how he did it but his feet squirmed on what must have been the woman's thighs and he flew upwards out of the grave, pushing Barrington out of his way. He was trembling with fear and disgust, he crouched on the grass, facing Barrington, both of them on all fours. The words wouldn't come, he was gibbering.

Words came to Barrington easily enough. 'Look at that bloody dog,' he said, 'I'm livid.'

'Jack,' stuttered Joe. 'Jack...'

'I know, bloody woman in white...'

'Listen, there's a dead woman in the bottom of this grave, I saw her arm...she's another woman in white.'

It must have been his police background but Barrington didn't doubt it for a moment. He sobered up immediately and, carefully, levering with his arms, his feet spread, he lowered himself into the grave.

Joe was sick then, there, where he was kneeling. When he'd finished he crawled to the mound of spoil, covered in its sheet of plastic grass, and sat on it. The dawn was up and Joe could see beyond the churchyard wall.

After about five minutes Barrington came to sit beside him. He pulled the vodka bottle from his jacket pocket. 'It's a Norland nanny,' he said at length, 'in her uniform, white and brown. Not been dead many days...three or four perhaps. Strangled by the look of it.'

He took out his mobile phone and rang the police. 'We'll have to wait till they get here,' he said. They both drank from the bottle. A couple of swigs each and it was finished. The silence of the night gave way to the noises of early morning; a distant car leaving the village; an owl dipping home and the beginning of the dawn chorus, the songs of the birds becoming louder, and then louder again.

Barrington slipped the bottle back into his pocket. 'It was the nanny from Harrison's Farm,' he said, 'the one called Helen...the one Vernon Minge said had gone missing.'

*   *   *

The next day Joe had several visitors, and the first, Norah, was the best of them. Joe had got into bed at about five o'clock, with the sky clear and the grey turning to gold in the east, his head thumping with the vodka.

The police had turned up at the churchyard in two cars, slithering to a halt on the gravel of the track that led to the front of the church. They came through the second of the two kissing gates, moving fast and business-like. Joe had been apprehensive; the police always tended to suspect those who found the body, and now he was doubly suspect – he had form and he had already killed two people.

The coppers knew Barrington well, they were all from the Thames Valley police where Barrington had spent his working life. It must have been for that reason that Joe was hardly questioned.

'He lives next door to me,' said Barrington, putting an arm around Joe's shoulders. 'He'll be there in the morning even if I have to nail him to the floor...I know we were pissed but he'd have had to be a magician to get out of my sight at any time during the night.'

'It'll depend on when she was killed, won't it?' said the inspector in charge as he watched his men tape off the scene of the crime and tie the kissing gates shut.

A woman constable drove them over to Milton Magna. Joe's door stood ajar and he was so pleased to get home that he leant with his forehead resting against the coolness of the stone wall, calming himself after the adventures of the night. Barrington had marched past him with a gruff 'Goodnight,' no doubt anxious to get to bed himself just as soon as he could. Joe pulled himself together, pushed at his door and was on the point of crossing the threshold when he heard a bellowing from the direction of Barrington's cottage.

His first thought was that Barrington had fallen over again and hurt himself. He ran along the twisting path, behind some bushes, and came to Barrington's front door to find him shaking his fists at the sky, his face staring upwards, still bellowing like a bull enraged. Lying on his doorstep, blood trickling from a head wound to form a halo, lay a dead dog, neatly shot.

Barrington could hardly speak. 'Two bloody dogs in one night,' he hissed. 'That woman's taking the piss out of me. I'll get her if it's the last thing I do. I'll wring her bloody neck.'

Joe couldn't find the energy to share Barrington's anger. He could only think of the dead girl they had found. 'Jack,' he said. 'I'm sorry about the dog...but we found a murdered nanny tonight...I mean, that's terrifying...after all, a dog is only a dog.'

Barrington turned a face of bitterness and hatred in Joe's direction. 'It's not the dogs, Joe, it's not the dogs. It's what this killer is doing to me, to the village. There'll be a score of coppers onto the nanny killing...but there's only me to sort this out...only me.'

Joe shrugged. 'Try to get some sleep, Jack,' he said, 'we're both exhausted.' With that he returned to his own house, went upstairs and pausing only to remove his shoes, threw back the duvet and got into bed.

Norah was there waiting for him, naked. He didn't realize it at first, not until she started undressing him. 'You've been out with that Jack Barrington,' she said. 'You smell like a brewery.'

'Oh no,' moaned Joe. He could hear the despair in his own voice. 'I need to sleep...what the hell are you doing here...?'

'My husband has to get up at four,' she explained, 'gets into the sorting office by four thirty...I can never get to sleep afterwards...he doesn't come home till three in the afternoon.'

Joe let his head fall back on to his pillow and fell into a delicious slumber. When he awoke he felt like a deep sea diver with a huge helmet clamped to his head, inside which everything was throbbing. He was wearing lead boots too.

Norah was massaging his face with cold cream, stroking his temples. Her touch was exquisite and gradually the diver's helmet around his skull loosened. She ran her hands over his chest and his thighs and kissed his nipples. Norah was an enthusiast; she put her heart and soul into sex, it was the centre of her life. To her it was a religion, but far more satisfying than the gift of faith.

Joe had always found it bizarre that whenever he had been drinking his randiness increased in direct proportion to the hangover he was carrying: force five, nothing much; force eight and he awoke with an erection; force ten, which was what he had that morning, and the erection was like a girder, indestructible. Norah found it and sighed with delight. Joe lay back, halfway between pain and pleasure – not a bad place to be, he decided. Norah clambered on and crouched so that she could plant lascivious kisses all over his face. It was good, very good, and Joe let his senses drift away until he became weightless.

When she'd finished with him she lay by his side and stroked his face again. Joe blinked but the day was coming through the curtains and the light was too fierce for him. The jazz-bird was singing, mocking again. 'You're good,' said Norah.

'I didn't do a thing,' said Joe, 'I just provided the wherewithal.'

'Some wherewithal.'

'I gotta go to sleep,' insisted Joe. 'Life's too fast in Milton Magna. I feel ill, give a guy a break. Have a shower and go home...what's the time?'

'I never have a shower afterwards.' Norah laughed. 'I'd miss the trickleback. It's seven o'clock.'

'Trickleback?' queried Joe.

'Oh, Joe,' said Norah.

'Norah, don't tell me what I think it is you're going to tell me.'

'I know the human body and all its corners.'

'Why don't you go home?'

'The world is divided into women who like sex at night, most of them, and women who like sex in the morning. You'd think it would be a class thing, but it isn't. It cuts across class. Just because you have to go out to work doesn't mean you don't like sex in the morning. I had a Spanish waiter once, he called it 'el mañanero'…Carlos the God I called him. My husband loved his early morning swim…as soon as he came back from the beach, reception buzzed me on the phone and Carlos was out the window at the speed of light – so romantic.'

'So trickleback?' Joe's mind was cloudy with sleep.

'Sperm doesn't stay up there for ever, you know. It trickles back, down the leg, and if it happens when you're out shopping, or sitting at dinner with your husband, or taking drinks in the garden, it is unbelievably exciting. It reminds you of the love-making you had earlier, reminds you of your lover, where you did it, your bed or his, or someone else's – like when the neighbours are away and you have the key. Your whole body warms, you fall in love again and it's like making love one more time. Yet another experience you men can't have…it's wonderful.'

'I got all the way to forty years old and never knew about trickleback,' said Joe, and fell asleep.

*   *   *

The next visitor was Sylvie. She brought him his tea and marmalade toast.

'What's the time?' asked Joe, too lazy to raise his arm to look at his wrist watch.

'Ten o'clock,' said Sylvie. 'I let you sleep on a bit. I heard that you were out last night with Mr Barrington, up to no good. You traipsed mud all up the stairs, and your clothes are all over the floor, and they're covered in mud too. What were you up to? The gossip's all over the village, they can't talk of anything else in the shop. That Norah's no better than she should be. That poor girl, murdered, and you finding her. Lovely girl she was, that Helen, in her uniform and all. Such a thing to happen here.'

Joe pulled himself up in bed and reached for his tea.

Sylvie went on. 'Who could have done such a thing? There's

police cars everywhere, coppers asking questions. Harrison's Farm nanny it was, no smoke without fire, eh? Viscount Lewknor 'ad a nanny too, but she didn't stay long, something dodgy there I can tell you. And what about his father, he's an odd one, old Hazelmere, limping about, nasty fish eyes, all watery, he's got skin like the underside of a slab of cod. Wouldn't like to meet him on a dark night down a dark alley...Anyway, I've made you a lovely beef casserole for tonight, and I stocked up the fridge, you could have a nice tuna salad for lunch, nice and light, would be good for your liver, needs a good clean out after the drinking you did last night, I shouldn't wonder. You had quite a session in the Plough, so I heard. Bet you were singing too, waking up law-abiding citizens...'

'Oh, God,' said Joe, 'could I have another cup of tea before I get tarred and feathered by the Parish Council?'

*   *   *

A couple of plain clothes policemen were next. Hopkins and Cope. Joe was relaxing in the sitting room, unable to do much more than breathe. Sylvie had gone and he had drunk four or five cups of tea, now his head was nodding and he was fighting to stay awake. There was a knock and Joe went to the front door. He could see they were coppers, he'd met enough of them. 'Mr Rapps,' they said, almost together. 'Detective Inspector Hopkins,' said one. 'Detective Sergeant Cope,' said the other.

Joe let them in and conducted them to the sitting room and invited them to sit in armchairs.

'Last night,' said Hopkins, 'can you tell us what you were doing in Haseley churchyard at three o'clock in the morning?'

'Hasn't Mr Barrington told you?'

'We want corroboration.'

'We were looking for the person who's been shooting village dogs.'

'Shooting dogs.' Sergeant Cope shook his head. 'We could do with such a person in Thame, there's dog crap everywhere.'

'It was Barrington's idea. He is determined to solve the mystery,' said Joe.

'Didn't do too well when he was on the force,' said Hopkins, 'they retired him early.'

'We went to the Vivaldi.'

'Funny place to look for a dog shooter.'

'We didn't stay long, we got thrown out.'

'Sounds like Barrington.'

'We saw a woman in white.'

'In white?'

'Yes, only in the distance, flitting along by a hedge.'

'Flitting?'

'Then we went to the Plough...we had a drink or two, and we saw the woman in white again and chased her but she disappeared at the back of Hazelmere Court. Then I fell into the grave, banged myself on the head, and...'

'You found the body?'

'Yes, I was sick. I'm not good at bodies. Never seen a dead body before.'

'Not quite true is it, Mr Rapps? I believe you were in a road crash three years ago.'

Joe took a deep breath. It hadn't taken them long to get round to the accident. He had form so he was a likely suspect, or at least he was someone who had to be investigated.

'I did three years in Wandsworth for that. It doesn't make me a nanny strangler.'

Hopkins was on to it in a flash. 'How do you know she was strangled.'

'I don't,' said Joe. 'Manner of speaking, internal rhymes, 'n's and 'a's in both words.' The two policemen looked at each other. They knew a know-all when they found one.

Then Joe remembered. 'Barrington said so. He went down into the grave to have a look at her.' Joe shuddered. 'I couldn't have done it.'

Sergeant Cope changed the subject. 'What are you doing in Milton Magna?' he asked.

Joe knew that if he told the truth the answer would sound even more ridiculous than the answer about dog shooting. Oh, yes, a stretch limousine picked me up outside the prison, and a Bishop brought me down here and a billionairess gave me a house, a car and ten grand in the bank, oh, yes, and a housekeeper as well...Better not say that. 'I had to go somewhere,' said Joe, 'I stuck a pin in the map.'

'Did you know anyone here?'

'No.'

'It's suspicious, to say the least. A house, money in the bank, a Saab in the garage. We need to know where this wealth came from, Mr Rapps. Was there money laundering going on? Did someone in Wandsworth ask you to do some favours? Sunshine Leary, for example.'

'Sunshine Leary would crack my head open like a walnut, on the slightest excuse.'

'The money, Mr Rapps, where does it come from?'

'What has this got to do with the murdered girl?'

'That's just what we're trying to find out, Mr Rapps, and we're hoping you can tell us.'

Joe knew he could say no more without getting in deeper. He needed to ask the Countess what he could tell them.

'I'm not going to say anymore, not without seeing a lawyer.' Joe spoke primly like a virgin.

The two policemen sat stony-faced and silent. The silence invaded the room. Then eventually: 'You've never seen the murdered woman before?'

'Well,' said Joe. 'I dunno.'

'Did you look at her closely, to see if she was still alive?'

'Look at her closely! I was out of that hole in the ground like a rocket. I was scared witless.'

The two policemen stood. They nodded at each other as if they had both decided that Joe was a cretin and as transparent as cheap glass.

'Well, Mr Rapps, you are not to leave the village, and we want your passport.'

'Now?'

'Now. And we'll be back soon. An autopsy is being performed...that will help us.'

Joe crossed to the writing desk, opened it, took out his

passport and handed it over. 'I was going on holiday,' he said. It was a poor joke.

'Not back to India,' said Cope, and Hopkins laughed, cruel and cold. "Fraid that will have to wait.'

*　　*　　*

Joe had been exhausted by the interview. He felt as if the blood had been drained out of him. His bones had gone soft, the marrow steamed and soggy. He made a cup of Darjeeling to revivify himself and took it out to the arbour. He needed the view to refurbish his soul, to carry him away from an extremely ugly world. He had begun to see Milton Magna as a refuge, a place of beauty. Now with the discovery of the nanny's body and the arrival of Hopkins and Cope there was an awful chance that it might become like everywhere else.

He sipped his tea and tried to relax but then someone moved silently into the periphery of his vision. His heart leapt in his rib cage and he spilt half his drink over his trousers. There was a man at the edge of the arbour, a slight man wearing a crumpled grey suit and a dog collar.

He was about five feet six inches tall with fragile bones. His hair was gingery, sparse on his head. His eyes, as far as Joe could ascertain, were colourless, and while making every attempt to look at Joe those eyes weren't up to the job. They flickered all over, from arbour, to bench; from grass, to bush. It was a glance that was apprehensive and nervous, guilty even. His eyebrows were sandy like his hair, and there was dandruff on the shoulders of his suit. The skin on his face was patchy, like he was suffering from scurvy, and he was badly shaved, or perhaps not shaved at all. He was holding a large bike by the handlebars, an old roadster, painted black. The bike was too tall for its rider and mounting and dismounting must have been a problem for him.

The man hesitated. He looked around for somewhere to lean his bike. Finally, he chose a bush and let the machine fall into it. Then he turned and his voice, when he spoke, grated against the senses, like rusty corrugated iron.

'Meredith Baker,' he began, 'vicar of St Mary's, Milton Magna; St Peter's, Haseley Magna, and St James's at Milton Parva. Services are ambulant, you know, each Sunday in turn.'

The last thing Joe wanted was another visit. 'Hello,' he said.

'Yes,' said Baker, sitting down without being asked. 'You've been to India. How exciting!'

'Yes,' said Joe. 'I brought some good teas back with me. I could do you a lovely Darjeeling.' He was wondering when Milton Magna would run out of people ready, if not eager, to visit him.

Baker shook his head, beamed and glanced at his watch. "Tempus fugit," he said. 'Do you know, I don't usually do this, but I rather fancy a glass of Scotch, that is if you have any...I hardly ever touch it but I've just cycled from the hospital, sixteen miles there and back, visiting the halt and the lame, and I feel a bit halt and lame myself, in need of reinforcements.'

Joe set off for the house and the Reverend Baker continued to talk during Joe's absence, not stopping for a second, and was still talking when Joe returned with a generous tumbler of whisky. The clergyman didn't seem a bit put out by the size of the glass and clasped it eagerly in both hands.

'Oh, "gaudeamus igitur",' he said, as he raised the glass to his lips and took a good pull at it. 'Let us rejoice...I came back in good time today for a funeral at Haseley, but it's been postponed, the churchyard's all roped off by the police. But you know about that, you're the one that found the body. Strange isn't it? I mean finding a body in a grave when it's not supposed to be there. God knows when I'll get the funeral service in now, not for days, I shouldn't wonder. There would have been two bodies in the same grave...it is permitted of course as long as you have permission, but apparently this second body was an interloper, manner of speaking, and put in first. Saves money, I suppose – do you think that was behind it?'

'I think,' said Joe, 'that someone was trying to hide a murder.' He thought about a hair of the dog for himself but then decided against it. He'd better stick with tea.

'Do you really?' The vicar screwed up his nose in thought. '"O tempora! O mores!" What sad times we live in. Dirty work at the cross roads. "Pulvis et umbra sumus", we are all dust and shadow.'

The Reverend Baker went on talking, nodding his head, gazing about him, alighting on different subjects as the mood took him. 'You have a lovely house here, Mr Rapps. The view, just off the main road, spacious without being ostentatious, south facing. The vicarage is a bit poky, you know. You must have been upset last night, they told me in the shop. A hive of information that shop, if one can say a hive of information.'

'A honey pot of gossip,' suggested Joe.

'Well, "carpe diem"', said the vicar. He looked into the bottom of his empty tumbler, but said nothing.

'Would you like another one?' asked Joe.

'Well I shouldn't really but now the funeral's been cancelled...'

Joe rose and went into the kitchen. He thought again about a drink but made himself a mug of tea instead. His head was still tender, his brain a white sauce with a few rotten leeks in it. He poured another big one for the vicar.

Again the vicar was still talking to himself on Joe's return. Joe didn't mind, he did it himself all the time. 'It's an odd part of the world,' the vicar continued, 'between Haseley Magna churchyard and Hazelmere Court.' He took a swig from his glass. '"Nunc est bibendum"...now is it time to drink...A lot of people fleeing from Chalgrove field killed there, heading for the church, but didn't make it. Hunted down and slaughtered, thick with blood that ground, so an extra body, nice and tidy in a grave, doesn't make an awful lot of difference "sub speciæ æternitatis".'

'Yes,' said Joe.

'I think that in the future people will ask to be buried with their mobile phones so that they can send text messages from the other side, but where will they charge their batteries? Now there's a thing.'

'Yes, indeed,' said Joe.

'Such a pity they dropped Latin from the curricula of our schools. I ask you, referendums, stadiums, bacteriums. What next? Criterions I suppose, addendums. I was so upset the other day when someone I was speaking to, my interlocutor, didn't know what a "quid pro quo" was. Strange, eh, in a capitalist society?' The Reverend Baker placed his glass on the ground before him and cracked his knuckles one by one. Then he retrieved his drink and sipped at it, closing his eyes in pleasure.

'So who killed all these Chalgrove people?'

'The Civil War,' said the vicar. '"Bellaque matribus detestata." Wars detested by mothers. After the battle, the vanquished were hunted down. Ghosts everywhere, not that I'm supposed to believe in ghosts. That's odd too. I am allowed to believe in the after life but believing in ghosts is frowned upon...And have you ever thought that ghosts are never seen naked, always in clothes of the period? Do you think there's a theatrical costumiers on the other side?'

'Seems likely, now you come to mention it.'

'There's a long yew walk between Haseley Magna church and Hazelmere Court. It's very dark, even on a summer's day, at night it's most forbidding. At the time of the Civil War a young lord and his wife dwelt there, but the lord owed his loyalty to the king and set off to fight for him. He was absent two long years and she stayed there alone. At that time a young rector lived in a small cottage just below the church, where Latchford Lane slopes down, and at first...'

'Perhaps another whisky, vicar,' suggested Joe.

'Well, I shouldn't really, but it is very moreish, isn't it? So the young rector...'

The vicar was still talking when Joe returned. This time Joe had succumbed and had provided himself with a glass of Aligoté.

'...so the young rector comforted her in her loneliness, read prayers to her and although he was a man of the cloth they fell in love... "Amor vincit omnia". Eventually the war came to an end and the husband reappeared, safe in his body, but changed in spirit, cruel and hard and unforgiving. He had seen and done things that no man should have seen and done. He found his wife with child and he slew her, and the unborn. The young rector heard of the husband's return, he rushed along the yew walk to protect his mistress and his child. "To be in love and to be wise at the same time is not granted, even to Jupiter," as the Romans said. He was too late. He ran from room to room in his lady's house and found her lying in a pool of blood, her simple dress of brown and white torn and stained with gore. The young man went berserk with anger and despair. He seized a pike from the wall and not finding the husband within he dashed from the house and along the yew walk, back towards his cottage, back towards the church. The husband was by this time striding in the opposite direction, hunting the cleric, his sword already blood-stained, looking for revenge, looking to kill him. Then he saw the rector and he cried out: "She's dead, and your bastard too, gone to perdition, unbaptised." And in the dark and gloom under the trees the rector ran full tilt at the husband and slew him quicker than it takes to tell, and then he fell upon his weapon and died, and that is where the bodies lay until the servants came. That is why that area between the church and Hazelmere Court is heavy with the smell of death. If you were going to find a body anywhere in these four villages, that is where you would find it, at Haseley Magna. Murder loves it there.'

'Brown and white, the dress,' said Joe. 'How do you know?'

'It's in the records of the inquest,' said the vicar, 'in the records of the church: brown and white.'

'That's the colour of the Norland nanny uniforms,' said Joe. He felt cold fingers touching the nape of his neck, the hairs stirring.

'Once every hundred years,' said the vicar. 'This really is excellent whisky.

'Every hundred years?'

'Crime passionel,' said the Vicar, 'one in the eighteenth century, one in the nineteenth and of course one in the nineteen-thirties, a farmer found his wife in suspicious circumstances with the Lord of the Manor, promiscuous they were in the nineteen-thirties...plus ça change...Too much time and money on their hands, those that had time and money of course. The murder in this century has come earlier than in the other centuries. The police really ought to come and see me...Perhaps I'll go to see them this afternoon, I have to anyway about my funeral. Not mine, you understand, the one I was to officiate at. Poor old Mrs Clutterwicke... "O lachrymae rerum".

The vicar rose to his feet, pulled his bike from the bush where he'd let it fall, and turned it in the direction of the path. He seemed none the worse for wear after his three double whiskies, though his scabby face was glowing red in patches. 'Come and visit me at the church,' he said. 'It's a delightful building, dates back to Norman times. We've not long had the bells rehung. You'll hear them on Sunday morning – cost over thirty thousand pounds. Our Mr Griffiths was very good, and the Countess Woronzov was most generous, in fact most generous to all our three churches. You must try one of our whist drives...and one of our quiz nights. You're tip-top at general knowledge, I'll be bound. But above all you must come to the village fête in a fortnight. We'll soon find something for you to do...that's really why I came to see you, I forgot...You could do the wellie wanging, wellies provided of course. You'll do that for us, I feel sure. You have an air of authority.' The Reverend Baker threw back his head and laughed, showing the inside of his pink mouth. Then he pushed his bike up the path and around the side of the house, talking most happily.

*   *   *

Joe leant back and stretched his legs. He let a moment or two go by, then he gathered up the dirty glasses and tea cups and, leaving the view with reluctance, took them into the kitchen. After that he spread two slices of brown bread with butter, picked at the tuna salad that Sylvie had left for him, and drank a glass of Pouilly Fuissé.

Through the bedroom window, as he chose his clothes for the evening, the late afternoon sun released a dusty light into the house, a sort of cathedral light, calm and gentle, as if passing through stained glass, making the antique furniture and carpets look pale and golden. How easy it was, Joe realized, to fall in love with a house.

He spent a long while in the shower, changing the temperature of the water from hot to cold, refreshing himself after the excesses of the night and the questions of the day. Later, and in his dressing gown, he went downstairs to the sitting room and found Erica Sands-Lindsay lounging in one of the armchairs, reading the village Bulletin.

'They'll have to do something about these dead dogs,' she said, 'it's getting beyond a joke.'

Joe sat opposite her, relishing the enchantment he felt. He'd first seen Erica as the naked nymph emerging from the river, now here she was sitting in his house, casually dressed: fashionably faded jeans and a white blouse with its two shirt tails tied loosely at the front. No socks or stockings, just bare feet in cream coloured moccasins of soft leather. Her strawberry blonde hair was, like everything else in the house, catching the evening sun. She leant forward and placed the Bulletin on the coffee table. Her face invited Joe to look at her, her expression welcomed him in.

'I just wandered over,' she said. 'I've done enough studying for today so I thought I'd see how you were getting on.'

'Well, of course,' said Joe, allowing himself to compare her to the Countess. Both had a very English beauty in terms of colouring: they were both tall and exquisitely formed, but one cloaked her brilliance in haughtiness, whereas Erica exuded warmth and affection. She made you want to get close to her, to touch her. Joe was faced with the eternal dilemma of men – was the woman simply being a friendly villager, or was she curious about him, encouraging him?

'Can I get you anything?'

She shook her hair in refusal, knowing exactly what she was doing with the sun that she had trapped in it. She pointed to a jam jar on the table. 'I'm being neighbourly,' she said, smiling. 'I've brought you some of my home-made marmalade, to welcome you.' She leant back in the armchair. 'And I wondered if you were doing anything for dinner tonight. I've got some wild salmon, fresh vegetables, a Chablis...I like cooking.'

Another person who knew his taste in wine; someone must have put a list on the village notice board. Joe allowed himself a secret smile and once again did not attempt to reflect on what was happening to him – just go with the flow. Could he manage a night with this woman, that is, if that's the way it was to turn out? The previous twenty-four hours had been tough – on a bender with Barrington, a dead body, two dead dogs and, at the end of it all, Norah to finish him off. Then the police. He thought seriously of ducking this invitation, thought of pleading fatigue, post-traumatic stress. He thought of it but only for about thirty seconds. He couldn't; it would be against everything he stood for.

Joe tried to keep the excitement out of his voice. 'Why I'd love to,' he said. 'I may not be excellent company though, I had a very hard night...we found a dead body you know. I'm still shaking a bit.'

'Yes,' said Erica, 'I want to hear all about it. I promise you it will be restful, I haven't asked anyone else.'

Joe nodded. What was she planning? Were naturists more promiscuous than others? He hoped so. He tried to remember if he'd ever slept with a woman as beautiful as Erica. The answer was simple – no. What was the saying? "I've never been to bed with an ugly woman, but by God I've woken up with a few."'

Erica got to her feet in a lazy motion that appeared to take no muscular effort. 'That's great,' she said. 'Seven for seven thirty. Noilly Prat for apéritif? Fine.' She walked to the front door and Joe followed her into the garden; they looked at the view for a while. Barrington came towards them from the direction of his cottage.

'I'll look forward to it,' Erica turned to go. 'You must tell me about India too.'

'Of course,' said Joe, and watched her walk away. It was graceful, her walk and, having already seen her naked, he didn't have to imagine her with no clothes on. He wanted her desperately, even for ever.

'Bloody gorgeous! I could leave the straight and narrow for her.' Barrington was standing at Joe's shoulder, watching what Joe was watching. The two men stood silent for a while and dreamt the same dream together.

'What about the dog?' asked Joe. 'Whose was it?'

'Don't remind me,' said Barrington, and his face hardened. There was a determined hatred written all over it. 'I'll get her,

I'll get her. It was Harry Pearce's, over Milton Parva. Nice old boy, and a nice little dog, mongrel, bit of collie in it, was once a sheep dog I think. Bright little thing, as dogs go. Anyway, I took it over to him and we buried it in his garden...he was crying, you know. I will get her.'

'What about the body in the grave?'

'No problem,' said Barrington, off-hand. 'As I told you before the police will have thirty or forty men on that job. As far as the dogs are concerned there's only me.'

'I had a bit of trouble with the police.'

'Don't think you were the only one, they spent a lot of time with me too. They hated me, Hopkins and Cope, when we worked together. I mean, they gave me nothing but trouble. I was senior to 'em, you see. Trained 'em, and that got up their noses. Now it's pay-back time, so they really put me through it...they are odious creeps.'

'Yeah, but ultimately you're one of them, and you haven't got form – I have. They didn't like a thing I said...what was I doing here, why come to Milton? What was I up to? And they're coming back.'

'Oh they'll be coming back, make no mistake. But you'll be all right if the autopsy's all right. You were inside until a couple of days ago. Your alibi is watertight. It's Vernon Minge they'll be after. He collects nannies, doesn't he?'

"Course I'm in the clear. I was in Wandsworth for three years. I know nothing about Minge's nannies.'

'They're going to dig up some of the more recent graves in all three churchyards, just to see if there's something there that shouldn't be. They reckon that whoever put Helen in the bottom of that grave might have done it before. They're going to check on every nanny that's ever been here, see if they're back in their own homes or working somewhere else. Norland nannies, especially, something about the colour of the uniform.'

'The vicar told me a story about the Civil War – a woman murdered in Haseley Magna, and in a brown and white dress. He said there was a crime passionel every century, and brown and white was connected with every one.'

'Well, he's a bit of a loony, the vicar. Never mind the Civil

War, two bloody dogs done last night, two more flags on my map. It's beginning to look like the Normandy Beaches. That assassin, whoever it is, certainly enjoys the work.'

'Well, you can cross those people with dead dogs off your list of suspects, can't you?'

'Seems reasonable,' replied Barrington, 'but I keep an open mind. It could be to put me off the scent...kill your own dog and get yourself off the list of suspects... The dog could be diseased, blind. There's a deal of cunning in the human mind, evil also.'

'It's horrendous,' said Joe.

'For the dogs, it certainly is.'

'No, for the nannies.' Joe was about to invite Barrington into the house when the phone rang. Barrington moved on up the path. 'I'll be off. How's your hangover?'

'Force ten,' said Joe. 'See you later.'

He picked up the phone in the kitchen. It was the Countess.

'Mr Rapps,' she said. The voice was lemon sorbet at its coolest. 'I want to talk to you about our little business affair. I've ordered dinner for us at the Vivaldi. Eight o'clock sharp, and my Chateau Latour waits for no man.' She replaced the phone, the line went dead.

Slowly Joe put the receiver down. Dammit! He'd have to cancel Erica. She wouldn't be pleased, but on the other hand, it might aid his cause if she was given to believe that she wasn't the only pebble on the beach. Joe knew that the Countess could not be disobeyed. She wasn't used to it. A couple of Alka-Seltzers for his hangover, and a couple of pints of water. He'd need to be on form, and he'd have to phone Erica immediately.

* * *

Erica took the cancellation in her stride. 'It's the Countess,' explained Joe. 'I can't really get out of it, there are reasons. Perhaps we can make it another evening, soon.' Erica laughed. 'I can't compete with the Countess,' she said, 'We'll make it some other time. I'll look forward to it.'

Joe walked slowly through the village. He was wearing

another of his magnificent suits; dark grey this time, an apple green tie and cufflinks with his monogram etched into the gold. The warm air caressed him, and the sun laid shafts of light across the house fronts; every blade of grass and every leaf on every tree was distinct and clear.

It was a ten minute walk before he came to the square columns that formed the main entrance to the Vivaldi. It was a Jacobean Manor with tall brick chimneys and mullioned windows. The drive was long, bordered on each side with flower beds, trees and shrubs. Joe could only guess at the number of man hours it took to keep such extensive grounds orderly. There was a stream, the ornamental lake where he and Barrington had sat waiting for the woman in white to reappear, a gazebo or two, little bridges and arbours, benches set in quiet corners and hammocks slung between saplings. It was perfect, more like a fifteenth century embroidery than anything else.

The gravel sounded rich beneath his feet. In Joe, gravel had always given rise to envy; an energetic emotion. Toffs were always annoyed by envy, they felt they didn't merit such treatment; the politics of envy they said, was evil, but only because it threatened them. No matter. Joe had been happy with envy. It was envy, initially, that had given him what drive he'd had, made him want to do things, got him into the film business, earned him good money and shown him the world.

But although he owed his start to that emotion, he had never let it consume him. Not through any conscious effort of will on his part, but simply because he'd come to enjoy life too much and too fast to find the time to think about his lack of status. Eventually his envy had diminished until it had disappeared, and then at the end had come prison, convincing him that the quiet life was best, reposeful reflection was all he needed. His only desire was to retire from the business of earning a living. On that daily treadmill you were obliged to undertake work you didn't want, occupations that were below you, demeaning pursuits that were vulgar wastes of time, while the people who embraced that vulgarity beat you to the cash at every turn – and worse, climbed into positions of power that gave them complete control over your life and what you did with it. That was the

paradox: work for the money that gave you freedom and you
became as vulgar as the next man; avoid the vulgarity, and you
couldn't afford the freedom. Joe sighed; what was it that
camera-assistant used to say when crawling over some factory
roof, or climbing into the bowels of some stinking merchant
ship? "There's no substitute for inherited wealth." True
enough.

Joe entered the main door and went directly to the reception
desk. The girl smiled at him.

'The Countess Woronzov-Zinoviev,' said Joe, basking in the
music of the name.

The girl increased the voltage of her smile. There was a bell in
front of her and she gave it the slightest of touches and one
clear note rang out. A porter in a red coat appeared.

'The Venice rooms,' she said, and smiled yet again. Joe was
impressed. It was obvious that receptionists at the Vivaldi were
subjected to a special operation on their facial muscles to give
them extra voltage in their smiles.

He followed the porter deeper into the hotel. He saw the
restaurant before him but they did not enter it. They went along
a corridor, up a small flight of stairs, and followed another
corridor. Suddenly Joe realized – he was being entertained in a
private dining room.

The porter stopped at a wide door, knocked and then opened
it, standing back so that Joe could enter. He stepped inside and
the door closed behind him. The Countess was standing at the
window, gazing at the westering sun. She turned and gestured
Joe to a seat. On a low Moroccan table was a silver wine bucket
with a bottle of champagne in it: his favourite, of course – Louis
Roederer, Cristal Brut, the white bottle.

The Countess knew how to stand; even motionless she made
Joe's blood race. She knew what to wear too. The dress was
long, a soft indeterminate colour, brown maybe. It fell to her
ankles, touching her body like Joe wished he were touching her
body. It had sleeves to the wrist, and a low neck which revealed
a diamond necklace, a simple design, but blazing with half a
million pounds worth of light, and two rings that shone with
the same kind of power. Again Joe felt that he was seeing

eroticism incarnate.

Then she moved from the window and it was impossible not to think of wanting to make love to her. She lowered herself into an armchair, as if carrying something precious.

'Gerard,' she said and Gerard appeared, a genie from a lamp. Joe glanced about him. This was more than a private dining room, it was a whole set of rooms. What he could see of them was impressive: more Persian carpets and elegant antiques. Topinambour must have employed some very talented interior decorators.

Gerard opened and poured the champagne for the Countess to taste. Gerard had a contained red-bloodedness in his movements, but he was well-mannered and gave the impression of being gentle. Joe sensed that he was not a man whose fruit gums you should steal.

The Countess tasted the wine, said nothing and her glass, then Joe's, were filled. Gerard replaced the bottle in the bucket and left the room, but not by the same door that Joe had used to enter.

'Does he go everywhere with you?' Joe asked.

The Countess smiled and raised her glass. 'Gerard would kill for me,' she said, and Joe knew she meant it literally, no metaphor about that. Joe tasted the champagne. It was the best.

'Is he Russian?' asked Joe.

'His grandfather came to Paris at the revolution, a White Russian. He was an aristocrat and, like many of those aristocrats, he became a taxi driver. Gerard has done well for himself: he was born in Paris, brought up in England, speaks half a dozen languages fluently...but in his heart he is Russian.'

'Whatever that means.'

'It means that he is used to the hard knocks that life can bring, and knows how to fight them...I understand you made quite a night of it last night,' said the Countess. 'Inspector Barrington is obsessed by the dog mystery. I suspect he is more interested in that than the death of the poor girl you found.'

'Well, he thinks there might be a connection. You know, dead dogs, dead nannies. By the way, the police want to know why I am in Milton Magna, where I got the house and the money.'

'Tell them a half truth. I have employed you to make a film for me, we are discussing it. The house is part payment.'

'Very well. Do you have a dog?'

The Countess shook her head. 'Life's too short to open tins of dog food. I travel too much.'

'Then you could be a suspect.'

'Not really,' she laughed. 'I'd get Gerard to do it, he's very good with guns.'

Joe laughed then. 'Yes, why keep a dog and bark yourself.'

Halfway down the second glass of champagne a waiter appeared and bowed. Dinner was ready. Joe stood and followed the Countess through the door, watching her body. It made him tremble, just looking. How could one village have two such women in it? Erica Sands-Lindsay, a true English rose, and this aristocratic lily, both of them moving like they'd invented flesh and blood.

The table had been laid with care. There were rosebuds lying between the place settings and polished semi-precious stones had been strewn from one end of the linen tablecloth to the other. There were two candelabra, and the candles gave a yellow light that was reflected in the plates, the decanters, the silver cutlery and the crystal glasses.

The waiter helped the Countess into her chair, and Joe sat. There was a card with the menu on it: foie gras, and Chateau d'Yquem; Italian water ice: pears and Parma ham, with a Latour. Then a roast of wild boar, and a Gevrey Chambertin; another water ice; cheeses and Chateaux Margaux; baked apple with caramel, and vintage Calvados.

The Countess deployed her napkin. 'I hope the choice meets with your approval. We needn't rush. It looks to be a great deal, but remember, it's nouvelle cuisine.'

'Very well,' said Joe. He allowed himself to wonder what Danny The Drugs was eating in Wandsworth that night. What he said was: 'Do you often eat here?'

'Well, yes, as a matter of fact. I own the place.' She let the remark sink in. 'Topinambour ran into some money troubles a couple of years ago, borrowed too much too quickly, the usual thing. I kept it going for a while, now I have a seventy-five per cent share. It's rather nice to have it opposite. I call it my local cafe – the Silver Spoon as distinct from the Greasy One.'

The meal went slowly, very slowly. It was certainly the best and longest that Joe had ever eaten. The wines were superb. He remembered that Barrington had told him that the Margaux at the Vivaldi was eighteen hundred pounds a bottle. The whole meal must be costing a king's ransom.

The Countess made polite conversation but then there were two waiters in and out of the room continuously; 'pas devant les domestiques' would be her rule. How was he settling in? How was the house? Did he like the car? Had he made any plans for the future?

Joe shook his head. 'Thanks to your generosity,' he said, 'I don't have to rush into any decisions. For the moment, I am happy where I am. For me, Milton Magna is an enchanted isle.'

The Countess waited until the coffee was being prepared. She rose, Joe also, and they returned to their armchairs, and the coffee was brought to them.

'Colombian,' she said, 'and a forty year old Calvados.' She thanked the waiters and watched as they closed the door behind them. 'Our conversation the other evening didn't get us very far,' she began. 'I think I have one or two things to say that might change your mind. On reflection I didn't treat you well...a million is not very much these days, Mr Rapps. I understand your reluctance, but I want you on my team. I promise you the endeavour is not as dangerous as you might think it is, the feasibility tests have been exhaustive. It has been discussed and planned, as I said, by some of the keenest minds in the country, and we have help coming from the highest quarters.' She raised her hand to stop Joe interrupting. 'I think two million can achieve twice as much as one million, don't you? I am offering you two million.'

She let this remark sink in as well. Joe felt his mouth go dry; twice as dry as when the Countess had offered him one million. The silence went on. The Countess picked up her coffee cup. Joe looked up to a space halfway between his head and the high ceiling. He was expecting to see the Cheshire cat, grinning. He saw nothing. Two million would certainly give him the distinguished life style he wanted, but the scheme was crazy. What good was two million if he was inside for twenty years, or however much porridge you got for kidnapping the heir to the throne? He'd be sixty by the time he got out.

'We're going to come to an agreement,' said the Countess. 'We have to.'

'This caper scares me,' said Joe. He could hear his voice shaking. 'I'm not a crook. I wouldn't know what to do if it went wrong.'

'First,' responded the Countess, her voice toughening, 'it won't go wrong. You will have plenty of back up, a whole organization has been preparing for this operation for three years. And behind that organization is a legion of Russian friends of mine who will protect you and make sure you get out of the country, if that becomes necessary…but it won't.'

'You know I had trouble with Sunshine Leary,' said Joe. 'I can't go into London, I killed his daughter and his son, in a car accident. I was drunk.'

'I know,' said the Countess. 'But I can stop Sunshine Leary, in fact I already have. Money can achieve almost everything, "pecunia vincit omnia" as our vicar might say. Why do you think you are still alive, Mr Rapps? Leary would have killed you on the steps of Wandsworth Prison if it hadn't been for my money, and my Russian friends. They run a network a little stronger and richer than his. Leary will do what he's told.'

'You?' said Joe.

'Yes. I couldn't stop him giving you a hard time in prison, but I did keep you alive.'

'That's fine and thanks a bunch, but what happens if you suddenly decide that I am 'persona non grata', as once again our vicar might say. You could let Sunshine Leary off the leash at any time.'

The Countess nodded. 'Yes indeed, but I won't, you have my word on that, unless of course you refuse to join me. You have four good reasons for coming on board, Mr Rapps…two million pounds, an absence of Sunshine Leary, and keeping in my good books.'

Joe didn't answer. He lowered his head into his hands. He was a pawn in a game that was way beyond him. There was perhaps safety in flight, but how far would he get with the Russian Mafiosi everywhere, and them with access to limitless funds?

The Countess got to her feet, walked to the door, turned and came back to look down at Joe. 'Relax and listen,' she said. 'You have done many royal interviews on camera. I'm just asking you to do one more. You will have really good people with you, experts. There will be no danger, and there will be plenty of time to get away. You will be substituted for a *bona fide* film unit; you take their place and their papers. You are the director/cameraman, there will be a producer, a recordist, a video assistant and an electrician. Come on, you know what royal security is like, very superficial.'

'Well, I only know it from three years ago.'

'It hasn't got much better: a little, but cosmetically only; odd balls getting into Windsor garden parties, "Fathers' Rights" protesters getting into Buck House, pro hunt people running around the Palace of Westminster. You let me worry about security – Clarence House or Buckingham Palace, it makes no difference. It's not your responsibility. All you have to do is take the place of a film unit and do an interview yourself. You go in with the equipment, and you come out with the prince. But that's enough, I cannot tell you any more...just in case...though I have to point out that if you talk to anyone at all about this, you won't live long. And that really would be out of my hands. Behind me there are people from the very top.'

Joe could see his fingers trembling. 'I tell you we wouldn't get down the stairs. And these others who'd be with me, can they be trusted? who are they?'

The Countess laughed, like a young girl without a care in the world. 'Hand picked,' she said. 'They will take care of you. Gerard will drive, he's the best at what he does. The producer, he was one of my husband's Russians, a good man, cool and calm, a rock in a crisis. He's in charge. Then the recordist, a professional like yourself, but before that he served on the Royal Family protection unit, knows what he is doing. The electrician is one of Leary's men, was once a film electrician at Ealing studios, and worked for Leary on the side. They all know the ropes. We need one film person to be director-cameraman, someone who's done it before – that's you, a final touch of verisimilitude.'

'Why me?'

'Why? Because you are just what we need: experienced in photographing the royals, you are at ease with them, and you've filmed a lot in the Palace; and, above all, we knew that you would be obliged to help us.'

'Guns?'

'No guns,' said the Countess. 'There'll be no need, it will be simple and silent...I'm telling you no more now, but come over to the house with me, I'll show you something that will make you change your mind.'

As they were moving to the door Claude de Topinambour entered, portly in evening dress, his stomach pushing hard against his jacket, the wave of his hair flowing backwards over his skull. He affected not to recognise Joe from the previous evening.

'Ah, Contessa,' he said, every word slippery. He bent low like a Japanese diplomat on the eve of Pearl Harbor, and looking no more trustworthy. 'I hope everything was in order.' The Countess smiled. She dwarfed the Belgian in every respect – mentally, intellectually and physically. It was Sara Bernhart meeting Stan Laurel.

'As always,' she said.

Topinambour turned to Joe. 'Et monsieur?'

Joe tipped his head slightly to one side. 'Excellent,' he said. 'A vast improvement on last night.'

Topinambour ignored the remark, as if Joe had spoken a language he did not understand. 'I'm so pleased,' he said and stood away from the door.

'I'll bring Barrington next time,' Joe added and was gratified to see that the muscles of Topinambour's face could barely maintain his maître d'hotel smile; it was cold custard shifting beneath a wrinkled skin.

Joe was swept down the stairs in the wake of the Countess.

The diners were out of the restaurant now, relaxing in alcoves and small, discreet sitting rooms. Joe relished the glances of envy and admiration that came his way – who was this man enjoying the company of such a beautiful and distinguished woman? There was a lot of money looking up at him; this was the other side of envy, the pleasurable side. This is what you got when you'd arrived.

*　　*　　*

Gerard was waiting with a car. The Mercedes. 'My shoes,' said the Countess, 'are no good on gravel.'

They drew up at the porch and, as the Countess disembarked, the door to the house opened, and Joe followed her in. Just inside the hallway stood a man whom Joe took to be some kind of a butler. He was large, good looking, fit as a flea, and definitely Russian.

'This is Alex,' said the Countess. 'You will get to know him better in due course. He will be the producer for the interview.'

Joe nodded at the man. The Countess must be in command of a whole regiment of minions, he decided, and all of them fiercely loyal.

They climbed the stairs and entered the huge sitting-room where Joe had been entertained before. Despite the warmth of the evening a heavy log glowed red in the Adam fireplace.

'I like to watch the burning of it.' said the Countess. They sat in the armchairs facing each other and a carafe of sparkling water was brought for them.

'You were going to show me something,' said Joe, just wishing she would take him to bed and talk to him there. 'You were going to convince me, not that I think I have any alternative. I wouldn't get very far if I ran.'

'No,' she said.

'Why do you want to kidnap Charles? What do you hope to achieve?'

The Countess possessed a great deal of charm, but now she threw it from her. 'Revenge,' she said, 'revenge. I loved Diana. I knew her before she was married. An unworldly girl, all goodness, all love. But once that man got his hands on her she was changed, her life ruined. And once she had produced a couple of heirs to the throne she'd outlived her usefulness. She was trapped...then she was murdered because she was in the way of an adulterous liaison. She was a marvellous woman, but for Charles she was too beautiful, too charming, she took the limelight and left him the shadows. She was breaking new ground, taking the royal family in new directions, giving rise to great love from the public. She was adored, he was hated, and still is by a large section of the population...they want rid of him. Eighty-five per cent of the British public believe Diana was murdered, and that there was a conspiracy against her, a conspiracy that left the way open for Charles and Camilla to marry. It was just too pat. And falling in love with a Muslim as well – she had to go.'

'Do you really believe that?'

'Of course I do. I've had teams of researchers looking into it for years, and spent a great deal of money. I haven't gone into this lightly. There is so much that is louche in the affair. Her campaign against land-mines threatened the arms industry, she was seen as a trouble-maker. Was Henri Paul, the driver, drunk or was he drugged? And the white Fiat that was seen in the road tunnel at the Pont d'Alma...it was tracked down by an Al Fayed investigator, was it not? And it belonged to a pretend paparazzo attached to MI5. It was later found on French Army land and the photographer had been burnt to a crisp in it.'

Joe sat quiet. He had not imagined that the Countess could be so venomous, or that anger could shine out from her so clean and clear, like the light from her diamond rings.

'And there was an MI6 officer who created a scandal when he stated that Henri Paul was in the pay of MI6, and he also said that he had seen files showing an MI6 plan to kill Slobodan Milosevic during a visit to Geneva. A strobe flash gun was to be shone at the driver, causing him to crash. Several witnesses said they saw a flashing light shortly before Diana's car crashed into that concrete pillar in the underpass.'

'I don't know,' said Joe.

'Of course you don't, you aren't in possession of the facts.

Why do you think people all over the world worship her, and form groups so that they can come together and exchange their views, tell their thoughts? Those people in the chapel you saw, to them she was a goddess. They worship her and cry for revenge. She brought happiness into the lives she touched, she gave us life; Charles gave us death...but she will live forever, like Helen of Troy. Had she lived, she would have gone on to do great good – she had a spiritual side that people clove to, but she was a lamb to the slaughter and she died at thirty-seven – a tragedy. I loved her, loved her from the moment I met her...she was a woman above all others. Her memory cries out for vengeance.'

'But even if you get him out of Clarence House, what are you going to do with him?'

The Countess hid her face in her hands for a moment, took a deep breath then took the hands away. The anger in her face now mixed with sadness.

'You don't have to worry about that, it's not your concern. There are all kinds of things we might trade him for...demands we can make...we'll see.'

It had been a long meal with good wines and Joe was beginning to feel ready for sleep, but he wasn't allowed to feel sleepy for long. The door to the room opened and Alex entered and stood to one side. From behind him a figure in a dark suit appeared and began to walk towards the Countess. It was Charles, Prince of Wales.

* * *

Joe sprang to his feet. Confused. He knew what to do in the presence of royalty, he'd done enough of it, but what was Charles doing here? Was he an accessory to his own kidnapping? Had he had enough? Was he planning to disappear with Camilla and lead the quiet life tending his garden? Joe dismissed the thought; that wasn't in his character. Like Auntie Margaret, Charles was far too keen on the trappings of royalty, the money above all, and the power the Windsors weren't supposed to have but wielded in ample measure.

Joe watched the prince advance down the length of the room. His walk was the walk, the tilt of the head, that constipated expression; the tie sitting perfectly on the shirt, held in position with a safety pin. It was Prince Charles down to the slight scar on his face, centuries of blue blood, curdled with privilege.

Joe bowed as the prince approached. Charles passed between Joe and the Countess, she didn't stand but smiled, watching Joe. Charles stood in front of the fireplace and rested an elbow on it.

'Good evening,' he said, and the voice was perfect. 'how was dinner at the Vivaldi? An excellent place.' He held out a hand and Joe shook it. The handshake was firm. Joe could feel that he wasn't in control of his face, was, in fact, searching for an expression. The Countess laughed.

'Don't look so surprised,' said Charles. 'I'm here often, a safe house in Oxfordshire, away from those media people, aren't they just awful?' It's very convenient for Camilla too – nobody, but nobody knows we are here, and the servants are so discreet. The Countess is a true friend. If she didn't have everything already I would give her Hampton Court.'

The Countess laughed again and waved a dismissive hand. Prince Charles bowed to her and began the long slow progress to where Alex waited. The door opened and the two men disappeared through it.

The Countess crossed her legs; there was no stocking noise. It was spring and her legs were bare. 'There, Mr Rapps, is the reason why you will get away from the palace, and you won't be stopped on the way down the stairs. They will not know, for half an hour at least, that Prince Charles is not in the building, and half an hour is enough to spirit your little film unit away.'

Joe stuttered. He could hardly pronounce his words. 'He's impeccable,' he said, 'he's as good as the real thing.'

'Better,' said the Countess, 'as far as I am concerned, much better.'

'Where did you get him?'

'It took a lot of work. We searched for a couple of years until we found the right candidate. There are a lot of them out there, but we wanted someone who was intelligent too, and this one is, more so than the prince himself, which isn't difficult. But he wasn't flawless. There have been two years of intensive training, watching videos, speeches, voice coaching. Hours and hours with people who have worked with Charles, secretaries, drivers, policemen from the protection squad...and quite a lot of plastic surgery.'

'It ought to work for long enough, half an hour should do it,' said Joe, 'it's amazing.' He sank slowly into his armchair.

The Countess nodded. 'I'm convinced that even if Camilla had him in bed she wouldn't know the difference, unless there's something intimate we don't know about. Such a squidgy business sex, brings us all down to the same silly level. I tell you if I had a magic wand I'd turn Prince Charles into the Tampax he once desired to be.'

'You really hate him, don't you?'

'To the death,' said the Countess. 'I am tired now. You have been hard work, Mr Rapps. I know you have no real option but I want you to join us in a good spirit. What do you say now?'

'I think it will work.'

'There is no changing of minds at this stage. You may not falter. If you do you will not get very far. I know you have little time for the royal family, but you might lose your nerve.'

'They're a carbuncle on the body politic, spoilt brats with small brains and too much money. I will be terrified, but I'll see it through. There's nowhere to go but with you, and I believe you when you say two million, I just do.'

'You will be given instructions on the eve of the expedition, simple instructions, and the number of an account in Geneva in your name where a million pounds will be deposited. Immediately after the expedition a further million pounds will be deposited in the same account. Then you are free to do what you wish. You can stay here, or you can leave the country for a place where Sunshine Leary will never find you. Your utter silence is assumed. You talk, Mr Rapps, and it will mean you dying.'

Joe nodded. 'I can see that. When is it for?'

'The day after tomorrow. Now I must sleep. Gerard will drive you home, or you may walk. Goodnight.'

Joe couldn't help himself, it seemed so natural. He stood,

took the Countess's hand, bent low over it, and kissed it, and he understood in that moment why men would kill for her.

* * *

As reliable as the sun rising Sylvie came in the following morning with his coffee, toast and marmalade. 'Got some lovely eggs when you come down.' She smiled and gently drew the curtains. 'Another lovely day,' she said, 'the thrushes are singing, you should have heard them at five this morning, there was a gorgeous sunrise. I done you a lovely fish pie for dinner. I enjoy cooking for you, it's good to cook for a man who's so appreciative.' She left the room and Joe pulled himself up and leant against the bedhead; the aroma of the coffee was all around him and made enjoying the day seem a reasonable option.

He gazed out of the window, enjoying the view up to Cuddesdon. Had he dreamt it all? Was there really a million pounds going into his account and another million to follow?' What would it do to him, so much money? At twenty it would have ruined him, but he was forty now and he knew that two million wouldn't turn his head or lead him into stupidity. Money makes you immortal, at least for a while. It gives you power, completes you as a human being, shows you your true potential. It arrests time too, briefly, like making love does. He sipped his coffee, and decided to stop thinking about the Countess as a possible paramour; Erica was a possibility. After he was through the next couple of days he would invite her to a picnic of the gods down by the river, that is if he wasn't back in Wandsworth by then.

The thought of doing more time petrified Joe, and there would be no leniency for those who had attempted to kidnap the heir to the throne. But panic or not there was no backing out now. The Countess had laid it on the line – let her down, or speak out of turn, and he'd be found floating in the river Thames, courtesy of Sunshine Leary. Joe shivered in the warmth of his bed. The look-alike decoy would certainly be a help, just half an hour's start should do it. Where would he go afterwards? Strangely enough, for a London boy, his preference would be to stay in Milton Magna, but could he? Was there an extradition treaty with Brazil or not? He'd have to find out. Sunshine might not find him there, but MI6 would, if they wanted to.

* * *

He finished his coffee and was on the point of getting up when the phone rang. It was the Countess. 'I'm sending Gerard along,' she said. 'He has something for you. You leave the village at 04.00 tomorrow morning. All you have to do is be ready. You tell no one. In any event, you will be back by lunchtime.'

She rang off. Joe took his shower and went downstairs. As he arrived Gerard appeared at the open door with a large manilla envelope in his hand. He held it out to Joe and gave one of his curt little bows. He was dressed as usual in his dark suit. Joe wondered again if he was the Countess's lover. Gerard didn't stay, nor did he say anything. He turned at once and disappeared. Joe went into the kitchen where Sylvie was putting his eggs into the egg cups.

'Four minutes,' she said. She'd already cut the soldiers. 'I know you men,' she said, there was a gurgle of mirth in her voice. 'My husband's just the same, he can't do without his soldiers.'

'How's your grandson?' asked Joe. He attacked the eggs. Boiled eggs always brought pictures of contented childhood afternoons to his mind's eye. The eggs were fresh, the yokes molten gold, the butter, salt and pepper mingled on his tongue.

'My Tom, he's lovely, and he's growing so. I can't believe he's six already. It seems like only yesterday she was carrying him, my Sarah, that is. He's good at school, bright little button he is, love him. They're lovely at that age.'

She left the room and when Joe heard the sound of the Hoover upstairs he opened the envelope and drew out a print-off of the details of his Swiss bank account; the secret number had been written in for him. There was a telephone number too, a code word and the balance; one million pounds.

There was another slip of paper with a typewritten message on it: he was to be ready to leave the village at the time already stated; he was to dress as a film director on his way to interview royalty – formal suit not necessary, but he was to wear a jacket and tie. 'You are not to give a moment's thought to Sunshine Leary,' the message continued, 'he knows you will be in London, but only for the morning. He will not interfere.' That was all.

Joe finished his second egg and poured himself another coffee; in spite of the danger promised by the following day he found himself grinning – he was, after all, a millionaire.

He spoke out loud to the empty room: 'If my mum could see me now.'

*   *   *

Sylvie had gone. Joe sat at the kitchen table with his second pot of coffee. He was going to do nothing that day except think of the morrow. There was a knock at the front door but as it stood wide open Joe did not move. Whoever it was would come in anyway. He was right. He heard a 'Hello' and Vernon Minge stepped into the kitchen and, without being asked, sat so that he was facing Joe. Joe reached behind him and took a cup from the dresser, filled it with coffee and pushed it across the table, closely followed by the milk jug and the sugar bowl.

'You don't look good,' said Joe.

It was true. Though as immaculately dressed as ever – red felt jacket, cream trousers, pale pink shirt and flowery tie – Vernon's face looked haunted, as grey and as bloodless as an empty car park. His eyes were sunk into sad hollows of mauve, the sexual spark of them extinguished.

'They had me in Thame police station all day yesterday,' he said. 'I'm scared, really scared. They really think it's me, I'm sure of it. I tell you, I'll never ever seduce another nanny.'

'Well, that's a pity,' said Joe. 'What can I do for you?'

'My wife's giving me hell, and I had to get out of the house. I can't go anywhere else in this village, I know everyone too well, there's too much side to them. Even walking down the village I could feel the looks from behind the lace curtains, poisoned arrows striking me between the shoulder blades. I know you aren't carrying any prejudices, you don't know me well enough. I wanted a breathing space...thanks for the coffee. Have they been on to you?'

Joe nodded. 'They tried to make things difficult, but they couldn't, not really. I must have been out of the country when she was killed.'

'India. Lucky you. Wish I'd been somewhere. Baghdad would have been nice and quiet.'

'Was it Hopkins and Cope?'

'Yeah, all the usual stuff. I tell you, Joe. I may call you Joe? It's not easy, knowing that someone you made love to, frequently, has been strangled and dumped in someone's grave. It makes you shiver. Even my wife thinks I did it. She hates me...everything's come out, you see...the other women as well. You should see her face...no, better if you don't...Medusa with heartburn.'

'So what did they ask you?'

'When did I see Helen last, where did we do it, how did I get away from the wife, hotels, Travel Lodges, getting into her room. Barrington had told them about me and a ladder. They kept those damn straight faces, they didn't even laugh about it. They said I could have killed her anywhere and dumped her body anytime. It's all circumstantial, but until they've got a proper time of death I'm their number one suspect...I hope I can remember where I was that day, or night.'

'Well at least they let you out.'

'Oh sure. They've taken my passport, not that I've got anywhere to run.'

'What are you going to do?'

'I'm going to stay in college. Cornelia, my wife, is unbearable. There's no living with her at the moment. Can you imagine a voice like fingernails on a blackboard? Hour after hour. That's it, and never stopping for breath. I'll be based in college, I told the cops, but if I have to come out here I'd appreciate it if I might use your place as headquarters. You could visit me if you come to town. I've got a fine set of rooms, St John's College, you could stay. You can see Crebillon's sofa...you can try it out.' Vernon laughed weakly, a watery laugh.

'I'll put you up,' said Joe, 'whenever you like.'

'I mean, you don't believe I had anything to do with Helen's death, do you? The way people in the village have been looking at me – "no smoke without fire". I'm going round the bend.'

'No, of course you had nothing to do with it,' said Joe, well aware that he had no proof either way. Vernon did collect nannies and that was odd enough in itself.

'I'm terrified. A long sentence in jail would finish me. They do dreadful things to you, don't they? The inmates I mean, extortion, beatings, male rape.'

'I wouldn't know,' lied Joe, 'but it certainly ain't Beatrix Potter. But don't worry. You didn't do it.'

'There have been miscarriages of justice before.'

'Yes,' said another voice. Barrington stood in the doorway. 'There certainly have. Joe reached for another cup and filled it with coffee. Barrington sat. 'Just thank your lucky stars they got rid of capital punishment. You might be taking the eight o'clock walk.'

'Anything new on the dogs?' asked Joe.

'If I catch her,' said Barrington, 'she'll be taking the eight o'clock walk. She's made me a laughing stock.'

Vernon banged the table with his fist. 'How can you two even think of bloody dogs when the fuzz are trying to pin a murder on me, and my wife has got chapter and verse on every peccadillo I ever committed. I'm in serious trouble here and all you can talk about is dead dogs.'

Barrington pointed his finger, shoving it close to Vernon's face. 'There's a maniac out there and she's shot three dogs in a couple of days, one on my doorstep even. It could be humans next, the psychological progression is obvious. I may well be preventing a murder.'

Tears of frustration welled up in Vernon's eyes. 'Why can't you help me, Jack? You know the game, you know me, I'm not capable of this kind of thing. Have a word with Hopkins and

Cope.'

'They wouldn't take a blind bit of notice of me. I'm old and worn out as far as they're concerned. I trained them when they joined the job, that's difficult for them to handle, and we never got on. If I came down on your side they'd think I had an axe to grind. It would make them even more suspicious of you. I'm afraid you're on your own, Vernon.'

Vernon stood suddenly. 'I'll be in college if anyone wants to contact me. Come and visit, Joe.' It was an entreaty. Then without a goodbye or a wave of the hand, he was gone.

Barrington drained his cup and stood, ready to leave. 'He's in a mess, that Vernon. I know his wife, she'll have given him hell. Never stops yammering, it must be like standing under Niagara on a rainy day.' He yawned. 'I've got to get to bed, been up all night, and I'll be up again tonight. Will you come with me, Joe? No vodka, I promise, strictly teetotal.'

Joe shook his head. 'I'm busy tomorrow and got to get a good night's sleep. Afterwards maybe.'

Barrington gave a thumbs-up and left. Joe leant back in his chair. Talk of nannies and dogs had fatigued him enormously and pushed thoughts of the next day, and what was to happen in it, to the back of his mind. Now those thoughts came rushing back and the cold blood of an abject fear surged through his stomach; he closed his eyes and screwed them tight. Had he been a praying man he would have prayed, for just as long as it took.

*　　*　　*

Joe cleared the table of coffee pot and cups and was about to see what Sylvie had left for him in the fridge, when there was a noise at the front door and Hopkins and Cope entered the kitchen. They were big men in loose suits, and they filled the room. Joe did not offer them coffee but indicated that they should go into the sitting room. He went with them, sat on the sofa and they took armchairs.

There was a small silence while they arranged their thoughts, then: 'Have you seen Vernon Minge today, Rapps?'

'He was here a little while ago. We had a cup of coffee with Barrington.'

'How was he?' This was the other policeman. Joe thought it was Cope.

'Who, Barrington?'

There was an intake of impatient breath.

'Vernon Minge.'

'He seemed nervous. He'd come out to get away from his wife...he said he was going to stay in college for a few days. He said you guys knew.'

'We've been to his college,' said Hopkins. 'He wasn't there. Now you're saying he isn't here.'

'He was.'

'Did you know Minge before you moved here, before you came out of Wandsworth?'

'Of course not.'

'We still don't know why you came to Milton Magna, Rapps.' Was this Cope? 'Of all the villages in England you came here, where there's been a couple of murders.'

'A couple?' Joe sat upright and looked from one policeman to the other. There was no expression on their lumpish faces.

'We found another body, Rapps, another missing nanny in a grave that wasn't hers. Milton Magna graveyard this time; same uniform.'

'Good God!'

'Yes,' said Hopkins. His mouth was a slit in his chin. 'It's all very peculiar. Are you sure you didn't know Minge before you came here? You've got form, you know, Rapps. We'd like to know why you came to Milton, and where you got the money for this house, and the car in the garage...Whatever's going on here we're sure you've got something to do with it.'

'Look guys, the Countess Woronzov bought me this house, and the car. She wants me to make a film for her, about Russia, it's part payment for the job. She's so rich she wouldn't even notice the price of this place...ask her, check it out.' The two policemen looked at each other and Joe felt another influx of cold blood into his intestines.

'Did you have any day releases from Wandsworth when you

were there?' Joe closed his eyes. Was this Hopkins or Cope now? His mind was so cluttered he wasn't sure which was which. 'You know, working, rehabilitation...you could be in Milton in an hour and a half, quicker even...You and Minge could get up to things in a day, and you could be back in your cell at night, all innocent.'

'Rapps and Minge! Not exactly Burke and Hare, is it?' said Joe, 'more like Abbott and Costello.'

'Don't get intellectual with us, chummy.' They said it almost together. They stood, and turned towards the door. 'If you run into Minge before we do you'd better tell him we want to see him. The sooner we have a little chat the better it will be for the both of you.' They nodded their heads in unison and left.

Joe felt weak; there was an onset of trembling in his knees and elbows. He made his way to the arbour to warm his lifeless brain in the sun, it felt frozen. He needed the view too, to make him human again, to bring him to a small quiet place where he could be calm and unperturbed, a place where his world would stop spinning. The procedure was just beginning to work when Vernon Minge appeared from the end of the garden, entered the arbour and sat beside him.

'You damn fool!' Joe was incandescent with anger. 'What the hell are you doing back here? They're after you – and me, they think we're in this together. They've found another nanny, in another grave, Milton Magna this time – musical tombs, and you are their number one suspect...I don't want you anywhere near me, you've got bird flu, aids, mad cow disease...fuck off. Get someone to represent you, a top class defence lawyer. They're trying to prove that I knew you before this, that we murdered the nannies together. What on earth would I have to do with murdering nannies?'

'Or me?' Then without warning Vernon dropped his face into his hands and wept, huge sobs of despair.

Joe let him weep. He felt sorry for him, whether he'd committed the crimes or not. This man was on the brink of losing his grip. In a kinder tone Joe said: 'They will want to see you again, you know.'

Vernon uncovered his face and turned it towards Joe. It was

wet with tears and lined with sadness. 'Oh, Joe. I can't face them. I'm going to slip back into college, just for tonight. I'll see them tomorrow. It's so peaceful at St. John's. The college will get me a barrister, the porters will say I'm not there if the cops follow me. I need a quiet night...I wish they'd get the autopsy done.'

'Autopsies,' said Joe.

Vernon got to his feet. 'I'll go now, thanks Joe. You've been good. I'll see Copkins and Hope tomorrow. I didn't do it, you know, I didn't do it. Sleeping with a nanny is one thing, strangling one is a bit different. I've been into a lot of things but not necrophilia.' With that Vernon walked away up the garden path and disappeared around the side of the house.

Joe sighed, he was doing a lot of it. It only needed the police to falsify the records at Wandsworth Prison, the day release records for example, and they could put him in Milton on the day of the murders if they so wished. Joe sighed again and looked at the view for sustenance and reassurance, but found none. One way or the other the beauty of the countryside that he had come to admire might be torn from him in the next couple of days, and there was nowhere he could run.

*   *   *

Joe was awake before his alarm clock rang, before the dawn chorus. The world was still dark beyond the curtains. He lay in the warmth of his own body for a while. The grinding sensation of fear was already at work in his guts. He was about to do the stupidest thing he'd ever done in his life, and he'd done a few. Climbing over a roof that was being demolished beneath him just to get a series of shots; leaning out of a helicopter with someone hanging onto his legs; lying down under a locomotive as it drove over him. Any of those could have killed or crippled him but this latest exploit could be much worse: it could put him in jail for life.

It was like being in one of those trashy novels of adventure he'd read so many of at Wandsworth. Death and disaster on every page. But that was not where he wanted to be, his desire was to wake up in some low key, tender, Joanna Trollope romance where the main concern of the characters was the solidity, or otherwise, of their relationship, or how the second marriage was working out. Or in a small scale Anita Brookner saga as it resounded to the mighty clash of tea-spoons on a Sunday afternoon. That would be the game. Instead of which he was into a royal kidnap with the Black Widow, the Russian Mafia and a taciturn hatchet-man called Gerard.

He slipped into his bathrobe, went to the kitchen and made coffee and two slices of toast. While he waited for the bread to brown he put the previous night's plates into the dish-washer. He took honey and butter from the cupboard. The crunch of the toast was loud in his head, resonated in his skull. He thought about what he should wear. Film Director normally meant an old jumper and battered trousers with lots of pockets, but this was jacket and tie. There was a light grey tweed upstairs and a pair of dark grey trousers; stacks of shirts to choose from, and a regiment of ties. He'd better take a shoulder bag as if for the script, a book, a pad and his view-finder.

He showered, dressed and was ready by three forty-five. He thought about another cup of coffee but decided against it. There was too much shake in his hands already. He took several deep breaths for the sickness in his stomach and waited. The Countess had said he'd be back for lunch.

He heard footsteps down the path, a tap at the door. Joe glanced round the kitchen as if for the last time. He looked into the sitting room too. How many days had he been here? Four was it? It felt like as many months. It was a good house and he wanted to stay in it. Then he thought of the racks of wine in the cellar. If he did get back that afternoon he would open something special.

The tap at the door came again. Joe swung it open and there was Gerard standing in the pool of light thrown by the security lamp. Joe suddenly thought of Barrington. It would be awkward if he returned to find Joe going out at four in the morning.

'Barrington?' queried Joe.

'He's indoors. He was back at two. I was watching for him.'

'Lucky he didn't see you, he might have thought you were the dog-killer.' Gerard ignored the remark; it was obviously not worth answering.

The car was a large Mercedes. Joe couldn't make out the colour. There were three men on the back seat, Gerard indicated that Joe should sit in the front. The men said nothing as Joe took his place; not a nod, not a good morning. He sat, closed the door and leant his head against the head-rest, hoping that this would relax him. Gerard slipped behind the wheel and drove through the village and up to the M40. He drove well, nothing flashy, just good. Joe could feel the surge of the power rising through the leather cushions and into his back, pushing his spine. Closing his eyes Joe tried to imagine that this morning was like a thousand other mornings when he'd been picked up by a car and driven through a pale dawn to a studio or to an outside location. Only then he would have been going over his script, or giving the crew the shape of the day.

He felt something drop into his lap. Opening his eyes he saw a brown envelope. A reading light came on in the dash.

'From the Countess,' said Gerard.

Joe opened the envelope, which had not been sealed, and took out a sheet of paper, closely typed on one side:

You are a Freelance Director/cameraman: employed today to shoot a fifteen minute interview with Prince Charles about his forthcoming visit to Russia. You have done it many times before. Ostensibly you are in charge.

Gerard, you know; totally reliable. He will act as your assistant.

Alex is sitting behind you; he is Russian but completely bilingual. Used to work for Moscow TV in one of my husband's companies. He knows what to do. He will help carry in the lights.

The man in the middle: the recordist, Colin Vinten. Until three years ago he worked on the royal protection unit of the Metropolitan Police, before that on the police film unit. He now works for me.

The third man is the electrician. Harry Hutton. Worked in the film business for years, now works for Sunshine Leary. As you know Sunshine doesn't want you in London but for today you have permission.

Your crew will be taking the place of a freelance film unit, sub-contracted to Moscow television; five people. They have a rendezvous point in Mortlake: the cameraman's house, at 07.00. Their transport is a Range Rover and a transit van for the lights. By the time you arrive outside the house those five men will have been taken care of. They are to disappear for a certain time, then bribed to keep quiet. It's silence or death, though both is never bad. You will pick up the security passes at Mortlake, photos to match.

The interview was to have been at Clarence House but has now been changed to the Palace. Why, does not concern you – a royal family matter. You will enter by the side entrance in Buckingham Gate. The cars will be stopped at the entrance, your passes checked, and the vehicles. Once you are inside there is little if any supervision, as you know. Nothing has changed much since you last filmed in the palace.

You will go up in the lift to one of the two rooms situated behind the front balcony. You will get the equipment installed and ready. As you again know everything has to be perfectly ready two hours before the arrival of the Prince so that he is not kept waiting for technicalities.

Once the Prince is in the room you will proceed as you have on many previous occasions, and engage the Prince in polite conversation. Gerard will act as general assistant when and if necessary; Vinten will put the mike on the Prince's tie and run the cable. That is it. Once that has happened the others take over; they have rehearsed it a hundred times and I have made sure they are well practised.

Joe folded the sheet of paper, and replaced it in the envelope. He folded that too and was about to put it into his shoulder bag when Gerard held out his hand.

'I'll take it,' he said, and Joe passed it over.

The car was now passing the High Wycombe exit. There was

still a total absence of conversation and Joe couldn't make up his mind if that was a good sign or a bad one. He didn't want to talk anyway. Having one of Leary's men sitting behind him was enough to paralyse his brain. He'd heard of 'Knuckles' Hutton; he was a hard little bastard.

*　　*　　*

The rest of it was dreamlike. Drifting shapes: a dance, a ballet without music, predestined.

They came over Chiswick Bridge and did a hard left and drove along by the side of Mortlake Brewery. Joe thought of the Boat Race but it wasn't that type of innocent day. The street lamps were still on and the sky was grey. They turned right eventually, went over a level crossing and turned immediately left. The name of the road was Eleanor Grove. A cul de sac.

The car halted at the end of it. Gerard parked and got out. The others also disembarked and Joe followed suit. Someone appeared out of a transit van, came over to Hutton and gave him a couple of keys, then got into the Mercedes and sat. Hutton went to the transit and started the engine. It ticked over like a sewing machine.

Gerard crossed the road and climbed into the Range Rover. The security passes were on the dashboard. Alex and Vinten followed him, and so did Joe. Gerard checked that everyone was in the car and started the engine. Another sewing machine. He put it in gear and headed off, back down Eleanor Grove. The transit followed.

The whole business had taken no more than two or three minutes. Joe broke the silence. 'How many times have you rehearsed that?' he asked. There was no reply. Joe wanted to ask what had happened to the original camera crew: drugged, bribed or killed. With the Russians and Sunshine Leary in the mix any one of those three choices would not have been a problem. It was a question not worth asking.

The Range Rover and the transit set off in the direction of the river. They drove slowly; they had all the time in the world. As for words – still nothing. These guys did not do repartee. After all, what was there to say?

*   *   *

Getting into the Palace was just as Joe remembered it. The two vehicles drove slowly up to the side gate close by the entrance to the Queen's Gallery, and halted at the barrier. A policeman in uniform came to the driver's window. Other figures could be seen beyond, between a couple of small outbuildings. The passes were handed over and the policeman took them away. Two other policemen watched. Joe knew from experience that they wouldn't be the only ones watching. There might even be armed marksmen, out of sight, a possible addition since the last time he'd done this.

They waited a while. Another policeman went to the transit van behind. The same process. There was tension inside the Range Rover; a quiet full of strength. No one, except Joe, seemed nervous.

Joe stared out of his window. A cat walked across the yard. A man in an army uniform came and went. The policeman returned, he put his head halfway into the car. held up the passes, looked at the photos, compared them to the faces and asked each person his name.

'All right,' he said when he'd finished, 'you've done this before. Pull ahead and park over there to the left, the door's in front of you. Through that and into the lift. There'll be someone there…don't stray.'

The vehicles moved forward, turned and backed into the parking spaces, ready for unloading. The crew disembarked and Hutton came out of the transit. A man in green overalls shoved through the flapping sheets of rubber that shielded the loading bay, rather like the back entrance of a seedy hotel. 'Through there,' he said, 'the lift's down on the right. Then it's up to the East Gallery. I'll show you where it is.'

It was hard work unloading, but then it always was. Twelve silver cases and two long boxes, at least two and a half feet wide, carrying the lights. Everyone lent a hand as film crews always did. Again not a word, as if the merest utterance would have shattered a spell and given them away.

There were two trolleys to get the boxes as far as the lift and it took two journeys to get the gear upstairs. Once there, they found themselves in the East Gallery, on the Upper State Floor. There were steps down to the left, leading to the main entrance, and the ballroom was somewhere further along.

They wheeled the trolleys along a corridor, past a series of offices on the right, the offices of the master of the household. One or two people looked up from their desks, but that was all. Not a smile, not an eyebrow of greeting. Royal Apparatchiks, they were used to scruffy film crews and they didn't like them. Joe glanced at the paintings on the walls; it took his mind away from his fear. He was always impressed by the small painting of Richard III and the huge painting of Charles I by Van Dyck. It pleased him that all those royals had came to sticky ends: Bosworth Field, execution in Whitehall, not to mention Edward II with a red hot poker up his rectum, and the Duke of Clarence, head first into a butt of malmsey – some hangover! Now it was Prince Charles's turn.

'Humph,' Joe spoke aloud in the hope that one of the snotty functionaries would hear him: 'When the revolution comes we'll all have a Richard the Third in the loo.'

* * *

They were shown into the room in which the interview was to take place, one of the small sitting rooms behind the balcony that looked down over the statue of Queen Victoria. There was no supervision and they were left to get on with the work. They stood and looked around them: there were two high windows, giving onto the balcony and curtained with yellow drapes, a writing desk between them. A picture of Frederick, Prince of Wales, young and pale, hung between the windows and above the desk.

There was a connecting door to the next room, a picture of flowers. There was even a fireplace with an electric coal fire, above it a picture of chickens, dogs and a tortoise. On the mantelpiece a blue clock and a bouquet of porcelain blooms stood under glass. To the right of the fireplace was a bureau in walnut, inlaid with gold. Another clock, French, occupied a rosewood stand. It was decorated with a statue of Father Time and a cupid. Two turquoise vases were encrusted with parrots, peacocks and more flowers. In the middle of the room was a yellow sofa, two armchairs, one yellow, one lime green. It was a bilious room in expensive bad taste, like one of Her Majesty's hats.

Gerard and Joe unloaded the camera and screwed it to its tripod and checked that it was functioning. Hutton opened one of the light boxes, put the lamps on their stands and ran the cables from the power points. Alex sat in a chair as a stand in for Charles, and Joe lit him. Vinten loaded the recorder with its cassette and made sure it was running properly, then did a colour balance, on the monitor. They switched everything off, and switched everything back on again, then everything off. A young woman popped her head round the door, bright and officious. She had a voice you could slice carrots with.

'I'm Jenny,' she said. 'The Prince will be here at exactly ten o'clock. You've got him for half an hour, not a minute longer.' She flashed a smile with years of falsity in it and departed.

The next two hours were not good. The room was claustrophobic, and Joe was sweating. Alex and Gerard were good at waiting. They sat in the armchairs and stared silently at the pictures on the wall. Vinten was more agitated. He walked up and down the room, stopping occasionally to stare from the 'waving' window as he called it. Hutton sat on an aluminium box, his head in his hands, gazing at the carpet. Joe could feel the tension, brittle enough to break. He left the room and walked the corridors on that floor, back to Richard III. The portrait, though small, had something haunting about it. The expression was cold and full of power. Had he had the young princes killed? Why not? In those days killing royals was an everyday occurrence, cousins or brothers, it didn't matter. What a shame the habit had been lost. Joe moved on to the ballroom, walked up one side and down the other. He shook his head; how vulgar these rooms were. But even the concept of monarchy itself was vulgar. He glanced at his watch: it was time.

The tension in the room had eased, it was five to ten and there was only the deed to be done, no time for reflection. Alex stood by the door, Hutton stood by the control board of his lights, Vinten sat by his recorder and Gerard waited. The room was silent: too silent: Joe knew it didn't look right: he needed to get them talking. They needed to look more relaxed, more natural.

'Lights,' he said, and Hutton switched on. 'Get the mike ready.' Vinten ran the cable forward to the chair. Then it began. The woman, Jenny, appeared at the door. 'We're ready,' said Joe. She disappeared and a minute or two later the Prince entered the room, his right hand fiddling with the opposite shirt cuff. He smiled, affable. Alex, as the producer, approached him, smiled and nodded by way of a bow.

'Good morning your Highness,' he said. After that it was in order to call him 'Sir'.

The Prince was in a very good mood. He smiled and came further into the room. He was wearing a light grey suit, and brown shoes, a white shirt with a broad, green stripe in it, and a tie that was regimental in its pattern. There was the scar on his left cheek. Suddenly Joe thought about the clothes; what would the lookalike be wearing? If he was dressed differently to the Prince that could scupper the whole plan. Escape would be out of the question, and they wouldn't even get as far as the lift. The pain in Joe's chest became more acute.

The crew moved towards the Prince with just the right amount of deference and hands were shaken all round, words exchanged. Charles hesitated as he came to Joe.

'Now I've seen you many times before,' he said, 'we've worked together on these things...but not for a while.'

'I've been in India, sir,' answered Joe.

'Ah. Anywhere interesting?'

'I was in Kerala for six months, and then I ran a TV studio in Delhi.'

'You must have enjoyed that.'

Joe smiled. 'I did,' he said.

The Prince moved towards the designated armchair and stood by it. Alex beckoned Vinten forward with the lapel mike, the clip and the cable. The Prince, practised in these matters, undid his jacket so that the cable could be hidden under it. While he waited he told a story about the room they were in, a story about an Indonesian doctor who had been lodged there, a member of someone's retinue. He had been found in bed the next morning with three women.

'I don't know how they do it,' Charles said and Joe thought 'Squidgy' and 'Tampax.'

The Prince sat, and Joe, with Hutton's help, made the finer adjustments to the lights. Alex moved a chair forward and sat to the left of camera, the list of questions in his hands. Jenny popped her head around the door, saw that everything was progressing as normal and went away. Joe ran the camera; 'Speed,' he said.

Alex went into the first of his questions and they filmed for maybe ten minutes. Joe had his eye to the view-finder all the time; the Prince was relaxed and professional. 'It's looking good,' Joe said, in a break between questions.

'The mike needs adjusting,' said Vinten, 'it's slipped a bit.'

Joe switched the camera off and Gerard moved to the side of the Prince and moved the mike, so as to point it more directly at the Prince's mouth. Joe ran the camera again. Gerard moved behind the Prince, took something from his pocket, a small syringe shaped like a pistol, and shot it into the Prince's neck. A look of alarm came momentarily into Charles's eyes but it only took a second or two and the Prince was unconscious. He slumped forward. Alex rose and pushed him more or less upright. Gerard removed the mike.

Hutton moved over to the door and stood by it to stop anyone entering. There was a movement behind Joe and Vinten opened the second light box and the lookalike appeared. He stood and stretched his limbs. Joe was astounded. He was wearing exactly what the Prince was wearing; same suit, same shirt, same tie, and same shoes. Alex and Gerard lifted the Prince and laid him carefully in the lighting box and closed the lid. The face of the lookalike was pale. He took a few deep breaths. 'I need a pee,' he said.

'We thought you might,' said Alex and handed him an empty two litre water bottle. 'It's only nerves. Hurry up.'

But there was no hurry. The whole thing had taken no more than a few minutes. Once the lookalike had finished peeing he sat in the chair and Gerard put the mike on him. Joe fired up the camera, trying not to notice that his hands were shaking, and Alex asked the lookalike a question or two, just to get him settled and into the role.

'What will interest you most?'

'Oh, St. Petersburg,' said the Prince's voice. 'I'm so glad it isn't called Leningrad any more...The Hermitage of course, the grave of Dostoevsky, and strangely enough, The Aurora.'

There was a knock at the door and Joe switched off the camera. Hutton opened the door and Jenny came into the room. She ignored the technicians. 'We've got fifteen minutes, sir,' she said. This was the lookalike's first test. He passed it easily. 'Yes,' he said, 'I'll be there.'

'Wrap it,' said Alex as soon as the woman had gone and the men moved without instructions. The lights came down; the camera was loaded into its box, the recorder, the monitor and the mikes too. During this activity the lookalike sat in his chair, crossed his legs, folded his arms and leant back. He looked totally relaxed. Joe could not understand why he seemed so calm. Maybe it was because this was his big chance. He had impersonated Charles in night clubs up and down the country, done weddings and birthdays, then the Countess had discovered him and transformed a superficial impersonation into perfection. This was his Oscar winning performance.

He was a very brave man, thought Joe, as he stowed the tripod. He had to give them half an hour to get away, then he would be arrested and put through the mill. The anti-terrorist branch wouldn't give him an easy ride.

Suddenly they were ready to go.

'All right,' said Alex, 'let's do it.' He glanced at the lookalike. 'Okay?'

'Yes,' said the voice of Prince Charles. 'Don't worry, I'll give you plenty of time.'

They gathered together at the door and pushed the trolleys from the room and back along the gallery. Twice they loaded the lift and sailed down to the dirty corridors of below stairs. Joe was trembling, his knees the weakest part of his whole body, and his sphincter muscles not as tight as they should have been. He expected to hear shouts at any moment, the clang of alarm bells or steel gates clattering from the ceilings like portcullises, and men appearing with AK 47s in their hands and balaclavas on their heads. But there was nothing: just the cold faces of lackeys staring.

In a moment they were out in the yard, sliding the two lighting boxes carefully into the transit. The rest of the gear went into the Range Rover. Two policemen watched them, another two stood at the gate and opened it as the vehicles moved forward.

It had indeed been dreamlike. A few seconds later they were out into Buckingham Gate, out into the traffic. It was eleven o'clock only. The Countess had been right; they would be back in Milton Magna for lunch. Joe breathed again, leant back, let the sweat dry on him, and began to think of the wine he would choose when he got back to Pegswell Cottage – maybe the Cheval Blanc.

*   *   *

It got easier. Hyde Park Corner, along the south side of the park, and then a right into Kensington Palace Gardens, a road that Joe had always known as Millionaires' Row: palatial houses set in enormous gardens, some of them embassies, some belonging to men who made Croesus look like the inhabitant of a cardboard box. Joe had done interviews in a few of them. The Russian embassy was up here, and the French.

Gerard swung the car into the drive of a white painted mansion which had a turret on each corner. The transit was close behind. There was a massive gate of iron which swung open as the Range Rover approached, and the two vehicles drove very slowly into the grounds and to the back of the house. The garden was joyous, surrounded by tall trees of great height, fresh in their springtime leaves. The herbaceous borders were a gardener's fantasy made into flowers. There was a fountain and a few white marble statues, and in the middle of the large and perfect lawn stood a helicopter, the pilot already in place.

The Range Rover halted near the helicopter, the transit too. Everyone disembarked. Joe studied the rear of the building and saw only shuttered windows. A staircase swept down from a rear terrace but there was no one to be seen. The helicopter pilot sat without moving.

Hutton and Alex went to the rear of the transit and pulled one of the lighting boxes out and loaded it into the helicopter. Gerard beckoned to Joe and gestured for him to climb aboard. Gerard followed and closed the door. The engine kicked into life and the props turned, picked up speed, and then the aircraft rose, violently, nose dipping.

Looking out of the window Joe could see that the others below were not even glancing up. They returned to their vehicles and disappeared inside them. Then the beautiful garden was lost to him and the helicopter climbed above the roofs. Soon there was Holland Park, Hammersmith, the river, the M4 and the M25: then Henley and the Chilterns, the shadow of the helicopter flitting over the hills in the strong sunlight. That's all it took.

*　　*　　*

The helicopter lurched in over Milton Magna; the chimneys of the Vivaldi came into view, then the tower of the church and the straggling village High Street. They dropped closer and Joe saw the size and solitude of Chiltern Hall, the wall around the estate, the sprawling fields behind. The helicopter spun on its own axis and plunged onto the helicopter pad. Gerard slid out of his door and the rotors slowed and stopped. He jerked his head and Joe followed him across the grass towards a gate set in the boundary wall. Half a dozen men passed them, hurrying in the opposite direction: they would be going for the Prince.

Through the gate was a gravel path which led to some stone steps, which in turn gave access to a conservatory that was built along the back of the house. The conservatory was wide and long, possessing a tiled floor, and it was furnished with a huge oak table, armchairs, potted plants and shelves of books. A door led into the house proper and Gerard shepherded Joe through it and into the main hallway and up the wide staircase. At the top he knocked on the door of the vast sitting room and Joe heard the Countess say, 'Come in.' Gerard motioned to Joe that he should enter, then he went back down the stairs.

The Countess was standing at a window that overlooked the garden and the helicopter pad. Joe advanced a yard or two, then stopped. In the midday sun, blazing the whole length of the room, she looked lovely still. A billionairess with those looks. It wasn't fair. She was as good in profile as she was full face.

At last the Countess turned, and glanced at her watch. 'I said by lunchtime,' she said. 'I heard, everything went well.'

It was only then that Joe came to a full realization of the enormity of what he and the others had done that morning. His mind had stood static for a while, not daring to think. They had done what they had set out to do and had got away with it; and this woman standing before him had planned it all, to perfection. Everyone had done the right thing at the right time. She was remarkable.

She smiled at him and stepped over to a bureau on which stood a slim computer screen. It was already connected. Joe went with her. She touched a few keys and Joe's Swiss account came up on the screen; Credit – two million pounds sterling.

She smiled again. Her smiles weren't for other people, they were smiles of contentment for herself, enjoying the power she wielded. 'There are two things I can do,' she began. 'I can transfer this money back into one of my accounts, right now – two or three touches.'

Joe knew the blood had gone from his face, he heard it cascading into his boots.

'Or, I could have you killed.'

'I could see my union representative about this.' The joke

didn't manage to stop Joe feeling sick. He said nothing more, there was no point. Whatever she decided she would do. She walked to the fireplace and stared at it. Silence. Her power over Joe was total and, perversely, it made him want her more. Wasn't there a tale in the Arabian Nights where the Sultan's wife chose lovers from amongst her slaves and then had them thrown into the river in a sack? The Countess could kill Joe twice; take back the money and then throw him in the river. A dog's chance and no chance.

She turned, elegantly. 'If you can forget what happened this morning,' she said, 'neither of those things will happen.' She joined her hands and a diamond ring caught a handful of sunlight and threw it at him. 'I haven't made my mind up about you yet.'

Joe had never sensed death so close. That premonition of mortality he'd had outside Wandsworth Prison the night of his release had settled on him like an old black crow, and was still on his shoulder.

'But what about the others. They could talk just as easily. Why should I even think of it, there's no mileage in it for me.'

She studied him closely. 'Alex and Gerard belong to me,' she said. 'They know what happens if things go wrong.'

'And the film crew we took the place of?'

'Ah yes, a road accident this morning.'

'Vinten?'

'Vinten has three children, he is very fond of them, now he is very rich, and he is ex-protection unit...he too knows what could happen to his family.'

'Sunshine, Hutton?'

'They have worked with us before, they have a good track record and they too have been made rich beyond the dreams of avarice. What is more, they wouldn't dare upset my Russians. They wouldn't die easily. They are sensible men...that leaves you. No wife, no children, no friends to speak of.'

The silence came again. Joe had no answers.

Then: 'What I like about you,' she said, 'is your ordinariness. You don't think being brave is worth it. Your cowardice is an asset, it is a very sensible human response to life. In this case it will probably save you. If there is a whisper, the slightest whisper from any source, you will be considered the guilty party. I believe you will be silent, others may not.' She touched her hair and sunlight escaped from the diamond again. 'You thought you would sleep with me, didn't you?'

Joe swallowed. 'You're very attractive,' was all he could manage. It was the Arabian Nights again; she was going to take him to bed and have him killed. He prayed; 'If God lets me out of this one I'll never letch again.'

She laughed a little. 'I am not in the slightest degree flattered by your desires,' she said, 'but you are predictable, and it's the predictable in you that allows you to go home.' She moved to the door and opened it. 'Be very careful, Mr Rapps. Very careful. You will not see me again.'

Joe wanted to say something, anything, but nothing came. Gerard was waiting on the landing, leaning against the bannister. He didn't look at Joe but past him and at the Countess.

'He can go,' she said, and the door closed.

The two men went down the stairs to the front door. It was obvious to Joe that Gerard had been waiting to kill him if the Countess had given the word. Alex and another man were waiting; they glanced at Gerard, saw his face and then walked away, across the hall and into the depths of the house. Gerard opened the front door, gave that little bow of his and Joe stepped into the open. There was no goodbye, not even a smile of camaraderie, acknowledging a job well done.

Joe went out from under the porch. He felt unreal, a blob of ectoplasm beamed from one dimension into another. The sun shone clean and clear, high in a sky of sapphire, and yet Joe wouldn't have been surprised to see that sky all black, suffocating him.

Joe walked the length of the drive and didn't look back. Wasn't there another story in the Arabian Nights where the hero had been employed in necromancy by a beautiful princess, but when he returned to seek his reward the princess and her palace had disappeared, carried away by the powers of an evil spirit? He didn't want to know any more about Chiltern Hall, or who was in it. Looking over his shoulder might bring him bad luck.

Joe went on, out of the drive and through the gates, which opened automatically to let him pass. He walked up the slight hill to the village green. Two or three customers were sitting outside the pub, taking lunch, the sun sparkling amber in their pints of bitter. He came at last to the village shop and the telephone box, and then he stopped at the entrance to Pegswell Lane. He looked back down the village High Street. It was still unreal. The village had no connection with what he had done that morning. Milton Magna was a separate spinning planet with him spinning on it, but spinning so fast that nothing moved. He went into Pegswell Lane and towards his house, whistling the five notes for the jazz bird, but it did not answer. In any event the morning's adventure had been successfully concluded, he was still alive and he was a millionaire twice over – at least for a while.

*　*　*

He felt weak, the emotions of the morning had done for him. What he had told the Countess was true. He could never make a crook – he didn't have the cold courage. The Countess! He was glad not to be seeing her again. She came from the slopes of Mount Olympus and lived as she thought she would, like a Greek goddess taking sides at Troy – more full of human sin than humans themselves. Life and death, riches and poverty were all in her gift. It would be a good idea to put as much distance between her and him as possible.

He came to the front door of the house. It was unlocked. Sylvie would have left it open after her morning's work. He went into the kitchen and filled the kettle for tea. Someone came in behind him. It was the Vicar, the same suit, the same scrofulous skin, the same pale eyes, and the same hesitant smile hovering as light as a butterfly on thin lips.

'It's good to see you've taken on village habits,' he said, 'leaving the front door open, just like the old days.'

'Assam?' asked Joe.

'That would be nice.' Joe could see the vicar's disappointment; he'd been hoping for whisky, and he cracked his knuckles by way of protest.

'I came to see you about the village fête, next weekend. Amanda Fludd needs help on the bookstall. We thought you might be a pair of hands. She's a splendid lady, married to the Professor of Classics at Oxford.'

Joe warmed the pot and made the tea. He shook his head as if to clear it. Royal kidnap in the morning; tea with the vicar at lunch and a little chat about the annual fête. He waited for the tea to stew a little. There was a note from Sylvie: "Caesar Salad in the fridge and egg and bacon pie for the evening." Joe looked at the vicar. He tried to smile but he was still shaky. He could think of nothing but two million pounds and death.

He carried the two mugs of tea out into the garden, the vicar followed and they sat in the arbour. Joe thought that the village fête was the worst thing he'd ever heard of but, on the other hand, it might be a good idea to behave as naturally as he possibly could. Those people suspicious of him might give him the benefit of the doubt if they saw him selling second hand books at twenty pence a throw. And all hell would break loose as soon as the abduction of the Prince hit the news bulletins. Best stay where he was and keep his head below the parapet until the storm had passed.

He tried to smile again. 'I'd love to do the bookstall with Amanda Fludd,' he said. 'When is it?'

'This Saturday, at two o'clock. You'll like the fête. Though I say so myself it's the best in the country, the 'ne plus ultra.' Bric-a-brac, the Chalgrove brass band, races, a bouncy castle for the children, a cake stall, wellie throwing, a beer tent and a tea-room in the cricket pavilion. We've got our MP opening it this year. He's very famous, on television you know, very jolly. You must have heard of him, Percival Peachcroft. There's been some scandal about him, all newspaper talk – "dictum sapienti sat est" – a word to the wise is enough.'

'Where do the books come from?'

'Amanda keeps them in her old coach house. She lives in the

old vicarage, ten times the size of the red-brick place I live in. Those vicars had lots of children in the old days. They were always at it, I suppose, no television. "Faber est quisque fortunae". Every man fashions his own fortune.'

The vicar finished his tea and placed the mug on the seat between him and Joe. 'Well I must be off, "tempus fugit". I'm behind with my funerals, what with this police business, I've so many people to bury, ah well, "memento mori". Still I can catch up now, a busy few days with the old aspergillum. Phone Amanda this week and she'll tell you what she wants done. Five-five-seven is her number.'

'Where's your bike?' asked Joe.

'Yes, very good question. I left it somewhere yesterday and can't remember where. Someone will find it and bring it back to me. They always do.' He stood, bowed from the waist, went along the path and disappeared round the side of the house.

The moment he had gone Joe sped indoors, went to the television set, and switched on the twenty-four hour news service. If the kidnap had been discovered there would be both special and ongoing programmes. There was nothing: the prime minister visiting a new hospital; the same old contestants playing tennis somewhere; trouble in the Middle East. Joe fell back onto the sofa and cut the sound. Perhaps the kidnap had indeed been discovered but they, the Palace, were choosing their own time to reveal it; that would be likely.

There was a light knock and Barrington came into the room. He was jolly, pleased with himself. He laughed, and his stomach shifted under his shirt. 'They've found another nanny,' he said, 'just like the others, buried in someone else's grave. That makes three now. They'll get Vernon for it, mark my words.' He laughed again and took possession of an armchair.

'Poor man,' said Joe. 'Do you think he did these murders? I mean, three of them. It's unbelievable.'

'I dunno, he is a likely candidate. They'll question him until he breaks.' There was silence for a while.

'Scotch?' asked Joe. He had scotch and glasses on the writing desk, and the drinks were soon poured.

'I was out most of the night,' continued Barrington. 'Only just got up.'

'Find anything?' asked Joe.

'Nah.' He laughed at his own stupidity, but there was anger under the laugh. 'Not a thing. Whoever it is, is damned clever...there were two piles of dog-shit on my doorstep this morning. I will wring her neck when I catch her.'

'It might not be her doing the shit,' Joe suddenly thought out loud. 'It might be some smart-alec villager just winding you up for laughs.'

'It could be, but they're playing a dangerous game. Just let me catch 'em.'

'Where did you go?' Joe kept his eye on the television screen.

'All over. The Haseleys, Magna and Parva, Milton Parva...not a thing.'

'The Woman in White?'

'Not a sign, but I shall keep going until I find her. And what have you been up to?'

'Not much. I had a lazy morning, a bit of a walk, visited the church. The Vicar's just been. Wants me to help with the fête, the bookstall.'

Barrington gave a broad grin. 'We all have to help with the fête. It's a good day, you'll enjoy it. You'll see.' He put down his drink and hauled himself out of his chair. 'I've got to get on. I'm going to Thame. It's market day. We could have a drink there.'

Joe dismissed the idea. He was too jumpy and he needed to stay close to the television set. 'Thanks,' he said, 'but I won't join you. I'm expecting a 'phone call. Next time.'

Barrington hesitated at the door. 'They picked Vernon up at his college,' he explained. 'I wouldn't have thought he had the courage to strangle anyone, but you never know. I've seen stranger things in my time. Occasion and motive, he had both of those. It's a bit odd, isn't it, always going to bed with nannies. You never know with these academic types...too much book-learning can send you round the bend. They'll have him on remand soon...we'll have to go and visit him.' He smiled as if Vernon's plight was the most amusing thing he'd heard of in a decade. But all he said was: 'Cheerio, see you later,' and he left.

*   *   *

There were no more visits, and Joe left the television on all afternoon and all evening, watching as the day's light softened. There was no mention of the abduction or of the Royal Family. It was puzzling, and Joe couldn't shake himself free of anxiety. Surely MI5, the anti-terrorist branch, the Royal Protection Unit, all of them and more, must be aware of what had happened? The police lines must be buzzing with activity.

Was the Countess, and her retinue, already on the way out of the country? She'd had that look about her the last time he'd seen her. Were they taking the Prince out of the country with them? That seemed logical. And what were they going to do with him? The ransom would be enormous, but the Countess didn't need money. Was it really her sole aim to punish him for Diana's death? If so, how long would she keep him, and what would happen to him at the end of it all?

The lookalike must have broken under questioning by now. He didn't know the names of the film crew of which Joe had been a member, but he knew the Countess. That would have been enough for the authorities to trace them all. There could be a knock on the door at any moment.

Joe heated Sylvie's bacon and egg pie in the oven and opened a bottle of Cheval Blanc. He sat in front of the television, the voices and images acting on him like a drug, keeping him calm. The doors and windows were open; the wine was excellent. The May evening cooled; the jazz bird had returned and was singing its notes over and over again. Gradually Joe fell asleep, speaking out loud to himself before stretching out on the sofa – 'Now, that's what you call a hard day at the office.'

*   *   *

And so the next three days went by. Barrington came by late every evening as he set out on his endless search for the dog assassin, but Joe couldn't face going with him. His nerves were shot to pieces. He kept the television news channel on all the time. Nothing. Joe had never been so faint-hearted, he jumped at his own shadow, and he began to wonder if he was losing control of his mind; luckily there was one minor event that helped to keep him sane. Amanda Fludd telephoned him about the bookstall.

'I'm so looking forward to meeting you, Mr Rapps,' she said. 'I hear you've been to India. You must have dinner with us one evening and tell us all about it. The fête is such good fun, and I know you'll enjoy it. We have a gazebo to keep us dry should it rain, but bring a brolly. Make sure you are there by two o'clock, in time for the speech by Percival Peachcroft, and the Fancy Dress Parade. That's always the first thing – traditional, you know.'

And Norah came early one of those mornings, between four o'clock when her husband left for work, and the arrival of Sylvie at half past eight. Joe was only half aware of her slipping into the bed beside him: he warm and not yet woken to the dangers of the day; she cool from the dawn air, the freshness of the fields giving a fragrance to her skin. She stroked him awake and when he was ready she clambered onto his body. His hands rose to her breasts and she made long gentle love to him. 'Ah,' she said, 'and they say there's no God.'

And then it was Saturday. 'It's the fête today,' said Sylvie, when she brought his tea and toast that morning. 'Have you been roped in?'

'Bookstall, Mrs Fludd.'

'Oh, she's a lovely person. You'll like her and she'll definitely like you. She likes a good-looking man. I'll be there, I make the teas, in the cricket pavilion. You'll meet my old man, spends the afternoon in the beer tent. Did you see the news?'

Joe sat up, suddenly wide awake. 'No, what was it?'

'Our village was mentioned, that's all. Only because Percival Peachcroft is opening the fête. He's pretty famous, 'sposed to have been up to hanky-panky in London, with a journalist. I ask you, what larks, eh?'

Joe picked up his tea cup. 'Nothing else?'

'Not really, we were the most interesting bit. I've got you some smoked salmon for lunch, with scrambled egg, and tonight a navarin of lamb. You'll be ravenous after the day.'

Joe took his time that morning. He turned on the television and went through all the news programmes. Still nothing. He couldn't decide whether the absence of news was a good sign or not. He attempted to push the problem to the back of his mind, and almost succeeded. He bathed leisurely, chose a suit of yellow linen – just right for a fête in the south of England – a pale green shirt, no tie, and comfortable brogues.

By the time he got downstairs, Sylvie was laying out his lunch. She stopped what she was doing to stare at him.

'Oo,' she cooed, 'you do look lovely. Those women wont be able to keep their hands off you this afternoon. There's about a dozen widows lurking about this village, you know. You keep your distance. They'll make mincemeat of you – a single man, handsome, with a nice house and a private income, you're a bit of a rarity in this village...a rarity in Oxfordshire come to that. I tell you, I quite fancy you myself.'

At about half-past one Barrington appeared. He also was dressed to the nines: a blazer in broad stripes of red and black, white trousers and a wide brimmed panama. He was beaming and patting his belly.

'Best day of the year in Milton Magna, this is. Hurry up, now. We mustn't miss the opening speech. Percival Peachcroft's a bit of a wide boy, but all the Tories love him. He's so outrageous and funny too, you never know what he's going to say next. Just the job for this constituency – bats in the belfry: it's the Thames Valley air that does it.'

They walked away from the house, up Pegswell Lane and out onto the High Street. It was crowded: family groups pushing prams, villagers in clusters with their London friends, down for the big occasion. A few cars went slowly by, then a tractor pulling a flat wagon loaded with bales of straw to make a hollow square: behind that fortification were maybe thirty children in fancy dress: sunflowers, cowboys and Red Indians, space travellers, Catwoman and Superman.

Beyond the shop, and half a dozen bungalows further on, the

two men turned left through a five barred gate and onto the recreation ground – a large area the size of a football pitch. There was a cricket pavilion to one side, a long low building, which was the centre of activities. In front of it was a podium on which a sound system for playing music had been installed. There was also a microphone on its stand.

At least half the field was covered in brightly coloured tents, each one with bunting flying from the corners, and there were gazebos of green, gold and purple. There were also two roped off squares: one for the Fancy Dress Parade and the school dancing troupe, the other for the Chalgrove brass band. On the very edge of the field, set against a stone wall, was the beer tent, long and low. The open stalls were laid out closer in: white elephant, bric-à-brac, plants, cakes, home-made jams, tombolas and raffles and the book stall, all presided over by the women of Milton Magna, some of them aided by their husbands and children. The setting was a painting of England at its most delightful – tiny figures crowding the landscape, all got up in their Sunday best and their party dresses. The sun shone, the grass glittered, and tea and ice-creams were being served from a window of the pavilion.

'I'd better get to the book stall,' said Joe. 'What are you doing?'

'I'm helping in the beer tent,' answered Barrington.
'But not for long. They know it's the only job they can get me to do. Come over later when it all slows down. I'll buy you a drink.'

The book stall, with the books already laid out, was set under a pale yellow gazebo which lent a strange light to the faces under it; feverish and jaundiced. Amanda Fludd beamed at Joe; she was slim and angular, dressed in tweeds with her hair cut short. She looked like what she was – the wife of an academic: crisp, well-read and well-travelled.

'Oh, Mr Rapps,' she said; her voice was sisterly and her eyes friendly. She looked him up and down and liked what she saw. 'It's so kind of you to lend a hand, we've heard so much about you. This is my daughter, Tania, and this is Frances Goldsmith.' Joe shook hands with all three of them.

'It's so nice to have a man with us, it's normally just us girls.' Frances smiled and stared as deep into Joe's eyes as she could manage. 'The prices are written inside the books, and this is the float.' She pointed to a square biscuit tin. 'But we don't sell anything until the fête has been officially opened at two o'clock.'

A minute later there came a fanfare from the brass band, and the vicar stepped up to the microphone.

'My lords, ladies and gentlemen. It is my great pleasure to introduce our much loved MP, the Right Honourable Percival Peachcroft, so that he may declare this fête open. Pray silence for the Right Honourable Percival Peachcroft, and his "ardentia verba", those words that glow.'

Joe stood behind the barricade of books. The strolling crowd came to a standstill, as if for the minute's silence on Armistice Day. The microphone hummed, and out of the pavilion came the MP for South Oxfordshire.

He was of middle height, about forty but looking younger, solidly built, arms and legs thick. His summer suit hung loosely about him, the jacket swinging from his shoulders, his trousers baggy. His hair was reminiscent of August wheat and it sprouted out of his skull in every direction, windswept and wilful, unbiddable. His face was round, his eyes a blue glitter, restless, darting from left to right. He appeared shambolic, his speech also, but the voice was good, comfortable in its public school confidence and Balliol polish. Joe remembered the school – Eton.

Percival Peachcroft patted the pockets of his jacket and moved his head round in a hundred and eighty degrees like a searchlight. 'It's good to be here, I must say. My first visit to Milton Magna...not the last of course – election soon, and I shall be knocking on a few doors!' He paused for a while as if expecting a burst of applause. There was none. He fell silent for a moment. It was as if there were a multitude of ideas blustering through his mind at any given time, and he couldn't decide which one was the most important.

He went on. 'The vicar has told me all about the village, and the money needed for the bells...ah, not the bells, that's been done, hasn't it? Thirty thousand pounds! Remarkable, truly remarkable...What is it for, Vicar?'

The vicar whispered something.

'Ah yes,' continued Percival Peachcroft. 'It's the church central heating. Never mind. So, make sure you spend as much as you can, more than you can afford, and go to all the stalls. There are home-made jams, cakes – scrumptious they are – the bookstall, plants and white elephants...and so, with your permission, vicar, I declare the Milton Magna fête well and truly open.'

The bookstall did very well, and money poured into the biscuit tin. The sky remained blue, and large white clouds, like shapeless sheep, ambled across it. The brass band played continuously, and skittles clattered down. There was a maypole dance, wellies were thrown and children screamed on the bouncy castle. The Punch and Judy man was wildly popular and outside the Fortune Teller's tent stood a long queue. Milton Magna women flaunted their summer dresses and their men sat on shooting sticks, wore panama hats and talked sagely. The huge enamel teapots in the pavilion were no sooner full than they were empty, and the beer tent bulged with bodies, raucous talk and bursts of laughter.

Joe was changing a ten pound note for someone and being particularly charming to Amanda Fludd's daughter, when he heard the voice; a voice he recognised.

'Well, Joe, nice to see you out here in the country, behaving yourself, miles from London, doing good works.' The voice belonged to Sunshine Leary. Joe looked up. There was the heavy face, the full selfish lips, and a square forehead that was really a chunk of rock. Most frightening of all were the huge hands that looked like they could squeeze the life out of a fully grown Siberian tiger. There was no style to the man, but he possessed uncontainable power. Behind him stood his brother, rippling with the same kind of brute force, and behind him another man, a bodyguard.

Joe smiled and gave the change from the tenner to the woman who was waiting for it. He wanted to scream.

'Hello, Sunshine,' is what he said.

'Just came to see how you are, Joe. See that you're enjoying your stay. You look healthy. I hear you were in town yesterday…very naughty.' Sunshine laughed.

Joe knew that his face had gone out of shape. 'The Countess said it was okay, said she'd cleared it with you.'

'I know, Joe,' Sunshine went on, 'special permission…she told me you were on the job, but better not let it happen again…eh?'

'No.'

'That's right, Joe. Me and the Countess, we're old buddies, we've worked together in the past.' Sunshine picked up a book at random. 'I'd better buy something, I suppose, support the church. Give me this one.'

Joe took the book and checked the price: fifty pence, Then he took the twenty pound note that Sunshine gave him. The book had a green cover, the title in gold lettering on the spine – 'Death in Venice.' Joe's hands were moist, his mouth dry.

Sunshine was enjoying himself, letting the evil of his heart glitter in his screwdriver eyes; his lips tight over long teeth.

Joe scrabbled his hand in the biscuit tin for the change. Keep the money, Joe, for the church funds. But remember, just stay out of my way, no more trips to London. What's the book? 'Death In Venice' – a murder mystery, I like them. Mickey Spillane's my favourite.' Leary didn't wait for an answer. He walked away, and his two companions followed him.

'What a nice man,' ventured Amanda Fludd. 'Twenty pounds! You do know some interesting people. We should have him to dinner sometime…or lunch at the Regatta.'

'Yes,' said Joe, 'he's introduced quite a number of his friends to water sports, and not sculling either.'

'How nice,' said Amanda Fludd. Then: 'I think we can manage now, Mr Rapps. Why don't you explore? This is your first fête after all, and I'm sure you'd like to spend a while in the beer tent.'

*   *   *

Some nine hundred people lived in Milton Magna and most of them were gathered on the recreation ground. Joe pushed his way through the crowds, drifting this way and that. He inspected the white elephant stall. He threw at the skittles and missed, he chucked a Wellington boot, not far, and it wrenched his shoulder. He even bought a book of raffle tickets and guessed the mileage of a vintage car, wrongly as it turned out. He came eventually to a halt in front of the fortune-teller's tent, where the queue had disappeared and a banner across the doorway read "Sweet are the uses of adversity". He pushed a canvas flap to one side and entered the gloom of the interior.

He didn't recognise her at first. She wore eastern style robes, beads at her neck, jangling bracelets, a light silken shawl and a veil over her face, leaving only the eyes visible.

He handed her a five pound note when she asked for it and she took both his hands and held them in hers. Her eyelashes swooped.

'You have been married, but you were unhappy, you are no longer married – no children. You have been abroad, the orient, I see India...but you spent most of your time in a large dark building, lots of men in it.'

'A big film studio,' said Joe. He realized now that the fortune teller was Erica. He laughed awkwardly. Erica went on. 'You are happy here, very happy, you are not short of money, but you are worried, apprehensive, there are threatening elements in your life, and you can't seem to get free of them, but you must. You need to enjoy the coming years. You have recently achieved something extraordinary, but you must put it behind you. Your sex life is good, the woman is in charge, but then you enjoy that, it is part of your nature...you should travel for a while and then settle down with someone, enter into a more durable relationship. You need love, real love.'

Erica released his hands. Joe frowned. 'You know too much. Where did you get all that from?'

'I guessed most of it.'

'Oh yeah...You've been reading my mail!' Joe was peeved, and made no attempt to keep the note of anger out of his voice. 'There's something going on I don't know about.'

Joe fell silent and Erica's eyelashes swooped again. He knew he couldn't get to the Countess, but Erica was just as attractive in her own way. He let his annoyance fade.

'We were supposed to have dinner,' said Erica. 'Let's have a picnic instead, down by the river...we'll talk then. What are doing next Wednesday?'

'I dunno, you're the bloody fortune teller.'

'I'll telephone, to confirm,' she said, and Joe left the tent.

*   *   *

Joe blinked as he came out into the sunlight. But even as his eyes became accustomed to the brightness there was a flurry of rain and the wind squalled suddenly. 'Beer tent,' he said to himself, and within a second or two he had slipped through the main opening and pushed his way to the bar. The first person he saw was Norah, pulling pints, her face flushed with the heat of her work, a strand of hair swinging from her forehead and in front of her eyes.

'Have a beer,' said Barrington. He had left a group of villagers to join Joe.

'Could do with one,' said Joe. He looked about him while the drink was poured. The odours in the bar were redolent of love in hayfields. To provide seating, bales of straw had been placed around the perimeter of the tent, and the rich smell of them mingled with spilt beer, human sweat and cigar smoke. There must have been a hundred people present, mainly men, leaning on the makeshift counter or sitting in groups on the bales. 'It's very Thomas Hardy,' said Joe, 'do you think Henchard will come in and sell his wife?'

Barrington handed Joe a pint of bitter. The rain rattled on the roof. 'I dunno,' said Barrington, 'but I bet Vernon would like to sell his. Cornelia ain't easy.' He nodded and Joe's eyes followed the direction of the nod. Vernon, dressed in a seersucker suit of blue and white stripe, and wearing white Italian pumps, was in a corner of the tent, sitting on a bale, his elbows on his knees and his head held in his hands. He was staring at the floor. Beside him sat his wife, as hard as a hatchet, and speaking in sparks. Joe looked at her for a while to see if she was going to draw breath, but she didn't.

This was the woman who would play opposite him if he took the part of Silvius in the play. Cornelia must have been more than showy as a young woman, gaudy even. In fact, she still was, and Joe could see that she would have had a sure and certain tarty attraction for Vernon in his youth, and had doubtless been very dirty between the sheets. Her hair was dyed red, thick waves down to her shoulders; her lips were two splashes of scarlet. The face powder was pale, the eye make-up accentuated and blue. Strange things had happened to the creases round her mouth: the lines were deep and the muscles worn. She had the expression that newscasters achieve from pronouncing their words too carefully and too often. It was the hardness of her psyche working through to the surface of her skin.

Barrington laughed a hefty, half-drunk laugh, and patted his convivial stomach. 'Henchard wouldn't get much for her, I wouldn't give you tuppence.'

Joe wasn't listening. He glanced around the tent. Sunshine Leary and his entourage were standing at the far end of the bar. Sunshine raised his glass in Joe's direction and then turned his back. What was he doing in Milton Magna? It was more than likely that he had provided back-up for the kidnapping and had come for the pay off, or possibly he had made the journey simply to terrorize Joe, or kill him perhaps, now the capture of the Prince had been achieved.

Joe shifted his gaze. By the tent entrance stood Hopkins and Cope, watching everyone, their faces arrogant with suspicion. That reminded Joe.

'Vernon,' he said to Barrington. 'Is he still the number one suspect?'

Barrington let out a grunt of pleasure as if the mouthful of beer he had just taken was the best of his life. 'Nah,' he said. 'Hopkins and Cope couldn't hold him any longer. His alibis all stood up, and the DNA found on the bodies was not his. No, they've got to start all over again. You can't imagine how much pleasure that gives me. I tell you, Joe, I never had an unsolved crime on my watch, not one. Certainly not a murder, not even the theft of a bicycle. God knows what they teach 'em at police college nowadays. I'm loving it, just watching them as they get nowhere.'

At that moment Dudley Mackintosh, the editor of the Village Bulletin, entered the tent and elbowed his way to the bar. He came close to Barrington's shoulder and whispered something in his ear that Joe couldn't catch. Barrington's bonhomie drained from his face. He banged his glass on the bar, spilling some of the contents, and stormed across the tent, pushing people from his path, bursting through the entrance. Dudley Mackintosh followed him.

Joe smiled at Norah, but she was too busy to exchange even one word. She backhanded the sweat out of her eyes and shrugged. Joe moved to a straw bale and sat opposite a man he didn't know, but then recognised him; he'd been in The Plough at Haseley the night Joe had gone looking for the assassin with Barrington – it was Norah's postman husband.

'I think we met in The Plough,' said Joe, 'I was with Barrington.' Norah had told Joe his name – it was Tom.

The man was of a surly blood: it showed in his facial expressions, in the way he held his body, and the way he moved his limbs.

'Bloke's a bloody fool,' he said. His voice was like a hacksaw. 'Staying up all night trying to catch some bloody lunatic, what can you expect of an ex-copper? Coppers are the second criminal class, did you know that? Course you didn't...mind you, I've no time for dogs...been bitten more than once, just delivering the post. I kicks 'em as hard as I can, right up the arse.'

'Have you seen the television news today?' Joe asked, remembering that he ought to be worried.

'News? Why should I?'

'I thought there was a story about the Royal Family, and I was interested.'

'Don't start me on the Royal Family.'

Joe realized immediately that he'd said the wrong thing. Any subject but that.

'They're a waste of space, all of 'em. 'Bout time we gave them the old heave-ho. Spoilt brats, houses galore, all of which we pay for. Prince of Wales gets rid of Diana and then marries another one...from one bit of crumpet to another, yachts in the Med, fellatio on a felucca...did you know Charles has settled a million quid on each of Camilla's kids? That'll keep Parker-Bowles quiet, won't it. God knows how much of our money Charlie's settled on Camilla.'

'Well I'm no royalist, but what do we do with them?'

'What do we do with 'em? 'I'll be generous. Give 'em a million pounds each and send 'em packing. Confiscate their houses and palaces, turn Buck House into an art gallery, and take the jewels off the Queen. She only got them from the Saudis and such like because she's the head of state. Leonardo sketches given as pressies to the bloody Pope. As for the private fortune, so called, where did she get that from? Robber barons, the lot of 'em. Not taxed properly, are they? Did the Queen Mum pay inheritance tax? Did she buggery! When Diana died she left twenty-two million...where'd she get that? When she turned up she was penniless.'

Joe stood. This was a tirade he could do without. He found Hopkins and Cope at his elbow, looking boiled in their dark suits. The rain still pattered on the roof of the tent and the bar had become more crowded.

'You know we found a third nanny,' said Hopkins, 'in the churchyard at Milton Parvis.'

'We've checked you out, Rapps,' added Cope, 'and done some tests on the bodies. You're in the clear. You were in Wandsworth, and you weren't on day release. We've put your passport in your letter-box.'

'Lucky boy,' said Hopkins, grinning. Joe gave the grin a colour. It was green, and it made him angry.

'I'm not lucky,' said Joe. 'I'm just innocent,' and he shoved his way back to the bar, where he ordered another beer and let his anger cool.

'Might see you tomorrow,' said Norah, and then she was called away.

Joe turned from the bar with his pint of bitter and found himself standing beside the Bishop who was talking at one of his students.

'The Anglican church,' the Bishop was saying, 'is not cut out for fundamentalism, that would be far too energetic. Remember, my boy, that those who set their sights on the next world will readily accept the evil that exists in this one...killing for the cause is no problem to them, on the contrary, they are martyrs off to paradise, and yet our society is in a conspiracy to pretend that religion is beneficent...history shows us otherwise.

'Yet I love the Anglican church because it is uncontaminated by religion and believes that reason is a virtue. Anglicans love the beauties of this world, and they are in no hurry to leave it. God or Allah or Jehovah has got the other place sorted out, hasn't he? So what's the rush to get there?'

'Can I get you a drink, Bishop?' asked Joe.

'No thank you, Mr Rapps, I have a glass of water, you see. They don't have sherry here.' He did not introduce the young man, but continued talking.

'Now take the Lisbon earthquake – 1755 – or any other earthquake, come to that. If it was God's wrath, why Lisbon? Did that city have more vices, say, than London or Paris? In the eighteenth century they were happy to ask the question: "What kind of God is it that can allow such a thing?" Nowadays we are too pusillanimous. Divine intervention? Poppycock!'

Joe lifted his glass to his lips and studied the Bishop's companion: a good-looking young man, boyish, with a clear skin, and a gin and tonic nicely balanced in a graceful hand. There was a film of adoration over his eyes as he listened to the Bishop. He said nothing.

'The world is cowardly,' the Bishop continued, 'and very soon we won't be able to question religion at all...defence of human values or women's rights, for example, is already seen as religious hatred, and yet we need to fight for the abolition of religious schools...How can a reasonable person believe in an absolute truth just because it is written in a primitive book, be it Jewish, Muslim or Christian? We should concentrate on ridding ourselves of second-hand notions and false standards, and try to recover the old fresh view of life.'

The young man spoke at last. 'And salvation?'

'A deathbed confession,' said Joe, 'that's my plan.'

173

The Bishop smiled. 'Not original,' he said, 'it's Pascal's bet, isn't it? Though you might as well put your money on it.'

Joe felt a hand drop heavily on his shoulder and turned to find Oona behind him, her cheeks glowing from the heat of the tent and consumption of alcohol. She pressed her face against Joe's and he kissed it twice, once on each cheek, his lips tasting her sweat, feeling her bosoms against his chest.

'Silvius!' she cried. 'Have you seen your Phebe yet? She's here somewhere, over there with the red hair. You are going to be wonderful together. I've set the date for a first read-through, twentieth of June, my place. But I want you to come for dinner before then, say in a week's time, just the two of us, let the village talk. I'll ring you...'

'A drink?' asked Joe.

'I'll come back,' she said. 'That man from Radio Oxford is here and I want to make sure he does Duke Senior for us...or Touchstone perhaps. I'll be back, I promise.' She smiled compassionately, as if she saw and understood Joe's sexuality and was ready to satisfy all its desires. Then she headed into the press of bodies and was gone.

Joe turned again, searching for the Bishop, but he was no longer visible; nor was his acolyte. Instead he found himself face to face with a shrivelled man of about seventy-five years of age. He had fish eyes, as opaque as glue, and there was no way of looking into them. He was not tall, maybe five feet nine. His hair was sandy, his teeth an uneven brown. His body was scraggy, with elbows and knees poking against his tweeds like sharp kindling in a sack. There was an emptiness to his face.

'Hello,' said Joe. The old man ignored him. A younger man carrying a newly acquired pint of beer and a whisky and soda came from the crowd and stood by Joe.

'You are Mr Joe Rapps, aren't you?' he said. 'I'm Viscount Lewknor, and this is my father, Lord Hazelmere. He doesn't always know which conversation he's in, or which century.' He gave his father the whisky which immediately disappeared down his throat.

'Of course I do,' said Hazelmere, 'you whipper-snapper. I haven't kicked the bucket yet, wait your turn.'

Lewknor smiled at Joe. The affection for his father was obvious. 'He's led an extraordinary life, actually – tiger shooting in Bengal, mountaineering in Afghanistan. Gambled fortunes at Goodwood, and at Annabel's. Followed the route of Ulysses across the Mediterranean, in a galley, wrote a book about it. An Oxford man. The list is endless.'

'How amazing,' said Joe, 'truly amazing.'

'Working class,' said Hazelmere suddenly and unbidden. 'The damn working classes are getting too uppity.'

Lewknor transferred his interest to the other side of the tent. The rain had stopped and the sunlight was filtering through the canvas. 'Excuse me,' he said to Joe, 'there's someone over there I must have a word with. Could you please stay with my father for a couple of minutes?'

Joe nodded. Left alone with the old man, Joe was at a loss as to what to say. He need not have worried. Hazelmere launched into a defence of the House of Lords, and the principle of heredity. 'The aristocracy has had a monopoly of the best brains for some hundreds of years. When was Great Britain at its best? Why, in the nineteenth century, of course, when we had an empire. And who ran the empire? We did, of course. And because we had the money, we had the best women, in terms of brains and beauty. We bred better. Now what do they want to do? Fill the red benches with *hoi polloi*: little farts, bought men who will do what the government of the day desires of them…it's ridiculous. Look where the country is today, up shit creek without a paddle. Prime Ministers who went to grammar school. No style at all.'

'They'll die off soon,' said Joe. He looked down the tent, willing Lewknor to return.

'Die!' said the old man. 'We need the Commons to die, and the Lords to survive.' He gave a harsh cackle and his eyes became less opaque for a second. He shoved his empty glass into Joe's free hand. 'We can only hope for the best…there's a lot of death out there, and it's contagious, you know, death. It creeps up on you before you know where you are, but it won't catch up with me. I've got a private insurance, a whopper. They go on about this MRSA, but death is what kills 'em in the hospitals, simple death. You're a young man and I'll give you a tip, from a wise old man: stay away from people, they get you in the end. Carry an orange with cloves stuck in it…like for the plague.'

It was then that Barrington appeared at the tent entrance. He looked murderous. He pushed his way towards Joe, through the crowd, and while Joe waited for him to arrive Lewknor reappeared and bore his father off to a gang of landed gentry who were drinking heavily, and noisily, further down the bar.

Barrington's face was raddled with rage. Passion was shaking his body. 'It's coming down harder now,' he said. 'She's done another bloody dog, right here, on the day of the fête. Someone went behind the pavilion for a pee and found a dead Basenji. Comes from Manor Farm, Milton Parva, I know the animal…really intelligent breed, Egyptian hunting dog.'

'Oh, God,' said Joe. 'What can we do?'

'We've got to find the woman in white,' retorted Barrington. 'I'll do time for her, I will. Joe, get me a pint, they've cleared my glass away, I need to calm down. I want you to come out with me again tonight, give me a hand, and this time we'll be sober.'

*　　*　　*

Barrington came for Joe at about ten that evening. It was dark. They did the normal patrol: Milton Parva, Haseley Parva and back to Haseley Magna, and there they rested on a bench by the graveyard in the summer of the night. They were exhausted but it was pleasant where they were sitting, and they were both revelling in the beauty of the stars and the quiet of the planet. They were content; their eyes were half closed and they breathed deeply.

After a while they were almost asleep, but there was no mistaking the noise when they heard the kissing gate on the far side of the graveyard screech on its hinges. It must have been one o'clock in the morning. They sat without moving for a moment, expecting to see someone appear on the path between the tombstones. They saw nothing. Then they heard the soft expulsion of air in a silencer, then it came again.

'My God, we've got her this time,' said Barrington and leapt to his feet. He set off at a run towards the other side of the church and Joe hared after him. Near the kissing gate was a newly dug grave with, to one side of it, a mound of earth, covered in the usual sheet of plastic grass. On the ground lay a dead dog, a whippet Joe thought, and beside the dog lay the woman in white, on her back, legs splayed, very obviously dead.

'My God!' said Barrington.

Crouching beside both bodies was the scraggy figure of Lord Hazelmere, a rifle in his hands. 'Got the bastard this time,' he was saying. 'Got the bastard this time.'

Barrington and Joe came and stood by the old man. 'We'll have to turn him in,' said Barrington, a note of reluctance in his voice.

'Of course,' said Joe. 'But why has he killed the woman in white, and who killed the dog?

'Tigers,' said Hazelmere, 'man-eaters.'

Barrington knelt and peered at the woman's body, without touching it. 'Shot straight through the heart,' he said, 'bloody good shot. Dog as well. Hazelmere must have done both, you see. The woman hasn't got a gun.'

'Well, you may have found the dog assassin,' said Joe, 'but dogs is one thing, humans another. So many bodies since I came to Milton Magna. It's like the last scene in Hamlet.'

'Hoi polloi,' said Hazelmere, getting to his feet. He shook his rifle above his head and disappeared behind a large tombstone. A second later came the sound of him peeing.

'I dunno,' said Barrington, 'can't be any doubt that old Hazelmere did for her…it's a bloody shame though, him being away with the fairies. They'll shove him in Broadmoor, sure as eggs is eggs.'

The kissing gate clanged again, and Lewknor came along the path. He'd been listening.

'It doesn't have to be like that,' he said. He bent over the woman in white, put his fingers in her hair and, with a rough movement of the hand, removed her wig. He pulled the white raincoat completely open. 'No breasts.'

'Who is it?' asked Joe.

'Well, he said he was Lord Lucan,' said Lewknor. 'You see, in the old days my father was a gambling companion of Lucan's, Annabel's and all that, and it was here he came that first night, after he'd murdered his nanny...'

'Alleged,' said Barrington.

'...it was here he came, just while he got himself organized. Then he was off all over the world.'

'Lord Lucan, bloody Margaret!',

'I'm not at all sure it is him. It's a possibility, of course, and we've always called him Lucan. Whoever he was, he turned up about three years ago, destitute, on the run, claiming he was just back from Goa. He was about the right vintage, had all the lingo. My father believed him, and he's been hiding in the cellar ever since. We fitted it out for him.'

Lord Hazelmere reappeared, his unbuttoned flies wet, mooching up and down between the tombstones. '*Hoi polloi*', he mumbled, '*hoi polloi.*' He put the rifle over his shoulder like a sentry and began to march up and down.

'It was all right to begin with, having a so-called Lucan in the cellar, but then my father developed Alzheimer's, and "Lucan" became just as potty, tearing across the countryside at night, always at night, until at last neither of them knew who the other one was; and on occasion they didn't even know who they themselves were. "Lucan" became obsessed with gambling, needed to get into a gambling school. Well, there is only one big one in Oxfordshire...in some quiet rooms at the top of the Vivaldi. He dressed as a woman, and wore a wig to put people off the scent. I suppose he really thought he was Lucan, that's if he wasn't, you understand. In his nutty state, he thought it was the perfect disguise.'

'What did "Lucan" use for money?'

'Funny that, he always had money. It used to arrive reg'lar, cheques in the post, quarterly.'

'And who on earth did "Lucan" gamble with?' asked Joe.

'Oh, with Topinambour, and big wheels from London and New York...they could see that he wasn't a woman, but they didn't care who or what he was as long as he paid his debts.'

Lewknor paused. 'He's paid his debts now, all right. You see, I know that it was he who killed the nannies. According to my father, when he was still talking sense, that is, the real Lucan always had a thing about nannies, and this "Lucan" had taken that on board. He talked about nannies, dreamt about nannies, he was obsessed with nannies. He even began to steal clothes from our children's nanny...gave her a nasty fright when she found him in her room sniffing her underwear...you know. I was obliged to ask her to leave, and had to sweeten the pill with a considerable amount of money, just to buy her silence. My wife didn't like being without a nanny – she thought I'd been up to no good.'

'God Almighty,' said Barrington, 'is that why your father shot him?'

'Not at all. My father didn't even know about the murdered nannies, in fact, as you well know, nobody knew about them until you fellows found the first one the other night. It came as a shock to me, I can tell you, especially when I put two and two together. No, father's quarrel with "Lucan" was something else. He's been lying in wait for him for some time...'

Lord Hazelmere marched by on sentry go and then did a smart about turn, heading back towards the tombstones.

'Being out most nights, my father knew "Lucan's" movements, but he'd also forgotten who "Lucan" was, or meant to be. "Lucan" came across him shooting a dog one evening and beat the old boy up, seriously. You can't do that to a blue-blood like my father. I suppose "Lucan" found it easy to kill nannies. He couldn't stop himself, three of them that we know of, but he didn't like anyone mistreating dogs. Well, it's very English, isn't it, protecting dogs and ill-treating humans.'

Joe couldn't believe what he was hearing. 'Why haven't you been to the police?'

'Come on, Rapps. 'You and Barrington only discovered the first nanny a week ago. If I'd told the police my suspicions about "Lucan" I would have been in deep trouble. Hiding Lucan, if indeed it turned out to be him, my father and I would have both received hefty sentences as accessories to the original murder. I needed time to work things out. Now it's even worse

– they'd put my father away for ever, for *this* murder. It would be the end of him. I'd be inside as well and there'd be no one to run the estate. I tell you I was fast coming to the conclusion that I would have to kill "Lucan" myself. It seemed to be the only way out.'

'And why the bloody hell did your father start shooting dogs?' asked Barrington.

'Because he's back in Bengal,' said Lewknor, 'that's where he thinks he is, shooting tigers, out at night on the back of an elephant, shouting at the bearers.'

Hazelmere came by again, the gun in the crook of his arm this time. 'Yes, where are the bearers?' he asked. He went to the end of the church and stared at the stone wall.

'We'll have to report it,' said Barrington, no joy in his voice.

Lewknor squatted on the grass, away from the bodies, and invited Barrington and Joe to do the same. 'As you said, they'll put my father in Broadmoor, and I'll end up Wandsworth.'

'Not to be recommended,' said Joe, 'it ain't easy.'

'Consider, if you will, this proposition. If I promise you, as a gentleman, to see that my father is looked after, in a private asylum, secure, for the rest of his days – I have the very place in mind -the killing of the dogs ceases, doesn't it?'

'Yes,' said Barrington warily, 'that's all very well, but there's a body here and perhaps a very famous body. It won't disappear in a puff of smoke, you know. We have a social duty too.'

'I realize that, but I'm suggesting that we bury "Lucan" tonight. As far as the authorities and the general public are concerned, the real Lucan is already dead, so they won't be looking for him. If this body isn't Lucan then it's an unknown. But he's nonetheless dead, and as an unknown we can assume that nobody is looking for him either. There's a grave here, ready, and there's a funeral tomorrow. George Ashworth, one of my old farm workers – I've got to be present. So we bury "Lucan" deep in the grave, as deep as we can go, just like the nannies were buried. The police don't know he exists, and they've found all the dead nannies they're going to find. I'm told they've checked on all those who once worked in the area...and no one else is missing.'

'And how can you be sure of that?' Barrington asked.

'I play golf with the Chief Constable,' Lewknor answered. 'Even Minge is in the clear, as I understand it. Everything falls into place, don't you see?'

That's all very well,' said Joe, 'but that leaves three murders unsolved. What about Hopkins and Cope?

'Wait a minute,' said Barrington, 'wait just a minute.' A brilliant smile had illuminated his face, a furnace of a smile. 'It's a scheme that has a certain attraction. In all my years I never had an unsolved crime on my watch, but if we go ahead with this plan the odious Hopkins and Cope will have a real lulu on their doorstep...one that could ruin their careers for ever. They would never live it down. I like it.'

'But Jack,' said Joe, 'you can't.'

'Can't!' Barrington pointed at Hazelmere who had finished staring at the church wall and was once more marching up and down on guard. 'Do you want to see that old boy dumped in Broadmoor in a rubber lined cell, being beaten up as he gets loopier and loopier? I don't. And Lewknor here, who has done nothing but look after his dad and covered up for someone who may not even be Lucan. Why should he do porridge in Wandsworth or anywhere else? You know what that's like. Christian charity, Joe. Christian charity.'

'Some charity, ruining the career of Hopkins and Cope.'

'Joe, they're odious, always have been, the worst kind of copper.'

There was silence for a long while. Joe, yet again, couldn't believe where he was: one o'clock on a May morning, sitting cross-legged in a graveyard with an ex-copper, a Viscount, a dead dog, the corpse of an infamous runaway – possibly – and a Lord of the Manor wandering amongst the tombstones, saying *'hoi polloi'* every few seconds. Joe thought of his three years in Wandsworth and what hell it had been. He thought of Hazelmere being maltreated in a psychiatric hospital. After all, Lucan or "Lucan" had been punished, and Barrington was right. Hopkins and Cope were odious, and he owed them nothing. There was a certain kindness in doing what the other two desired. It was just bizarre that the decision should come down to him – little ordinary Joe Rapps. There was a special kind of air floating over Milton Magna, and there was little doubt that inhaling it made the inhabitants more than a trifle eccentric.

He broke the silence. 'All right,' he said, 'I'll go along with it.' Lewknor got to his feet. 'I'll never forget this,' he said, and went back through the kissing gate to get a shovel and a bottle of malt whisky. His father followed him, looking surprisingly docile.

* * *

It was still May and the weather held steady: blue skies, light breezes, and some rain at night. It was supposed to be the best May on record. Joe knew it was because he spent the days following his outing with Barrington watching the twenty-four hour news programme, and got a hundred weather forecasts as well. The only news about the Prince was that he was indisposed, some kind of summery flu, and had gone to Balmoral with Camilla to recuperate.

'Aha,' said Joe, speaking to himself. 'They're biding their time while they decide what to do.'

Apart from that there was nothing to upset him. He sat in his garden reading, and fell in love with the view every day. The strains of the previous two weeks began to fade, and he came to see a reposeful future lying calm and enticing before him. Even the madness of Milton Magna diminished too, given that there were no more dogs being killed, and nannies could now sleep safe in their beds or with Vernon Minge, depending on their taste.

He saw Barrington a couple of times. He was jolly and Falstaffian, guffawing and rubbing his stomach with affection. He'd been in touch with some old friends at Thames Valley Police Headquarters and had been delighted to learn that Hopkins and Cope were in serious hot water for their non-progress on the so called, 'Nanny Murders Case'. 'It's all over the local press too,' he said, 'they're having a field day. I've never been so cheerful.'

Norah visited a couple of mornings.

'Have you ever heard of Messalina?' Joe asked her. Norah hesitated in her undressing, her skirt caught round her knees, her breasts free of her brassière. 'No love, some queen was she?'

'A Roman empress who loved and enjoyed men, and indulged her every whim.'

'Well, no doubt she could afford to. We working class girls have to take it where we find it, not that I mean you ain't special, Joe.'

Joe was content. Sitting in his arbour, stretching his legs before him, he was happy to settle for what he had got. He didn't have to work. He could read, go to the theatre, he could play the country squire. That would do.

Three days of contemplating his navel and Joe became relaxed and ready to begin his new life. The phone rang on the evening of the third day. It was Erica. 'The picnic,' she said. 'How about tomorrow?'

'Fine.'

'Good, down at the swimming place, twelve thirty. Don't bring a thing, I've got it all organised, including the wine...no, that's okay, I know what you like...I'm a fortune teller, remember. It'll be by way of a farewell, I have to leave Milton Magna.'

'Leave?' Joe was astounded. 'But what about your D.Phil? You were the main reason for me staying here. I'm madly in love with you, you know.'

'Yeah,' said Erica. 'Me, the Countess...not to mention Norah. I'll tell you all about it tomorrow.'

＊　＊　＊

On the morning of the picnic the jazz bird gave its mocking call, putting Joe's life into a prospect of irony. Sylvie brought him his breakfast tray and sat on the bed for a while, as she always did. Real and comforting.

' 'Ad them two detectives in the shop this morning,' she said, 'asking questions about them nannies...they reckon it might be

someone coming in off the motorway, I mean you can get here
from London in an hour, and London's full of nutters, isn't it, I
mean crazy, not like here.'

'Don't bother to do me a lunch today,' said Joe. 'What tea is
this, it's good.'

'Co-op ninety-nine.'

'I'm going on a picnic with Erica.'

'She's lovely, that Erica, and so beautiful – but nice with it,
you know. Always a pleasant word to say. Not a bit snobby,
think they farts incense, some of 'em. She'd make you a lovely
partner. Don't rush things though, you don't want to scare her
off.'

Joe took his time getting ready: a good long shower, a light
cotton shirt, he thought the olive green one, and a pair of cream
trousers in cotton. For shoes, he chose a light pair of tan
moccasins. Erica had said not to bring anything but he took a
Puligny-Montrachet from the cool of his cellar, wrapped it in
several layers of newspaper, and slipped it into a shoulder bag
with a small corkscrew, just in case.

He took the Cuddesdon path out of Milton Magna, down the
slope of the field and up the other side; then along by the
pastures and over the Cuddesdon Road. It wasn't far to the
river and there Joe climbed the stile, paused for a long moment,
and leant against the fence.

The countryside around him rose and dipped like the
contours of a woman at rest, sinless and sensual. Filming
landscape had always made Joe think of his lovers, their
buttocks, their breasts. That's why making love in the open air
was so satisfying, it brought man and woman and the pathless
stars together, all in one body.

Joe stretched his arms above his head, pleased with this
conclusion. He was content. A divine woman waited for him
and it was a perfect day of spring too, a day that only England
could manage, a day when just being alive was a celebration,
when his heart swelled with passion for his country, and his
veins ran with Inca gold instead of blood. It made him feel
capable of achieving anything: capable of putting a ring of fire
around the earth, of understanding all books and all

philosophy; a day when he felt power in every breath he breathed, and every thought he thought. The world belonged to him at last.

Joe walked across the first field and into the second, to where the river curved and formed the swimming place and the mill race forked away to make the island. As he approached he saw that under the huge willow tree a car was parked, a Volvo estate, silver. From the open hatch at the back an awning had been strung to one of the branches of the tree, to give shade. Joe's heart beat a little faster. Erica was waiting for him, the picnic prepared, the wine cooled. He tried to think of another Arabian Nights' story to fit this scene but couldn't. Maybe Omar Khayyam – 'Come fill the cup and in the fire of spring, the winter garment of repentance fling…' That fitted the bill exactly.

As he neared the willow tree he could see that in the shade rugs had been spread. There were also two canvas armchairs, and a table for the wines and glasses, a raffia hamper, plates, silver knives and forks, and a box refrigerator powered from a spare car battery. And over that corner of Oxfordshire the sunlight, filtering through the foliage, shimmered. The sound of the river as it poured over the huge blocks of stone and into the swimming place, was subdued; there hadn't been any serious rain for a while. Indeed, it was too hot for the birds to sing, and there was little breeze.

Joe could see no sign of Erica, then her voice called. She was in the water, in the shade of the rushes, hard to see. 'Come on, Joe, it's lovely.'

'Dammit,' he said out loud. The one thing he'd forgotten – a swimming costume. Then he saw her clothes, every stitch, on the back of one of the chairs. It was the naturist in her. He removed everything he was wearing, and went to the bank, on the high side, and jumped in, stayed submerged for a while, then came to the surface and swam towards her. This was to be his day, he wouldn't even have to take her clothes off.

He came to her, by the rushes and laughed. 'I might have known you'd be naked,' he said. She allowed him to kiss her, not passionately, but lightly on the mouth, then she ducked under the surface, reappeared and swam towards the car. Joe caught up with her and they trod water for a while.

'How do you get a car down here?' he asked.

'There's a way through the farm, on the Milton Parva road. The farmer would do anything for me.'

'I bet he would,' said Joe, 'especially if he's over twelve years old.'

They came out of the water, up the slope of dried mud, and went under the awning. Erica threw him a towel and rubbed herself down. She loved being naked, Joe could see that. He felt awkward; he liked being naked too, but in bed or at very close quarters to the woman, so she couldn't see too much of him. Erica went to the boot of the car and threw him a sarong, crimson and black. She tied another around her bosom, pale blue with a dark blue Polynesian flower design on it.

'The real McCoy,' she said, 'pareos from Bora-Bora.' They sat on the armchairs and she opened the cool box. She put Joe's Puligny-Montrachet into it and took out a dish and another bottle, already opened.

'Starters,' she said. 'Lobster and Sancerre...that ought to interest you.'

'I haven't had Sancerre in a while,' said Joe, 'not a lot of it in India.'

'No,' she said, 'or in Wandsworth.'

Joe felt a cold hand touch his heart. This woman knew too much.

'I suppose Barrington told you that? You know an awful lot for a D.Phil student.'

Erica put a wedge of lobster onto a slice of French bread, gave it to Joe and poured him a glass of wine. The glass frosted.

'Don't blame Barrington,' she said, 'I'm not a student any more than I'm a fortune teller. They're a lovely mixture, aren't they? These two tastes. Very decadent.'

'Who are you, then. What are you doing in Milton Magna?'

There was silence as Erica made another rondelle and refilled the glass that Joe had drunk too rapidly. 'Be careful,' she said, 'don't drink too fast in this heat. Could make you pissed in very short order.'

'So?' Joe was careless and drank his second glass as quickly as the first.

'I work for the government.'

'The government! Inland revenue?'

'No, Joe. MI5.'

'Too young.'

'I was recruited straight from Oxford.'

'What did you study that made you so desirable?'

'Russian.'

Joe spread the next piece of bread himself. 'Why are you telling me this? Aren't you guys supposed to be the silent service, keeping stumm through thick and thin?'

She put what was left of the lobster back into the cool box and brought out a dish of cold roast beef, cut into thick slices, red in the middle, garnished with mayonnaise, and a green salad. There was a Château Batailley to go with it. She charged a plate and a glass for Joe and placed them on the table. There was more French bread and salted butter.

'Why? Because I'm leaving the country, and MI5 too, but the real reason is because I feel sorry for you.'

'Feel sorry for me?'

'And fond of you. You are such a simpleton, Joe. I feel kind of responsible. You've been dragged into this affair, and you are completely out of your depth. Unless I help you, you are going to drown.'

'Dragged into what affair?'

'Come on Joe, don't play the innocent. I've been in it from the beginning...Prince Charles...the Countess. It isn't over yet. It could get really dangerous, and you ought to be on your way out of here before it's too late.'

Joe cut a corner of beef, coated it in mayonnaise and forked it into his mouth. It was delicious.

'Go on.'

'There's a section of MI5 that looks out for the Royal Family, over and above the Police protection unit, especially the younger members. They are so brainless that we have to cover things up, clear up the messes, save them from themselves...I'm part of that.'

'But why are you here, in Milton Magna?'

'We knew all along what the Countess was planning, almost before she'd thought of it, three or four years ago. By coincidence I met her about then, socially, in Moscow. MI5 knew most of what was going on. We'd even infiltrated the Friends of Diana, world wide. We knew they were out for revenge. The Countess's idea began in a small way: just capture Charles, put a lookalike in his place for half an hour, just time to get away, hold him to ransom, make a video recording of him apologising for what he did to Diana. We watched the initial stages, kept pace with it and informed the palace.'

'Well, so why didn't you stop it?'

'It became complicated. Some of our guys were impressed by the lookalike, and thought it might be a good idea if the substitution went on a bit longer. You see Charles was giving everyone a lot of trouble...and not only behind the scenes. Selfish, self-opinionated, spending too much money, quarrels with his mother, the Camilla business...money for her, money for her kids, what he spent on Clarence House – nine million wasn't it? – he's like a modern version of the Prince Regent. Even some of his own staff call him Prinny. The establishment was finding him very tiresome, the big bananas in MI5 hate him, and some of them wanted to get rid of him permanently. They were convinced that there was a lot of evidence linking Charles to a conspiracy to murder Diana.

'Then things went a step further. Everybody knows that Diana's butler got his hands on a box of letters and mementoes, right, but there was more. Diana left another box with the Countess, much more valuable, and much more dangerous. It was dynamite! Its contents, so it was thought, would implicate Charles in some very devious doings. MI5 suspected that those contents proved beyond doubt that he was in the Diana conspiracy up to his neck...the Countess certainly believed so. Had those facts been made public it would have been the end of the monarchy. Once MI5 got a sniff of that stuff, and the Palace had been told about it, well that was the end of the line for Charles. He had to go. Brenda already knew that the monarchy was rocky...but this new bombshell blew her mind. She was livid. A right royal fury.'

'Brenda?'

'Her Majesty, to the trade…she knows how unstable the monarchy is, even after all the good work she's done. She is already concerned about what will happen after her. The populace shout for William to replace Charles, but what guarantee does she have that William will be any better than his father? *And* he's got dodgy Spencer blood into the bargain. Father and son could both turn out to be reincarnations of great uncle Edward Eight. Charles is more than halfway there. And the worst scenario of all, what if William meets an untimely end? Then Brenda would be succeeded by King Harry, and the previous one of that ilk wasn't too clever, was he? But her main concern at the moment is with Charles thinking that he has *carte blanche* to do whatever he bloody-well likes. He could bring the whole edifice crashing down round his large ears. And what would the populace do if they discovered he was definitely linked to Diana's death? Could be the French Revolution all over again. So a deal was done: the Countess would hand over the Crown Jewels Two, as her box was called, as long as she got Charles. The Countess wanted revenge. She knew Diana well – they were good friends for years, emotionally close, and Diana came to Milton Magna often. It was a safe house for her, Chiltern Hall, and they spent a lot of time together, they were fond…'

'My God! Are you saying…?'

'I'm not saying anything. I told you it was complicated.'

'So then?'

'So then, given that the Countess was in possession of information that could finish off the monarchy it seemed but a small price to pay – swap Charles for the evidence and get rid of the loose cannon. No one in the Firm liked what he was doing. He's such a bad tempered prig. So was it just a case of grin and bear it, for the royals, or do something about it? At the Camilla wedding, under that smile, Brenda was breathing fire, flames out of every orifice. I tell you, she would commit murder to save the monarchy…' Erica paused for a long while. Then: 'Even her son was not considered sacrosanct.'

'Why didn't MI5 just arrange another nasty car accident for him?'

'It was discussed, but decided against. Too much on William too fast and too soon. Better to have a Prince of Wales who did what he was told.'

Joe took another slice of beef and a second glass of Batailley. The river ran on; Joe was exhilarated by the faint sound of it, and the summery smells of the earth. The shade he sat in was broken into splashes of yellow sunlight by the slight movement of the willow leaves. The wine was perfection, and within touching distance was a near naked Scheherazade telling him outlandish stories. 'It's all very pretty,' said Joe, 'but I can't believe a word of it.'

Erica shrugged. 'So we were asked to go along with the Countess's plan, discreetly supervise it from afar.'

'But who asked you?'

'Ah well. I can only guess it came from the Palace, initially, from the very top and into the top of MI5, with no traces left.'

'That's ridiculous. You mean...'

'That's exactly what I do mean. The preparations were long, two or three years of it. The idea went from speculative to real, and the go ahead was given. The actual kidnap was rehearsed a hundred times, day after day. You'll remember that the lookalike was wearing exactly what Charles was wearing that morning. We couldn't have done that without inside help, and that's exactly what we had.'

'That did have me puzzled,' said Joe.

'The team was chosen very carefully. They waited for you to come out of Wandsworth. The Methodist chapel was bought and prepared. A special sound proof cellar was dug out underneath.'

'Is that where he is?'

'That's where he is, for the time being.'

'What will they do with him?'

'Well, the Friends of Diana are giving him a hard time at the moment, getting him to confess to all manner of things, all videoed for use maybe at some later date.'

'Will they let him go?'

'No, we've had clearance. The Firm has examined the lookalike; they like him, and he'll do exactly what he's told. He'll be a nice quiet Prince Charles. If he makes it as far as the throne he'll have extra training. If he dares to rock the boat, there will be another nasty car accident.'

'But Camilla, she'll know.'

'Yes she will, but she'll keep her mouth shut. Look, as a youngster she went round the block a few times, and back again. She was on the circuit – Charles wasn't the first by any means.'

'Virgins are nothing but trouble anyway,' said Joe.

'She'll do as she's told. She stands to lose a lot if she doesn't. The money that's been settled on her kids, not to mention on her. She's climbed the slippery pole, the *arriviste par excellence* – houses, cars, whatever clothes she wants, power and position. All she has to do is sleep with another man. She might even prefer the lookalike. He is a bit younger, and hung like a horse, so they say...we had him medically examined.'

Joe was dazed. He emptied his glass and filled it with fizzy water.

'And what happens if she spills the beans?'

'Another nasty car accident. If they happen often enough they'll seem beyond coincidence, more of a curse.'

'What about the two princes?'

'They won't relinquish one iota of their privileges. When it came to it, Princess Margaret didn't. She soon off-loaded the wing-commander.'

'This is the maddest thing I've ever heard. It's immoral too.'

'Yes indeed, but it will work. You are forgetting your Machiavelli, Joe..."It is not rational to be moral. The state must be kept stable, even if it means duplicity, or beastliness." Republicanism is on the rise, the monarchy is shaky, and we need a good dependable heir to the throne. Now we've got one.'

'So what will they do with Charles?'

'They could keep him in that chapel forever if they wanted to. But now we've had the final go-ahead, they'll smuggle him out the country, when the Friends of Diana have finished with him.'

'But where?'

'Anywhere. The Countess has estates all over the world. There are still salt mines in Siberia, you know. They might work him to death in one. That might satisfy her.'

'Poor Charles,' said Joe, 'the man in the iron mask.' He went back to the claret and took another slice of roast beef.

'Poor Charles be buggered, nobody wants him. Do you know what he calls us ordinary guys? "Grockles", that's what; odious and smelly lower-class erks. This new guy will do a better job.'

Joe rose from his chair and stood looking at the river. Erica pushed her chair out of the way and squatted on the rugs. The pareo slipped down from her breasts but she didn't bother to cover them. Joe squatted down to face her.

'I don't understand about the Bishop,' he said. 'Why did he play the messenger? His views are totally opposed to those of the Countess.'

'She had something on him, I guess. His acolyte maybe. There may have been some money involved too. He likes to live high.'

Joe nodded. 'Aren't you scared?' he asked. 'You're in possession of a lot of dangerous information. Between the palace and MI5 there's a lot of power sloshing around.'

'Well, yes. But I'm okay, in theory, though sometimes the grey suits at the top get nervous, and when they get nervous there are more accidents.'

'And the Countess, did she hand over the Crown Jewels Two?'

'Yes, once she had her hands on Charles. I arranged the transfer and took the box to London. She will have taken copies, just to protect herself, but the powers that be won't bother her, or her minions. She cannot be tempted by money and her men are loyal to the death. She'll be fine.'

'Sunshine?'

'They'll see how he goes. He'll have to be careful. One false move and he's gone.'

'That of course leaves me.'

'That's why I wanted to see you today. I shan't be here tomorrow, Joe, and you can see now what the dangers are. On the other hand you have two million in the bank and they may think that puts you beyond temptation. You'll have to be very quiet and never go near a newspaper office. Just spend your money slowly, without being flamboyant. Better still, jump in your car tomorrow and set off somewhere, dump the car as soon as you can, in case its got a tracker on it, fly to Brazil and settle down...But behave. I am seriously worried about you.'

'Where are you going? Couldn't I come with you?' Joe edged across the rug, getting closer to her. He touched the skin of her arm. She smelt of spring and summer, the river and grass. He had never wanted a woman as much as he wanted her.

'I don't quite know where we're going, though I know it is tomorrow. Once out of England I shall be well protected, even though my controllers do not like their people leaving. I am an exception, at least I hope I am.'

'"We", what does that mean?'

'I am going with the Countess, my protection. You see why you can't come...poor little Joe.' She held his hand to comfort him. 'She and I are lovers...I was one of the reasons she got rid of her husband. 'Tis a mad world, my masters.'''

'Lovers, since when?' He took his hand away from hers and stared at her breasts.

Erica seized his hand again. 'Don't be jealous, Joe.'

He freed his hand once more, in a rough movement, sprang to his feet, walked a few yards up the river bank and stared at the water. He couldn't prevent himself feeling hurt, though he knew he was being foolish.

As he stood there he heard the sound of a voice, and from around the bend in the river, appearing like a vision from behind a row of willows, glided a punt, silent and serene on the water, its own reflection gliding along with it. On cushions lay the Bishop, a book in one hand, a glass of wine in the other. Standing at the back of the punt and poling with great expertise, was the handsome acolyte that Joe had seen in the beer tent at the fête. He was dressed in black trousers and a white shirt undone to the waist; his feet were bare. The voice that Joe had heard was the Bishop's, reading aloud to his companion.

'"Much have I travell'd in the realms of gold, And many

goodly states and kingdoms seen..."' The punt drifted towards Joe and the Bishop saw him, and began speaking as if their previous conversation had never ceased.

'Ah, Mr Rapps. Your sarong is delightful. I think the French might have got it right, you know. A real and positive separation between religion and the state, for religion is destroying us, insidiously, forcing us to take it seriously when it should be an amusing diversion, an entertainment. Why not woman priests? They wouldn't have to be virgins. Why not homosexual bishops? What difference could it possibly make? It's man's search for certainty that's the cause of all our trouble. He should read Keats and learn the joys of Negative Capability, "when man is capable of being in uncertainties, mysteries and doubts without any irritable reaching after fact and reason..."'

Joe raised a hand, confused, smiled, opened his mouth to answer, but by then the punt had drifted on under the guiding hands of the good-looking young man, and it quickly disappeared behind another stand of willows. A few more words hung on the air; '"O for a beaker full of the warm South, Full of the true, the blushful Hippocrene, With beaded bubbles winking at the brim, And purple-stained mouth..."'

As Joe stood there amazed Erica came up behind him and pressed her body against his, then she turned him so that he was facing her, slipped her arms around his neck and kissed him hard on the mouth. When she had finished she put her face into his neck, where it met his shoulder. 'Come on, Joe,' she murmured, 'let us part friends. I brought a bottle of farewell Champagne.' She took his hand, laughing, and guided him back to the awning. 'If I ever go straight, or want a child, I'll come to you, I promise.' They reclined on the rugs and Erica poured the Roederer, Crystal Brut. 'Remember what I say, Joe – The Establishment always wins. I'm leaving the country tonight, and you ought to be on your way by tomorrow at the latest.'

*　　*　　*

That afternoon exhausted Joe. He helped Erica load the car and then she drove him back across the fields, through the farmyard and back to the village. She dropped him at the top of Pegswell Lane. She got out of the car and gave him one last kiss. 'Do as I say, Joe,' she said, her voice a whisper, then she climbed back into the car and was gone.

Joe made himself a cup of Assam and took it to the arbour. The sun was halfway down the sky and the shadows were lengthening. The jazz bird uttered its ironic notes and once more Joe took in the view. The blackbird came nearer than it had ever been before and perched on a branch were Joe could see it quite clearly. He whistled the five jazz notes at it, and the bird replied at regular intervals.

'Just as crazy as the rest of the village,' said Joe, 'but then what would England be like without eccentricity?'

He drank his tea with pleasure. The blackbird was emphasising the drollery of his situation. Like the villagers had said he would, Joe had come to love Milton Magna, and now didn't want to leave. He would be content to look at this view for the rest of his life: the soft fall of the hillside, the climb to the row of trees on the skyline, the small old-fashioned fields with their hedges, the square tower of Cuddesdon church where the sun went down every evening; the crows wheeling in the sky. Beauty enough to render a man happy for ever. Yet, it was maddening. He had found a place in which to lead the simple life, but events were forcing him to leave, at least for a while. On the other hand those same events had gifted him enough money to do whatsoever he wished and, what was more, he had a place to come back to.

However his greatest joy came from the fact that he was out of the film business; he was no longer obliged to work. Three years in Wandsworth and a couple of weeks in Milton Magna had knocked all foolish desires out of him. He was a changed man. He could recognise simplicity now, and that was what he wanted. He was disappointed about Erica but Brazil was full of beautiful women and he only needed one of them to fall in love with him. What was the quote? "Men have died from time to time, and worms have eaten them, but not for love."

He stood and took one last look at the view. The evening was drawing in, the shadows under the trees darkening, spreading a sadness over the fields and preparing for the night. And the sadness of leaving Milton Magna crept across the garden and took possession of Joe too, bringing a darkness to his heart that was at one with the darkness on the hillside.

He'd leave immediately, he couldn't bear to wait for the morning. It wouldn't take him long to pack. His new wardrobe could be thrown into the back of the car, and he'd take a few bottles of his best wines. He'd go to one of those expensive country hotels in the Lake District while he thought about the future. Then he'd leave the car and fly to Rio. He'd never been to Brazil. Leave a note and a cheque for Sylvie. He'd miss her. He'd write to Barrington when he got there. He wouldn't have to write to anyone else, there was no one else. MI5 would know where he was, so would the Countess and Erica. She was right, don't try to hide, just play it straight. He squatted by the garden statue and touched its face.

'Goodbye, Mildred,' he said. 'I won't be gone for ever.'

The car was packed in no time. Joe took a last look at his house. Yes, he'd be back. It was too good to leave.

Joe jangled the car keys in his hand. He was looking forward to driving the Saab. He'd never had anything that expensive before, but he'd drive carefully, no more accidents, no more jail. He opened the garage doors and slid in behind the wheel. It was always a wrench leaving a good place. What was it his father's doctor used to say to people who complained about growing old, about dying? "If you don't have a sense of humour you shouldn't have joined."

Joe laughed and switched on the ignition.

*   *   *

The explosion was heard as far away as the village hall and the Vivaldi hotel. Barrington heard it, sitting in his kitchen, thinking about going for supper at the Plough in Haseley Magna. Some of his windows on the upper floor were blown in, and all the windows in Joe's house, on the side nearest to the garage, were completely destroyed.

The police came, Hopkins and Cope, but there was very little to find, not much left of the car or the garage, and even less of Joe. The coroner returned a verdict of unlawful killing by persons unknown and the funeral was held ten days later in the cemetery of Milton Magna. Only five people were present; the Vicar, the Bishop, Sylvie Cornish, Jack Barrington, and Norah. Within a month Milton Magna and its inhabitants had once more settled into a calm and normal way of life, where the monthly Parish Bulletin contained more than enough excitement to entertain and occupy its readers.